WAR IS HELL . . .

The lights, those ever-present, damnable lights on the Fraskan war room board, had been blinking for an interminably long time.

A tall, lean figure sat at the central console, gloomily studying the rapid series of printouts spewing forth. He looked like an eight-foot skeleton over which a tiny, thin layer of blue-white skin had been stretched to cover the entire frame.

Aruman Vard, Agent in Residence of the Fraskan Sector home world, paced nervously back and forth in front of the big board, disgusted with the information he'd been receiving and feeling helpless to correct the situation.

Every once in a while he would come back over to the command console and glance at the printouts and CRT displays . . .

There was little time to do what he knew he must as it was, yet he continued to put it off. One did not abandon one's life and homeland so freely.

SCIENCE FICTION IN THE GRAND TRADITION

Also by Jack L. Chalker
Published by Ballantine Books:

THE WEB OF THE CHOZEN

DANCERS IN THE AFTERGLOW

AND THE DEVIL WILL DAG YOU UNDER

THE SAGA OF THE WELL WORLD

Volume 1: *Midnight at the Well of Souls*

Volume 2: *Exiles at the Well of Souls*

Volume 3: *Quest for the Well of Souls*

Volume 4: *The Return of Nathan Brazil*

Volume 5: *Twilight at the Well of Souls:
The Legacy of Nathan Brazil* (forthcoming)

A JUNGLE of STARS

Jack L. Chalker

A Del Rey Book

BALLANTINE BOOKS • NEW YORK

Library of Congress Catalog Card Number: 76-15209

ISBN 0-345-28960-9

Manufactured in the United States of America

First Edition: November 1976
Second Printing: September 1980

Cover art by H. R. Van Dongen

This book is dedicated to the
Washington Science Fiction Association
for putting up with me and it for so long.

STEP ONE

1

PAUL CARLETON SAVAGE died for the first time on July 29, 1969, in a bit of characteristic Army brilliance.

Send eight men into unfamiliar territory, drop them by chopper into a little clearing in the otherwise impenetrable jungle; have them walk five miles to a second clearing, mostly in darkness, just to determine whether there really *are* that many VC in that particular grid on the map—and, by the way, find out if there are any NVA in the neighborhood as well, won't you?

Military intelligence, Savage reflected bitterly, was a contradiction in terms.

The bell rang and the chopper lifted into the air, the ground disappearing under him in a billow of dust.

Savage sat in the doorway watching the world go by beneath him. Below stretched a sea of green, broken only occasionally by large, dead areas where defoliants had been used. A few birds were visible down there, but nothing else seemed to be alive except trees.

He turned and looked back at the men riding with him. Most sat in their canvas seats trying to look as if they weren't nervous. Normally, this would be a split "A" Team—four Americans and four ARVNs—but there had been the usual foul-up and the only ARVN who wound up along was Sergeant Hao, a last-minute impressment when somebody found out he was born near the drop area. Savage, too, was a last-minute replacement even though he led the team; the Green Beret staff sergeant who had led the team for most of the year that it had been in Vietnam had gotten zapped by a sniper last time out. Newly commissioned Second Lieutenant Paul C. Savage had barely arrived at Firebase Hector when Colonel Matuchek came up with this delight—and noted on the new officer's record that Savage had led an "A" Team as a sergeant.

The air was cool this far up, and Savage felt a slight chill go through him. He wondered idly if it was really the air.

Off in the distance he could see a few wisps of smoke rising from the trees—possibly small engagements, but more likely the smoldering remains of recent encounters or perhaps signs that, down there in the green stew, people continued to live in the midst of the war.

Again he surveyed the group of men in the helicopter. Shadows obscured most of them, and he realized that he didn't even know all of their names. He resisted an impulse to give them a thumbs-up sign; every man knew that even the composition of the team for this trip was already so screwed up that unmitigated disaster seemed inevitable.

The pilot made a pass over the LZ without pausing; this was just to get an idea of what what they were getting into. The copter would continue on a lazy path around the area until dusk, never pausing long enough for unseen observers to guess where it might put down, if at all.

Savage pulled out his map and studied it once more, although he felt he already knew every detail better than the cartographers who had drawn it. He frowned. What he was looking at just didn't jibe with the scenery at all. Somehow, that sinking feeling in his stomach told him, the Army, as usual, had botched the map.

The chopper banked left and started losing altitude. The light was fading fast, and all inside knew that this was it. Each man instinctively checked his weapon. A tenseness was in each of them, and through each mind ran the thought, Is *this* the time that we land in the middle of them?

Suddenly came the forward push as acceleration

stopped; and they were on the ground, grouping near the trees. The blue exhaust flame of the helicopter shot upward until it barely cleared the trees, then was away. They had unloaded in less than five seconds and had made it to the trees without a shot fired. It had been a good landing. But their feet were soaked by the swampy ground at the LZ.

Sergeant Hao checked his luminous compass and they started off after him. Finally they were far enough from the LZ to stop. There had been no noise except the squishing sound of their movements through the marsh.

"Lieutenant!" one of the men exclaimed in a shocked whisper. *"My God—my map! I think I lost it at the LZ!"*

Suddenly that feeling was back. "Well, we can't go back and get it now," Savage snapped. "It's too damned dark to see anything, anyway. Let's just hope nobody else does—or they'll know we're here and figure out why."

"Shh!" Sergeant Hao shot at them. *"Somebody there!"*

They stood immediately frozen, most of them holding their breaths. Only a few jungle sounds filtered back to them through the dense foliage. They could hardly see each other in the gathering darkness, but each man's eyes surveyed the area, trying to spot what Hao thought he saw, heard, or felt.

There was nothing.

After a few minutes, they began to relax. Savage spread out a plastic ground cover and sat on it. With a disgusted sigh, he removed his boots and socks and started wringing the water out of the latter. Unless he was lucky, he'd have to walk them dry the next day. Pulling off the few leeches that had attached themselves to him in the dark, damp walk, he liberally spread mosquito repellent over every exposed area. The stuff stung when it went on over the leech bites, but served to cleanse them and settle them down to dull itches. Around him, the other men were doing much the same, except for Hao, who continued his watch, rifle at the ready, but was not as tense as he'd been a few minutes earlier.

All at once came the sound of firing from the direction of the LZ. Each man grabbed his weapon and felt, to make certain, that he had a clip in place. It was a nervous but instant reaction born of combat experience.

The firing was sporadic and not directed at or near them.

"What do you think they're doing, Harry?" one man whispered to another.

"Old Charley trick," Harry replied calmly. "Fire a few shots in all directions to see if and from what direction fire is returned. They just now found the LZ. Sloppy bastards."

After a few seconds that seemed much longer, the firing stopped.

"Think they found the map?" someone else whispered to no one in particular.

That, thought Savage, was the big question. The odds on their finding it were less than his own, because he knew it was there—but he was also keenly aware that, the way things were going so far, they probably had.

That map. He had looked at it a million times and its features haunted him. The eight-kilometer zone it illustrated showed clearly that they were in a valley, with fairly steep and mostly defoliated hillsides around. The exfiltration LZ was near the other end, and it was the only possibility for another ten or eleven klicks.

It was the best damned trap he had ever been in.

He took out his red-filtered flashlight and looked at his watch. 2215 hours. The contact plane would be over in less than fifteen minutes.

Suddenly a shot came out of the dark forest.

Sergeant Hao screamed and bent over double, the force of the blow pushing him back against a willowy tree. He collapsed to the ground and lay still.

The men were already fanning out, weapons in hand. Savage turned over two or three times, grabbing his own rifle as he did.

Another shot.

This time he saw the flash and started to call to the others, but they had already seen it. A withering fire produced by several M-16s all shooting on automatic in the direction of the flash ended the shooting in their midst, but there'd been no cry, no sound that any had found their mark. That sniper might still be there.

Whether he was or not, their position was known and they pulled out fast. Savage had gone about three hundred meters before he realized, by the stinging sensation of leeches attaching themselves to his feet and legs, that he was still barefooted.

They regrouped in a particularly dark grove and waited soundlessly.

Random firing, some very close, reverberated through the forest; but it was clear that Charley didn't know their location. That at least was a small stroke of luck—only one man had happened upon them, probably by accident, and if he was alive he had no idea where his quarry had gone.

Silence descended, but they could smell the rotten odor of *nuoc-mam,* the sauce made from decayed-fish oil that every Vietnamese was addicted to, all around them. It was so penetrating that often Charley's patrols would be betrayed over fifty meters away by the odor on their breaths. With Hao gone and the rest of the squad American, they had little doubt about where and from whom the smell was coming.

But from how many?

Only two or three men might be out there, or the team could have blundered into an entire division. The inky darkness and light jungle sounds made it impossible to tell.

Overhead they heard the sound of a plane's engines as it passed slowly by. The contact. There would be no call tonight. The next time possible would be at four the following morning. After that, it would be twenty-four hours at a stretch until they were either picked up or declared missing in action.

They didn't dare move in the dark, not with Charley out there. And so, after a tense half-hour with nothing happening, they settled down to wait out the night.

No one slept.

About a half-hour after midnight, they heard voices

whispering in Vietnamese. Whoever they had bumped into out there was still around.

Savage grew cold and his stomach tightened— someone was standing about two meters from him. He could sense movement even though he could not see clearly.

A new round of shots was fired into the air by the VC around them. None were returned, the men of the squad freezing like statues, their fingers poised nervously on their triggers.

The man nearest Savage now moved off, and the lieutenant was conscious of the movement of others toward the southeast. There appeared to be only four or five of them, but that didn't tell much about the size of the total force that potentially lurked in every bush and tree.

They were gone as suddenly as they had appeared, and the fetid air of the swamp somehow seemed fresher by the absence of *nuoc-mam*.

At about 0130, another volley was heard—off to the southeast—but pretty far away. Charley had missed them.

This time.

As they sat through the night watch, Savage became slowly aware that the squad was whispering to one another. But he could not make out what was being said. Once he admonished them for being so noisy, but after a short while the whispering had begun again.

At a little before 0300, one of the men crawled over to Savage's painful perch on a high clump of bush. The lieutenant looked at him in the gloom: a big blond fellow, well over six feet, and seemingly in the peak of condition. He would be ideal for a young German officer in a World War II film, Savage reflected, although the man's name was, incongruously, McNally.

"Sir?" he queried softly. "Can I speak to you for a minute?"

"Sure. McNally, isn't it?" Savage responded softly. "What's going on?"

"Well, sir, we been wonderin', well—uh, the contact time is coming up and we were, uh, wonderin' just what you were gonna tell 'em."

Savage shifted uneasily, considering the question and

the motive of the man who had asked it. It was certain that he was spokesman for the rest.

"I'm going to tell them what happened," he replied carefully.

"Yeah, but—what about gettin' us out of here?"

So that was it. He'd known it.

"Frankly, McNally, I'd love to get us out of here—right now. For one thing, my boots are undoubtedly staked out over there somewhere, waiting for me to get my brains splattered claiming them. I've got no desire to walk almost five miles barefoot. I'm not sure I'd make it."

McNally's face seemed to light up the gloom. "Does this mean you're gonna ask for exfiltration?"

"That's what's been worrying me. I'm pretty sure they've got a couple of men on the LZ, and that's the only way out. On the other hand, they don't know where the exfiltration zone is."

"Goddammit, sir, they've got our map! If we take all that time to get there, with you bootless and all, they'll have the whole goddam North Vietnamese Army waiting for us!"

"Now, wait. We don't *know* that they have the map, but we do know they know the original LZ. Playing the odds—"

"The hell with the odds, sir! Call 'em in! If we can't beat off this little force and get to the chopper, *then* we can still go for the pickup point. If we do it your way, we're dead for sure."

"Well, maybe that's what being an officer is all about, McNally. I'd say the odds are with my way—and we still have the mission, too."

"*That's* what it is!" the other spat. "You're gonna turn silver if you get us all killed and your feet ate off."

"No matter what you think," Savage replied, his voice even but touched with ice, "we'll play it my way. Go tell the men—and bring the radio back up here."

McNally turned with a snarl and returned to the others. Savage tried to make out their conversation while appearing unconcerned; he found it impossible to do either.

After three or four minutes he moved back to them,

every move painful from the legion of bites on his feet. The men watched him approach, looking very much like little boys in a dentist's waiting room—knowing something very unpleasant was coming. Knowing, too, that it was unavoidable.

"Well?" he said softly, standing in front of them, disregarding the risk a target of his size would represent. In those few short minutes he had resolved himself to dying, if need be, to keep the team together. He was somewhat surprised at himself, for he'd never been a particularly brave man, although always something of an idealistic one. But he had always had one hell of a temper.

"Who's got the radio?" he asked.

One of the others, a mousy little fellow who looked as if he was out of a New York street gang, reached around and pulled it out of the pack. McNally nodded and the little man put it down.

"We talked it over, Lieutenant. You ain't gonna send that message. You're gonna tell 'em to come and get us."

"The hell I am. This is a pretty shitty place to have a mutiny, McNally."

"We're all short-timers, sir. This thing's been a botch from the beginning, and I, for one, ain't gonna get killed this close to goin' back to the world if I got a choice."

"The rest of you feel that way?" Savage asked, glaring at each man in turn.

None answered; most wouldn't look directly at him. As Savage stood there, he slowly unhooked the strap and took his knife out of its scabbard. No one seemed to have noticed.

"We're playing it *my* way, *General* McNally," he sneered, and as he said it he reached out and grabbed the tall blond NCO by the arm and pulled him over to his side.

The knife was at McNally's throat.

"Now what do we do, *General?"*

"You don't do nothin', Lieutenant," said a voice behind him.

He felt a rifle barrel in the small of his back. Turning

slowly, without losing his grip on McNally, he saw that the little man with the radio had slid behind him, and cursed himself for paying so much attention to his own slick moves that he'd missed the movement.

"You're not going to shoot me, boy," he said confidently. "You'd have Charley here in a minute—if all this hasn't brought him already."

He felt the pressure ease, but it was replaced in a second by a sharp point.

"I got a knife, too," the little man said softly. "It's my favorite weapon. They spent fifty thousand bucks teachin' me how to kill people better with it. Why don'tcha just let Jonny there go and drop the knife?"

Suddenly all the determination went out of him. In frustration he shoved McNally away violently and then tossed his blade aside. He continued to feel the pressure of the barrel as a hand reached over to his holster and drew out his service revolver.

"Now pick up the radio," McNally ordered him. "It's almost 0400. And any funny business, and you're dead and *I* talk to them."

He felt numb, distant somehow, as he picked up the radio and turned it on. Isn't it stupid, he thought—these men probably just saved my life by doing this. And for forcing me to do what I want most to do myself, I damn near have to be killed.

"I'll make the call," he said resignedly, his voice sounding odd to his ears.

There was a quiet drone overhead and the muted HT-1 radio came to life, very quietly and tinnily.

"This is Artichoke," it said. "Acknowledge."

"Go ahead, Artichoke, this is Grasshopper," Savage responded mechanically, feeling somehow foggy, as if in a dream.

"Roger, Grasshopper, we read you five-by. Go ahead with message."

"Scout map in enemy hands, one dead, heavy enemy concentration," Savage reported. "Impossible to make objective. Request exfiltration at original LZ."

"Affirmative, Grasshopper," responded the tinny voice. "Can you do it in eighteen?"

"Ah, roger, Artichoke, see you soon. Out."

"Artichoke out. Good luck."

The radio went dead. Everybody around it relaxed, even though the toughest part was yet to come.

"Satisfied?" Savage asked McNally, who nodded grimly. "Well, we have only eighteen minutes, so let's get over there. My feet are killing me."

Santori, the little man, took away the point and they started off toward the LZ. No one moved to help Savage or to give him back his weapons. They walked slowly, deliberately, in dead silence, eyes on what they could see of the trees and swamp, conscious that they must make no betraying sound, no matter how much they felt like running.

They didn't smell any *nuoc-mam* until they were on the edge of the LZ. The sky had lightened considerably and they could see the perimeters of the clearing. The smell was not very strong—probably only one or two men left as a long-shot rear guard.

They waited in tense silence, trying to spot the unseen watchers.

The chopper was right on time, and touched down without incident. Nobody was kidding himself, though: the hidden eyes watching them would wait for them to break into the clearing, then open up.

Santori made one of them, and gestured.

"Now!" McNally shouted and they all went full-speed for the chopper. Santori fired just before he lept but was running too hard to see the man he hit fall from his tree perch. An AK-47 opened on them from the opposite side of the clearing almost simultaneously.

Savage was pushed ahead by McNally and ran for the open bay only meters away. As he did, he felt a sharp explosion in his back and went down almost as he reached the chopper door. Strong hands pushed him into the bay and he heard others jump in behind him. The chopper lifted off, bullets striking its sides.

"How many hit?" McNally called over the engine noise.

"Lost Sam and Harry," Santori yelled. "And *him*. No big loss, though. Bullheaded sonovabitch. Look at him lyin' there, like a big ape, bleedin' his guts out.

"Yeah," someone else put in. "Sorta like one of them cavemen or somethin'. Ugliest bastard I've ever seen."

The object of the comments lay facedown in an ever-widening pool of blood. He felt like a ten-ton spider was on his back, all the legs having equal and monstrous weight. He couldn't move at all, not even groan.

"He ain't gonna make it," someone remarked, but the words were a million miles away. He couldn't think anymore, yet he felt as if his mind were perfectly clear. Shock dulled the pain to a mild discomfort, and something told him that he'd be dead before he *would* feel the full impact of the injury.

He didn't give a damn any longer.

He was conscious of someone bending over him, but he couldn't see who, nor did it seem to matter. Mentally and physically, he was totally paralyzed.

"Sorry, Savage," McNally's voice came softly from the fog in his ears, "but no way was I gonna let you throw any of us in the clink—particularly me."

No one else heard the comment, and Savage could do nothing with it. For Savage there were no longer sounds, or sights, or feelings, nor even the acrid smell of the chopper. He was alone in his own private world.

The official records of the United States Army state that Paul Carleton Savage, Second Lieutenant, USAR, died in action aboard a rescue helicopter as the result of hostile fire on or about 0430 on 29 July 1969.

The first time.

2

HE WAS NOT aware that he was dead. This, on the face of it, was normal, as it meant a complete absence of sensation and he had had no previous experience of that sort.

The terror on his back was gone, lifted slowly as vision had been blotted out; but this brought no surprise, no shock that it was gone. It had lifted slowly, accompanied by that slow fade of all sensation, like a candle being gradually extinguished by carbon dioxide.

There had come a blankness, an absence of all colors, even black and white. He had had nothing to compare it to; such a concept could exist only in theory in the world he had left.

Bit by bit, he became aware of subtle differences, of tangibles in the void. As with the void itself, he had no frame of reference—*awareness* that there were other things, perhaps (or maybe "others") all around him. But it was as if, having been struck totally blind, deaf, and dumb, vision was returning.

Yet he could "see" only in this new, undefinable way which, lacking words or frame of reference, he could only experience, not comprehend.

What the shit is this? he thought angrily.

He remembered. He remembered the mission, the mutiny. He remembered that he had been murdered, not shot by an enemy.

Murdered? No, that couldn't be right. He was still— Well, he *was,* still.

The horrible thought struck him that he was in a hospital somewhere, deaf, dumb, blind, insensitive to the world—a living vegetable imprisoned in the wrecked shell of his body. It terrified him. He tried to shake, to move, to reach out, to prove it wasn't so.

Nothing happened. He had nothing to reach out with, or to.

He tried merely to lower his chin to his chest, to make certain that it was there—and was terribly afraid that it was.

It wasn't. He had no head to move, no chest to touch.

Absorbed in these thoughts, he failed to notice that more and more "somethings" were filling in the void. And something else.

Now he noticed it.

Voices— No, not quite. Thoughts—like random thoughts collecting in his brain. Other people's thoughts.

Gradually it was becoming apparent to him that he was not alone at all—that at least some of these other presences, perhaps a large number of them, were in fact other people. Some made no sense at all, but others radiated identifiable symbol connections. Many, most in fact, seemed to radiate the same panic that he had undergone only moments—hours?—before. A few were calm, resigned, or even expectant. Many were hopelessly insane.

Babblebabblebabblebabblebabblebabblebabblebabble-babblebabble . . .

It rushed in at him like a living force, exploding inside his mind. He fought furiously for control, taken offguard by the sudden attack, but the sea of thoughts came on, like giant waves, each greater than the one before. He tried to concentrate, tried to drive them off, stem the tide. No matter what happened, he had to lock them out, keep them away!

I am Paul Carleton Savage, Second Lieutenant, U.S. Army, serial number 214-44-1430AR. I am Paul Carleton Savage, Second Lieutenant, U.S. Army, serial number—

Babblebabblebabblebabblebabblebabblebabblebabble-babblebabbleBABBLEBABBLEBABBLE—

I am Paul Carleton Savage, Second Lieutenant, U.S. Army, serial—

BABBLEBABBLEBABBLEBABBLEBABBLEBABBLEBABBLE-BABBLEBABBLEBABBLEBABBLEBABBLEBABBLE—

A face formed dimly in his mind, laughing at him, mocking him. It said, "BABBLEBABBLEBABBLEBABBLE-BABBLEBABBLEBABBLEBABBLEBABBLEBABBLEBABBLE . . ." It poured out with terrible force in a thousand tongues, ten thousand—all different, all speaking at once of different things, running the entire emotional range. It was a deadly face.

"BABBLEBABBLEBABBLEBABBLEBABBLEBABBLEBAB-BLEBABBLEBABBLEBABBLEBABBLE . . ."

It was McNally's face.

Laughing, mocking, spewing out madness, it floated, weaved, and taunted him. An overpowering, unreasoning hatred welled up within him. *Not this time!* he tried to scream at it. *Not again! You will not destroy me again! Not again! You hear? You understand? You Will Not Destroy Me! You hear me, you bastard?*

BASTARD! Hear me? YOU. WILL. NOT. DESTROY. MY. MIND!

"Babblebabblebabblebabblebabblebabblebabblebabble . . ." it continued, in its madness; but the head had retreated as he attacked, the volume lessened markedly.

Hatred welled up in him; a fierce blast of hate shot out like a living thing from him and seemed to strike the bobbing figure.

It screamed and shrank.

He focused on the bobbing, weaving object. He faced it down as it continued to babble on in a chaos of random thoughts and tongues all at once; but it seemed to grow even more distant, hazier, so much so that even the torrent of thought that appeared to pour out of it was dampened to a quiet roar.

The thing bobbed and reeled. It swooped around, seeking an opening. It came at him from each side. It came at him from all sides at the same time. Focusing on it, he beat it back with the measure of his hate and pride, fighting it on a plane he could not really comprehend.

And now he was alone in the void once again, as if, in the midst of a cheering stadium, everyone but he was—in an instant—obliterated. One moment the enemy was there, all around him, on the attack. Then, in a time so sudden as to be immeasurable, everything was gone.

"That's pretty damned good," came a clear, sharp voice in his mind. "Who the hell's McNally, anyway?"

He would have jerked around if he'd had anything to do it with.

"Who? What—?" he tried to vocalize.

There was a chuckle. "Don't bother trying to talk. As you've figured out, you've got nothing left to vocalize with. Just *think* what you want to say and I'll pick it up."

Some of the intense emotion with which he had fought the thing was still in him. "Just who the hell are you?" he lashed out at the voice. "And what the hell is going on here?"

The Voice chuckled again. "Well, to answer the second question first, you're dead, of course. The enormous rush of thoughts you picked up were from the other—er—souls who died at the same moment. They'll come back, you know, when I let them."

Savage felt the lingering terror return. Somehow he could accept being dead, but not the continual battle he had just been through. Not *forever.*

"No," said the Voice, apparently hearing even those thoughts not directed to it, "not forever. You'll lose, eventually. Everybody does. Your self will crumble into that mass, which gets denser and denser as you naturally gravitate to those who've gone before—and are joined by those who've come after. Eventually your energy, your identity—your soul, if you will—all those thoughts and experiences that are *you,* will become one with all of *them*: a part of a collective mentality, a synthesis of mankind—in fact, of all living things that have ever existed or will exist on the Earth. That's the way things work."

"What are *you,* then?"

"Me? Well, you can think of me as God . . . an angel . . . or the Devil. Actually, I'm all of them—and none of them. For I'm not part of this synthesis but a product of a different one entirely."

"I—I really don't understand anything you're telling me."

As Savage said this, he was aware that, the longer he stalled, the longer he avoided the fate spelled out for him. The isolation in which he presently found himself was caused by the Voice, and could just as easily be lifted. He tried to imagine the horror he had fought—only ten times (a hundred, or a billion, perhaps?) more powerful. The Voice was right. He couldn't stand *that* off very long.

"What's happening to you is part of a process of nature as normal as the birth and death of a star, or the falling of leaves," the Voice explained in a tone reminiscent of a lecturing college professor. "It is as universal as the laws of motion, or gravity, or thermodynamics. Ultimately, the Synthesis produces a massive collective intelligence of enormous power—the collective power of God, as you might comprehend Him. Not all get to this point. Most races die out too soon, or external factors intervene. For some reason, no two worlds' maturity periods ever overlap."

"So what has this to do with you?"

"My race has passed to yet a higher synthesis, which even I cannot fathom. Only two individuals of the race are left, each incomplete, each weak in comparison with the whole. Both of us are driven to our duty, which must be fulfilled before we can join our people."

"Which is?"

"To ensure that the next synthesis occurs in time to stop the chaos that threatens always from without! To perpetuate, to keep the wheels of nature moving smoothly!"

"But what has all this to do with me, now?" asked Savage, puzzled.

"My brother is a part of me. We are a product of the same synthesis. Yet, it has been a long time, and without the greater synthesis to support us, we have devolved. We have become parasitic, material, and, as we have continued our separate lives, quite different personalities." The Voice became grim. "There is a war going on, Savage, and I am looking for volunteers."

Savage's mind whirled. Had the circumstances been any less bizarre, he would have dismissed all this as madness. Perhaps it was—he hadn't considered that.

The Voice interrupted his thoughts.

"The world lies below you, Savage—and above, and all around. It's your world and your destiny, and you shouldn't make light of it. We were a glorious people, Savage—and well yours might be, too. To be a part of that is the greatest glory that anyone can ever experience. We have *that* in common, my brother and I—we have both been at the pinnacle, in the company of, and part of, God—though we have fallen and are forever denied that again. We are both in Hell."

"So what do you offer me if I refuse that Earthly destiny?" Savage asked, knowing he would take any offer— and knowing the Voice knew it, too.

"You can't go to Hell, Savage, because you've never been in Paradise. The nature of what I shall do is such that you will be denied both. You will be forever in Limbo, never knowing any other experience, damned but never really knowing how much so. You would be condemned to live forever, and, as you will someday know, that is a *true* form of damnation."

Savage felt excitement well up inside of him. Condemned to live forever. But to *live!* To get out of *this!* And yet—Faust must have felt the same, and the Devil was the Father of Lies.

"What will I owe you in exchange?" he asked warily.

"Service—for as long as I might require it. I was attracted to you, as to the others I have recruited and will recruit, by the strength of your mind and of your will. By the force of the hatred that allowed you your victory, however temporary, over those that lately sought to consume you.

"While we have talked, I have taken a readout of your mind, your past, your personality and potential. You are certainly one of the men I need to aid me. You are a soldier. You were once a detective, before you were activated from your reserve unit. You are strong—far stronger than you know—and you are dangerous. I will realize those things you did not even know you possessed, and I will make you even stronger. And yours might—*might*—be the mission that wins the war. There are others like you as well, many others. But—I deny the glory of death to no man, for I could not do so even if I could guarantee his loyalty. The choice must be yours and freely made. Beyond this place—in death—is every mind of world history, from the one who discovered fire to the latest genius to pass on—and Hitler, too, and Stalin, and Genghis Khan. You can be part of them and *their* mission. Or of mine. You alone must choose."

"You know."

"*Say it!*"

"I'll work for you. I will accept your offer and abide by it."

"Very well. Restoration is a difficult thing—and a limited one. I must work with what I have, and not with what once was. Your body lies now in a morgue in Saigon, awaiting embalming and shipment to the United States. I can rearrange the molecules properly to make you live again, none the worse for wear—indeed, better than before—but I can work only with what I *have*. I do know where restoration can be done, and we'll get you there in due time."

"What are you talking about?" Savage asked nervously.

"McNally put a single M-16 bullet into your upper back, which shattered just about every bone in your torso. Child's play. It's a repair problem only. But the enemy sniper got you *after* that. Your right hand is still in the jungles of Area Five-C."

Savage paused for a moment. "So you can make me whole with what I've still got, but you can't regrow the hand."

"That's about it. Although, of course, after I'm through with you, should you lose the other one, it'll come back. Later on, I'll get you to a place of master biologists many light-years from here, where the hand can be replaced in a moment . . . But the injury will answer some questions, albeit weakly, about your recovery—and it'll get you out of the Army and home, where I need you."

"Okay I think I can live with it," Savage told the Voice, and somehow the remark sounded flip and funny—which it wasn't at all.

I can live with it, he had said. Or not live without it . . .

"Very well. It is done. The process is already in motion, and I have other things to attend to. I will contact you when you are ready."

"But how will I know you?" Savage asked, almost calling after the Voice. "To whom will I go?" He almost said: "To whom do I belong?"

"I call myself The Hunter, for that's as good as any, more descriptive of what I am and far less enigmatic than my brother's name, The Bromgrev, the meaning for which has escaped everyone. The Savage will recognize the Hunter: there is destiny in those linked names." The Voice paused for a second, then concluded, "It is ended. I shall see you in time."

Savage was alone once again, but now there was a change. He sensed that he was returning, going *back*, even though the term had no meaning. He also sensed the others, rising from their incubators and going to join this new, metamorphosed creature he knew surrounded him.

His world picture had been drastically changed. The Earth was one of many planets, perhaps millions, circling their suns, incubating components for the truly superior evolutionary creature of each world. Mystics through the ages had glimpses of the truth, but they could not comprehend—or did not want to comprehend—and misinterpreted what they had seen.

But there were still holes. Just what did these—gods—do? If the metamorphosis occurred repeatedly in nature, it was necessary to survival. But whose? And against what did it guard?

He would have time to ask the right questions now, he mused. All the time in the world.

There was light, but everything was blurry. He ached like hell, his right arm throbbing as he had never known before, his every cell screaming at what had been done.

He blinked repeatedly, and the scene came into focus, along with the fetid smells of the dead and its grisly contents.

He was in a human meat locker, stored with the rest of the dead until they could be prepared and shipped home by Graves Registration.

His lips felt dry and cracked, and he could not seem to generate any saliva in his mouth. Even so, he managed some movement, painful though it was—and managed to croak out one word in such a way that, if any had been able to hear in that terrible room, there would be no mistaking its intent.

"McNally," he said.

3

THE PAIN SUBSIDED gradually.

He was suddenly aware of the cold, and he struggled to get up. A stabbing pain went through him as he tried to rise by balancing himself on his right hand, and he fell off the little table on which he lay and went sprawling onto the floor. Pain tore through his back, rump, and the underside of his left arm. He shook his head violently from side to side to clear it, and looked at his left arm.

Parts of the flesh had been ripped away where his newly warmed body had touched the cold metal table. He stared at the damaged area for a little while. He couldn't take his eyes off it.

Slowly, methodically, and visibly, the skin was regrowing over the injured area. It reminded him somewhat of the stop-action photography of a plant opening and closing. As the skin repaired itself, the pain subsided, then vanished completely. Soon only a few flecks of dried blood remained to show that any damage had ever been done.

His back and rump no longer hurt, either.

So that was how it would be.

A sudden, sharp, incredibly intense pain struck him in the middle of his back, so severe and unexpected that he cried out in agony. Then, just as suddenly, it was gone. He heard a tiny noise of something hard striking the floor.

He looked down and stared at it.

It was a jagged, spent M-16 bullet.

Reaching out with his right hand, he was intending to pick it up and for the first time became fully conscious that all was *not* the same.

Like his arm and backside, the skin had grown over the area where his right hand had been. Only it wasn't there—his hand. Merely an ugly-looking stump, ending almost exactly at the wrist.

He exhaled, his breath causing tiny crystals to form in the air. The Hunter had said he could be taken to a place where he might get a new hand—no, *grow* a new hand, he'd said. Until then, it was something that could be lived with.

He got up and threaded his way through the stacks of bodies on their metal shelves until he reached the door. A thermometer at its side read 25°F. He felt the bitter cold, but it didn't seem to be lethal, just uncomfortable. His internal body heat, he realized suddenly, was being

kept at a high level. Where did the energy come from?
If from himself, it would be bound to do damage at
some later time—or run out.

This was Power. For the first time, he realized the
enormity of the forces with which he had allied himself.

He found the edge of a wheeled cart and sat down to
think for a minute.

The word "alien" came to mind—not the green-
scaled monsters of the science-fiction covers, but "alien" in its purest form. As rational, conversational, and
human as the Voice had sounded, it was none of these.

*"You can think of me as God . . . an angel . . . or
the Devil,"* this thing called The Hunter had said. But it
had admitted to having far less than God's powers or
omnipotence, and angels were surrogate humans. The
Devil had always been the most human of all.

And God created Man in His own image . . .

Alien.

He must remember that, always.

He decided to get out from among the corpses, if he
could. He got up and examined the door, not even noticing the same flesh-tearing sensation when he rose. He
knew now that it would go away.

The door had a bright red handle and there had at
one time been a decal superscription next to it in typical
military fashion, but the wording had long since worn
away. He pulled down on the handle. The door swung
open and he fell out into the hallway, a blast of warmth
bathing him.

A young soldier was walking up the hallway with a
sheaf of papers in his hand as Savage plunged out the
door and collapsed, half in and half out of the locker.

The soldier suddenly stiffened as if shot. He stared at
the apparition that had just come plunging out of the
dead locker at him. His eyes were wide, staring.

"Oh my God!" he said, and screamed for help.

Men poured out of nearby labs and offices and ran
down toward Savage and the still-immobile soldier.

Savage felt suddenly sick, dizzy, cold, in pain—
miserable. He groaned and passed out, oblivious to the
hands turning him over, lifting him up, and carrying
him to the examining table of a nearby autopsy room.

He passed into a deep, dreamless, almost coma-like sleep.

He heard the sound of a radio playing acid rock. The electric guitars seemed to be keeping time with the pounding in his head. He turned and moaned in agony.

"Hey! Doc! I think he's coming around!" someone yelled, and there was the sound of feet running up a tiled hallway toward his room.

For a few seconds, he thought he'd had the damnedest nightmare in all creation.

He opened his eyes to a typical gray-and-white military hospital room. Quickly, he lifted his right arm up and out in front of him.

The hand was still gone.

A young man in medical whites entered, followed by a similar man with sergeant's stripes on his white sleeves. The first man came over and stood by Savage's bed, looking at him. The sterile hospital smell, ever-present, was suddenly permeated with the odor of foul sweat and bad tobacco. The doctor had obviously had a bad night.

"Are you awake?" the doctor asked pleasantly. "Can you hear me?" He was almost drowned out by the radio playing in the next room. Realizing this, he turned to the medic and said, "Get them to shut that damned thing off, will you?"

The medic disappeared and soon they heard loud talking in an angry, argumentative tone, muffled by the walls and the radio. Then all was peace and quiet, except for some loud cursing from next door.

The doctor had not taken his eyes off Savage since he'd entered the room. Savage almost managed to focus on the doctor; he still felt lousy, which, if memory served, wasn't supposed to be in the script.

"Shee-it," he managed, more to himself than to the doctor, who smiled brightly at the comment. Savage noted that the two of him were merging more and more into one distinct figure.

"Can you hear me?" the doctor repeated softly.

Savage felt as if his mouth was full of cotton. He exercised his jaws and tongue, trying to get some moisture going.

"Yeah, I hear you, Doc," he croaked at last.

"Do you remember your name?" the doctor prodded. "Can you recall things about yourself?"

"Yeah . . . sure. Paul Carleton Savage, Second Lieutenant, U.S. Army, *et cetera, et cetera.* What the hell happened, Doc?"

The other man shook his head.

"I wish we knew. You are a medical impossibility, shot in the back and hand. The hand isn't serious, but the back— Jesus, man, you got scars a million miles long back there! I wasn't here when they brought you in last week, but I know all the reports said 'dead and gone.' "

"Well I— Did you say *last week?*"

The doctor nodded. "Oh, you were only in the meat locker for a few hours—fortunately, or the cold would've finished you. But you've been in a coma for over eight days. I wasn't sure if you were ever going to come out of it."

Something in the back of Savage's mind nagged at him. Only a few hours to bargain for a man's soul and accomplish a complete resurrection, yet eight days out cold afterward. Why? Instant healing, but eight days out and feeling lousy.

What might Hunter have done to him that took eight days?

"Savage? You O.K.?" the doctor asked, concerned about his patient's sudden lapse into silence and inattention.

Savage shook himself free of such thinking—at least for the time being.

"Oh, yeah, sure . . . Doc. Just thinking. It's not every day you come back from the dead . . ."

"That's an understatement. While you were out, I took every X-ray and did every test imagined—and a few I thought up. The bullet seems to have missed just about everything—except for one of only two or three spots in the whole torso where an AK-47 can hit and do so little internal damage. One chance in a billion. Almost no serious internal disruption—and the few that were there we cleared up in a three-hour operation. No complications. And that nice scar, of course."

Nice touch, that, Savage reflected. Just enough crumbs for them to make up their own explanation of how he survived. Plant a few clues and let the ignorant write their own script.

"One thing bothers me, though," the doctor continued. "I couldn't find that damned bullet! It's as if it dissolved in the body!"

Savage managed a shrug. "Well, I can't explain things if you can't, Doc. I'm just glad to be alive. Any other problems?"

"Nothing much—except the hand, of course. And some lingering effects of the cold you took for those hours. I'll keep you for a few weeks for tests and observations. Then we'll get you out of here and back home with an artificial hand."

He turned to go.

"Hey, Doc!" Savage called after him. "Where's 'here'?"

"Oh, yeah, that's right. You're in Markland Hospital in the Philippines."

The sergeant came back in and sat back down in his chair.

"You my watchdog?" Savage asked him.

The medic shrugged and looked sheepish. "Just part of the job," he replied.

"What's your name?" Savage asked conversationally.

"Cohen, sir."

"Well, Sergeant Cohen, relax and don't worry about me. Do you play gin?"

"I think I've played it once or twice," the sergeant replied playfully. "Maybe I can dig up some cards in a day or so."

"You do that, Sergeant, and I'll see if I can beat you left-handed."

He realized with a start that he felt really good. All of the dismal miseries were gone.

He had never felt better in his life. Somehow he suspected that the reappearance of a doctor would bring back just enough of them.

Who or whatever was looking over him was making certain that this medical marvel was convincing.

It had been almost four weeks since Paul Savage was murdered and the dead man was feeling fine. The tests had gone predictably; he'd had little trouble walking after the first time or two; and he was getting used to doing things with his left hand, although writing still came hard.

In fact, his progress had been so good that they had sent a man around during the second week to measure his stump and check his muscle placement and development. A day or two after that, they'd fitted him with a mechanical claw-like appendage and given him various exercises to increase his proficiency in its use and build up the necessary muscle coordination to use it. As he'd already read seven novels and now owed Cohen $1,-428.63 from playing gin, he was ripe for something else and spent almost every waking moment practicing. The therapists were amazed at his progress. By the start of the fourth week, he was using the metal claw almost as if he had been born with it.

His progress amazed him, too. Never in his life had he been able to concentrate so well, think so clearly, be so much in command of his entire body. He had always been far above most other people in intelligence, but now he found that he was able to put his potential to its fullest use.

Slowly, he began to think of himself as no longer quite human. Oh, same form, same memories. But subtly altered, a fine machine that was *of* the man but not the man himself.

Hunter had said something about being able to play games with his molecular structure. It was becoming apparent that there was more to it than that. He had been taken apart and redesigned—*engineered*.

For whom?

For what?

He began to wonder when he would be drafted. They seemed in no hurry.

On his thirty-fourth day after the resurrection, they pronounced him fit enough to go home. It was only when he went down to the out-processing section at the airport that it occurred to him that McNally and the rest of the squad were short-timers. A couple of bottles of booze and a session with a couple of personnel men he knew got him access to the files, and a little "officious" act scared the private in Records into punching the two names he'd pulled into the computer.

The clerk was a nervous little man who obviously hadn't been out of his air-conditioned office since reaching the Far East. Savage presented an imposing figure looming over the little private at his big console, the lieutenant's reflection in the CRT glass an intimidating reminder of himself.

Savage was over six feet, and powerfully built. His face was of almost the idealized gangster of the 1920s: rough, pock-marked from a severe adolescent bout with acne, and a long scar down his right cheek. His lips formed an almost permanent sneer due to a corrective hairlip operation when he was a baby, and his crooked boxer's nose added a further sinister touch. His bushy eyebrows were gray in color, like his hair, although he was barely thirty; and they met at the bridge of his nose. He looked more like a Neanderthal than anything else, and the extreme hairiness of his body had always made him the object of derision by his peers as a youth.

"Yaa! Yaa! Ape man!"

His cold, steely-blue eyes glared as the clerk punched in the names:

MC NALLY, JON OR JOHN F X
SANTORI, JOSEPH ANTONIO

The typewriter clattered on the output console and the clerk reached over and tore off the sheet, handing it to Savage.

SANTORI, JOSEPH ANTONIO, SP4, ASSIGNED FT ORD CA EFF 19 OCT 69
MC NALLY, JON OR JOHN, NO RECORD THIS THEATRE

"What the hell does it mean, 'No Record'?" snarled Savage. "I thought you had everybody in 'Nam in this thing!"

The computer operator looked apologetic and apoplexic at the same time. "I dunno, sir. Only thing I can figure is that you have something wrong in the input—name, serial number, or whatever."

"No, nothing's wrong," Savage growled. "I got my squad assignment sheet and I gave you McNally."

The little computer operator just sighed. He was always more comfortable with his machines than with people, and this was a perfect example of why.

"Look, sir, I can give you a printout on every McNally that's ever been to 'Nam, even on temporary duty. Also *Mac*Nally and any other variations you like. But the computer says that the person you're looking for just doesn't exist."

"All right, do that, then. I'm due to go home on Wednesday, and I'll be discharged soon after that. I want to know where that guy is before I leave."

The little man sighed and turned back to his console. In a few seconds, the printer typed out the information requested. Savage tore it off eagerly and scanned the sheet. About forty names were on the sheet, which also included their serial numbers, military specialty codes, assignments, and date of out-processing if they were gone.

None of them came close to McNally in the particulars. He simply wasn't in that computer.

Savage whirled angrily around and stalked out of the records center.

By the time he had hit the street and the hot, garbage-odored air of the Orient hit him, he'd calmed down enough to think it out.

The pincers at the end of his right arm took a cigarette pack out of his breast pocket. Almost as if he had always had the claw, he removed a cigarette and, with the lighter in his left hand, lit up and inhaled deeply. Oblivious to the heat, odors, and sounds all around him, he reviewed what he knew.

(1) McNally was real.

(2) McNally had been assigned to the mission and had gone on it.

(3) McNally had gotten out alive and had gotten back to the firebase.

(4) The Army said he didn't exist.

All of which meant that either the Army was lying or, for some reason, McNally was actually unknown to them. The former seemed the more likely, but—for what reason?

A strange thought hit him—and was gone, dismissed from his mind as too ridiculous to dwell on. And yet it sat in a dark corner and would not quite go away.

Did Hunter pick his recruits first, then murder them?

It seemed impossible. Incredible.

And yet Hunter had *known* Savage was dead, known to the split second when to come in, when to shield, when to make the offer . . .

Was Hunter that powerful? That devious? It implied an enormous temporal power on Earth as well. Things would have had to be arranged.

There were other possibilities. There *had* to be other possibilities.

Santori might know.

4

JOE SANTORI HAD had a good night. Tomorrow he was to be discharged from the Army, still whole and with nothing but three bitter years to show for it. *Out,* man! The barracks had thrown one hell of a party for him, and Christina hadn't just been a good screw, she was a superb *Italian* screw that almost made him wish he had a couple more weeks in the area. He was also, at this point, quite high, as he returned to the barracks from her apartment.

As he walked across the quad, he was whistling an

inane little song and his mind was a million miles from armies, barracks, and anything else less pleasant.

A man was leaning against the lamp post next to the barracks door but Santori paid little attention to him, taking him for one of the boys. As he drew closer, however, the figure took on a ghostly, shadowy shape and flicked a cigarette into the darkness, showering sparks. There was something grotesque about the man, Santori thought—sort of gorilla-like, yet oddly familiar . . .

As he approached to within a few yards of the figure, it spoke to him.

"Hello, Joe," came an oddly familiar yet unplaceable voice, a deep, rich, distinctive bass that, once heard, was never forgotten. "Celebrating?"

"Yeah, man," Santori replied. "It's all over now."

"I agree, Joe, but not for the reasons you think. Remember me, Joe?"

With that, the figure stepped full into the baleful half-light of the quad lamp posts.

Santori could never have forgotten the scarred face and huge, animal-like body he saw, His mouth flew open and he stepped back involuntarily and almost automatically made the sign of the cross. He continued to back away as the figure advanced.

"Don't run, Joe. It won't do you any good to run," said Paul Carleton Savage icily. "There's no hole deep enough for you to crawl into."

"But—but—you're dead! I saw—" Santori stammered.

"Yeah, Joe, I'm dead. You saw it. You saw McNally kill me, didn't you?"

"*I*—*I* never planned on killin' you, Savage," he protested. "I never thought the sonovabitch would *kill* you!"

"But I *was* murdered, Joe," commented the other, matter-of-factly, "and you are what the law calls an accessory."

Images of the quad, of places to run, of people to run to, sped through Santori's brain. But where can you run from the dead? he asked himself. Now, deep in the back of his brain, Joe Santori's survival self tried to shout out a fact, a very important fact. His right arm! He's got a claw hand! his mind exulted. And that meant—

All the terror suddenly lifted, leaving him drained and angry. "You ain't dead, Savage," he accused the looming figure. "Ghosts don't have no machine parts. McNally only got your hand!"

Savage shook his head slowly from side to side. "You're right—and wrong, too. I'm no ghost, Joe—but McNally got me square in the back with that shot. *And I want him for that.*"

"Well, go and find him, then. You know I didn't have nothin' to do with shootin' you."

"That's what I have to ask you about, Joe. You see, the Army says McNally never existed."

"The hell he didn't!"

"Right. Tell me what you know about McNally, Joe, and our business—yours and mine—will be finished," Savage coaxed soothingly.

"You ain't gonna press charges?"

"No way, Joe. I'm not even in anymore. Tell me about McNally, Joe, and I promise you no one will ever know what happened—then or now."

They were close together; the little corporal could smell stale tobacco and the remains of a pizza on the other's breath. It was somehow reassuring. There just wasn't any way Savage could be here—but there'd always been stories of crazy things like this.

"Can't tell you much about him, Lieutenant," Santori began. "None of us were regulars with each other, you know. We seemed to be just picked up if we was available, regardless of unit. Only three of us were from the same outfit. McNally was an add-on, like you. First time I ever saw him was during the mission briefing."

"You talked, though. Did he say anything about himself—prior service, names, wife, anything?"

Santori shook his head. "Nothin'. He talked all the time about how crappy it was to get picked for the mission, how we was all short-timers and all."

"You were? *All* short-timers?" The little man nodded affirmatively. "Everybody but me," Savage mused, more to himself than to Santori. "And you say McNally kept this up?"

"Yeah. Christ, Lieutenant, we was all spooked and sure we was all dead men by the time we hit the LZ."

"What about after? What happened then?"

"Well, McNally made his report in debriefing, then we both went over to the mess and had some coffee. He didn't talk much then. Well, hell, you know, after what happened and all. Just told me to stick to the story and all. Pretty soon this small chopper puts down and he says good-bye and goes over and gets in it. Zow, they're gone! Last I saw of him. I thought it was pretty weird at the time, but haven't thought about it since. Never saw or heard about him again. One thing bugged me at the time and keeps buggin' me, though."

"What's that?" Savage prompted.

"Well, if he was so set on killin' you, how come he pushes your body *into* the chopper bay instead of out of the way? I mean, if you'd rotted you couldn'ta come round like you did and maybe show the bullet was a frag."

Savage's eyes seemed to glow in the darkness. "He did *what?*"

"Pushed ya in, he did. A couple of the boys saw this, and figurin' McNally had a change of heart or somethin' they pulled you all the way in. If it hadn'ta been for McNally, you'd be worm bait in the 'Nam jungle right now."

Savage stood for almost a minute in total silence, lost in thought. Then, deep inside, something seemed to snap. His head, which had started to droop, shot up, and a glazed look was in his eyes.

"Tell me something, Joe," he said very quietly, without a trace of emotion. "That time you stuck that knife into my back—would you have used it on me if I hadn't given in?"

Santori thought for a moment, then shrugged. "Hell, I really don't know. I wasn't gonna walk any five miles through Charley country."

"Thanks, Joe," Savage acknowledged. "I think it's time we parted company."

With that, the big man reached out and grabbed the little man in a bear hug. Santori had not survived the streets of Newark to be taken that easily. Groaning, straining for breath, he still managed to get his pocket-knife out and stab the larger man in the abdomen. Savage cried out in shock and pain and momentarily released his grip. Before he could recover, Santori was back at him, stabbing him repeatedly. In shock, Savage lost his balance and dropped to the ground. Santori efficiently cut his throat, and blood spurted all around.

The victor sat down on the grassy plot between the barracks getting his breath back.

Suddenly it occurred to him that Savage had survived worse, and he reached over and checked the fallen man's pulse, even though blood still flowed and the body's eyes were open and glazed. Nothing. Savage, he thought with satisfaction, was finally dead.

He slowly rose and walked unsteadily to the barracks door. No one had heard. They would find the lieutenant in the morning, of course—but he would ditch the knife and burn the clothes. Tomorrow he'd be out of here, and there was nothing but that one bastard patrol to connect him to—

"It's not that easy, Joe. You should have known that," came a voice behind him, and he whirled suddenly around.

Savage struck him with the metal right hand, in the Adam's apple. Joe Santori died, eyes wide in disbelief.

Except for some blood on his clothes, there wasn't a mark on his killer.

Savage had barely gotten back to his motel room when his telephone started ringing. Since he had taken a great deal of care to make certain nobody knew he was there, his first thought was that it was the desk, on some matter. That anyone had connected Santori with "Robert Sanderson" in a motel forty miles away hardly even occurred to him.

He picked up the phone and said, "Hello?"

"Now that you've tended to personal business, Savage, are you ready to go to work?" a familiar voice asked cynically.

Savage almost dropped the phone. Although he'd never actually physically heard the voice before, there was no doubting who it was.

"Go ahead, Hunter," he said dryly.

"Okay," The Hunter began cheerfully. "First, you go into town and find P.O. Box 716. The combination's A–B, D–E, B–C. There'll be an envelope with some front money, an address, and directions from Dulles to your new office."

"Dulles?"

"Yeah. You're a Washingtonian now, son. Be there sometime tomorrow, won't you?"

"How are you so sure this package is there?" Savage asked skeptically. Hunter was just so *damned* sure of himself.

"Why, because I mailed it almost two weeks ago, of course," came the reply.

Savage felt that he was made of glass. "How long ago did you rent that box?" he asked.

"One of my people rented it—let's see—two days after you were killed would be about right. Why?"

"How the hell did you know I'd be here—in this town rather than another?" demanded Savage.

If voices could shrug, this one did. "Hell, man, I know how your mind works better than you do. If it makes you feel any better, it took my men the better part of a day to find the motel, though. But, you're kind of conspicuous, you know, once somebody looking for you has your general area."

"I don't think I like being so transparent," Savage commented. "Makes me nervous."

The voice chuckled. "Savage, old buddy, as you're going to find out, you're one of the *least* transparent beings in the entire galaxy."

Savage mulled the remark but didn't reply.

"Well," Hunter continued, "I have other things to do. I'll see you in person in Washington. Want that box and combination again?"

"I got it," Savage replied. "I'll be there."

He heard a click and the line was dead.

Savage slowly undressed and placed all the torn and bloody clothing in a laundry bag. He'd dispose of it tomorrow. No problem, really. He was certain that even if there had been forty witnesses to the killing, Hunter would have him free in no time.

He felt suddenly very tired, and flopped nude on the bed.

As he lay there in the darkness, he thought about the night's work. The McNally business still didn't make sense and he didn't dwell on it, but he was aware of a change within himself.

He had killed a man in cold blood in such a way that the other man hadn't had a prayer. One can't murder The Flying Dutchman. And he found it curious that he felt no guilt, no pangs of conscience, no remorse—no more than if he'd swatted a fly.

He had given the enemy better than that . . .

5

THE BOX CONTAINED a current airline schedule of Washington flights, a Xerox copy of directions on getting to an address on 16th Street in that city, and a certified check for $1,000. It was the latter that particularly interested him—it was drawn to the account of the SHW Tool & Die Company.

Steve Wade's parent company.

Wade was something of a legend among the powerful, although few people in the general public had ever heard of him. He kept out of the limelight, though not to the extent of a Howard Hughes. Wade was just not an outgoing person beyond his business, and he rarely if ever socialized. He was still, however, accessible—and he had been hauled up a few times by various congressional committees for meddling in some pricing schemes and making some questionable international trade deals. One national credit card magazine had profiled him as a "mover" and "shaker." Nobody really knew what he was worth, but his background had been profiled rather well in that article.

The son of middle-class parents, he had been an undistinguished scholar and a somewhat introverted youth.

Except for a small bald spot and obviously bad teeth, he'd kept his looks through the years—Savage could remember the tall but pudgy figure, perennially about twenty-five, peering out of the magazine's pages. After an unremarkable college career, he had finally graduated with a degree in political science and gone to work as a junior clerk in the State Department. Then, abruptly, he'd quit his job, borrowed capital from the wealthy parents of an old school friend, and started playing the stock market—with phenomenal results.

In bullish times, he had always seemed to pick the $5 stocks that zoomed to $45 in a matter of weeks, then always sold the day *before* they dropped. Bearish times found him making more killings selling just the right things short. As he'd been a failure at math in school and had, according to all reports, never been seen near a copy of the *Wall Street Journal* until his sudden plunge into the financial world, this was considered pretty unusual. Unusual, hell! It was the stuff of pulp fiction!

That Wade was very rich was beyond question—one of the richest in the United States, perhaps the world. But unglamorous, somewhat stuffy, never eccentric or colorful, and therefore of little interest in an age of men like Getty, Hughes, Onassis, and the like.

This explained a lot, particularly Wade's sudden rise from mediocrity and obscurity. This was another Hunter operation beyond doubt—a very convenient way of financing almost anything behind an effective blind.

Or did the "H" in SHW stand for "Hunter"?

On an impulse, he called a local newspaper's financial editor and asked.

It stood for Harold, and Wade never used it.

Somehow this was reassuring.

The plane didn't get into Washington until almost 9 P.M. due to the time difference, but he flew into National Airport instead of Dulles and therefore was ahead of the game, landing almost in the city instead of forty miles away. Because of his sudden affluence, he decided against cheap ground transportation and rented a car for his trip into downtown Washington. It was years since he'd been there, and the modern office complexes of Crystal City near the airport looked alien to him. He got on route I-95 heading into the city.

The capital never seemed to change. It was still a gigantic slum, islands of fresh-looking picture-postcard government buildings and monuments standing alone on grassy spots like oases in a desert of seedy row houses and tenements. He recalled his first trip to D.C., years before, as well as his shock at how those wonderful pictures everyone sees were mirrored in fact only if viewed from the proper angle.

Sixteenth Street, however, was different. Leading from the White House north, 16th Street had been envisioned by Washington's erratic French designer, Pierre L'Enfant, as a broad boulevard of stately homes, mansions, and foreign embassies, and it remained pretty much this way.

The address he had was pretty far out, almost in the area of Walter Reed Army Hospital. It proved to be a stately home in the Georgian style up on a hill away from the street. It had, however, no driveway so he parked, with great difficulty, on a nearby side street and walked around to it. Although the house looked like a private residence, and had no signs or other indications that it was not, there was the feel of an office about it—the half-door, oversized mailbox, carefully manicured lawn, and freshly painted exterior seemed too artificial and too carefully maintained to be someone's home.

He rang the bell, and was answered by a buzzing sound from the door itself. Realizing it had an electric lock, he pushed open the door and confirmed his suspicions about the place.

A fairly good-looking red-headed receptionist sat just inside and he could see a waiting room and a series of closed doors going down a long hall. A large oak staircase led off to the right. The sounds of several typewriters clacking away confirmed that this was a working area.

But it was pretty damned busy and full-staffed for nighttime.

The receptionist glanced up, and he saw in her eyes the usual reaction of people when they first caught sight of him—women particularly. Sort of the way you'd look at the bearded lady or Jo-Jo the Dog-Faced Boy, if you met them on the street rather than in a sideshow: a mixture of fear, apprehension, and pity. He had almost learned to ignore it.

Notwithstanding her transparent reaction, she put on her best receptionist's plastic smile and cheery voice. "Yes?" she asked.

"Paul Savage," he replied. "I was told to report here as soon as I got into Washington."

"Oh, yes, Mr. Savage. Mr. Wade is expecting you. Go up the stairs and all the way back to the end of the hall."

He mumbled his thanks and climbed the stairs. The second level appeared to be the same as below, but at the end of the hall he saw a set of double doors marked CONFERENCE ROOM. He glimpsed activity in some of the offices as he proceeded down the hallway toward the room: busy secretaries typing reports, a key-punch room, and some computer terminals.

Hesitating before the large double doors for a second, he turned the ornate, old-fashioned handle and went in.

The room was elegantly furnished, in the manner of foreign embassies, with lush carpeting, velvety drapes, and, in the center, a long table of walnut or teak around which were placed about twenty very plush chairs. He noticed a door with frosted glass leading off, apparently to another office at the far end.

Closing the doors made the room completely sound-proof. He could hear nothing but the rustling of his own movements: in fact, he thought he could hear his heart-beat. Tired from his trip, and feeling somewhat impatient, he plopped into one of the chairs.

The far door opened after a few minutes and Stephen Wade stepped into the room, sat down in the chair opposite his, and took out a cigar. With a gesture he offered Savage one, but the big ex-soldier shook his head. Wade lit his and leaned back, a smile playing on his lips as he studied his newest employee.

"Glad to see you, Savage," he began pleasantly. "While we've talked, we haven't actually met."

Savage sat straight up in his chair. There was no doubt about it—this was the same man he had talked to on the telephone . . . and someplace else.

"Yes, I'm Hunter," Wade confirmed. He took the cigar out of his mouth and studied it. "You really ought to try one of these," he said. "Real Havana. You must have my money and connections to get them."

Savage folded his arms and studied the man. In his appearance, nothing whatsoever suggested that Wade was anything other than what he appeared to be.

"I suppose you have a lot of questions," Wade prompted.

"Well," Savage replied, "almost everything I can think of is a question. You, for instance."

Wade's eyebrows shot up. "Me? I've told you all that before, if you remember."

"But where's the *real* Stephen Wade?"

Wade took a drag on the cigar. "Gone. Dead. He died the moment I took his body, of course." He said this so conversationally, so matter-of-factly, that a chill went through Savage.

"Why so shocked?" Wade asked. "You just killed a man for no purpose at all except petty revenge. *I* kill someone every sixty years or so—for survival."

"Santori was different—" Savage started to protest, but Wade cut him off.

"How? He was no threat to you. He could do nothing to you, whereas you were a constant threat to him. On the other hand, *I* have to make a serious decision on who to kill—or nature would make the choice random. You see, I'm a parasite. Unpleasant word, that, but correct. When *you* died, your body stayed behind—but the sentience, the animator part of you, did not. This 'self'—the soul, if you will, although robbed of its religious connotations—is basically electrical. You, me, everyone and everything animate anywhere in the universe, are all creatures of pure energy. We incubate, grow, and learn in these shells of ours, then are freed from them to join that great synthesis we talked about.

It's not too surprising: nature is a story of *processes,* of evolution. This is just a part of it."

"But not you," Savage said flatly.

Wade sighed. "No, not me—not anymore, anyway. The process, you see, continues on beyond the synthesis. My people, well, *continued*—I have no idea where or how or to what. I hope to find out someday by eventually joining with the next race to reach that point. In the meantime, natural laws bind me, the same as you. Lacking the awesome power of my people, I cannot long sustain my true form and nature. I need a physical shell—a wall plug to keep me charged up. Sorry, best explanation I can give."

"So what's this place?" asked Savage, changing the subject.

"My Washington headquarters, of course. A handy place—world capitals are where the decisions are made. I have to know those decisions. Particularly here. I have to know, ahead of time, if my organization has been compromised in any way, or if the government's into anything of mine I don't want them to be. You see, my headquarters are close to the United States."

"Your corporate headquarters?"

"Hell, no! Not the petty empire of Stephen Wade! *My* headquarters! Remember, I said I was fighting a war?"

"Yeah, I remember—but it wasn't too clear. Something about your fighting your brother for control of the universe or something like that. I assumed—"

"You assumed wrongly!" Wade cut in sharply. "It's a real war, Savage—a shooting war. Just like the one you've been in, only on a much larger scale. Look, come with me."

With that, Wade got up and walked over to the door from which he had entered the room. Savage hesitated a moment, then he got up and followed him.

The door led not to an office but to a small alcove with an elevator door. Wade took a key from his pocket and turned the lock that served as the call button. The door slid open almost immediately and he and Savage entered.

Instead of the usual panel of floor buttons, the elevator had a keyboard that looked very much like that on a touch-tone phone or a calculator. Wade pointed to it.

"About four years ago, we finished this project. We moved part of the house away and excavated here—had a hell of a time explaining it to the D.C. zoning board. We finally convinced everyone it was a secret government agency operation. There are so many that nobody knows what's going on, anyway. It was even easier in Moscow.

"This shaft goes down about four hundred feet. It's honeycombed down there—rooms of all shapes and sizes, mostly filled with computers and other electronic gear, including much that this world hasn't invented yet. And may never invent." He punched out a five-digit combination. "Can't be too careful," Wade explained. "Each story below the house is reached only by one of the two elevators like this one—and to make the elevators work you have to know the codes for each floor. Punch anything wrong and you're trapped in the elevator, which takes you down to a very nice jail and security headquarters and locks. The codes are changed daily, of course. Not unbreakable, but good enough."

The elevator was moving as he spoke, dropping down into the depths beneath the Georgian-style house. Finally, the door opened and they walked out.

It was a huge room, with busy men and women scurrying about and machines clacking. The center of attraction, however, was a huge representation, perhaps thirty meters square, that covered an entire wall. In front of it was a long, curved table with banks of phones, television units, and computer consoles.

To Savage, it was a movie version of the pentagon Situation Room, but the display was not of the United States or even of the world. It was something out of an astronomy textbook.

Pictured in millions of tiny lights was a spiral galaxy.

Although basically white-lit, large areas toward the galactic center were red-lit—and the red zones seemed to be growing. A small area off to the "south" of the red was now blinking. Savage realized that the blinking sector was probably several light-years in diameter.

"This is the Washington War Room," Wade explained. "Similar ones exist in perhaps half a million or more spots in the galaxy—and I have four more here on Earth, including the really big one at Headquarters, which is about thirty times this size. You *walk* on that one."

"What do the colors represent?" Savage asked, fascinated.

"The red represents the area now under The Bromgrev's direct control. The blinking area is the one the computers predict will be the next to go—the old Fraskan Sector. It took him almost a century to conquer his first territory. Another fifty years or so to reach its present size. But he's got allies now, and a hell of an organization. He could probably take half the key planetary systems in the next six or eight years. That's why things are getting so critical."

"Where are we on the map?" Savage asked him.

Wade chuckled. "See that spiral arm on the top left there? We're about two-thirds of the way out on it. Don't worry. We're so far away from The Bromgrev that we're in no immediate danger—and this is too young an area to be any kind of a threat to him, anyway. That's one reason we're here."

As they went back up to the conference room, Savage was silent, digesting what he had heard, organizing his questions. He had many left.

Seated once more, another cigar in Wade's mouth, Savage rekindled the dialogue—he was certain he would not have this chance again. Finally, he asked the one question that was at the heart of the matter.

"I'm overwhelmed," he began, "with the operation and the organization. I'm not too sure I understand the scale of, or even the reasons for, the war. But, then, that's nothing new. I didn't understand the last one, either. Which boils it down to the same question I had in Vietnam: What has all this to do with me?"

Wade grinned and blew thick smoke into the air. It hung there, almost heavier than the air, a blue-white haze.

"Since it's unlikely that you'll have to risk your neck in this war, it is not really very important to understand it. What your job is is a simple and somewhat screwy one—but not boring, I don't think." His face grew serious.

"You see," he continued, "while Earth isn't really in any danger of a massed attack, my headquarters *is* here—and The Bromgrev knows that. Even if he took Earth—which is unlikely, since our big guns are deployed and our defenses are too good to make the effort profitable—he couldn't get the Headquarters, anyway. It is, well, not quite on Earth . . .

"There exist other planes than ours, with different laws and frames of reference—yet coexisting in the same time and space as we. They are pretty much barren, lifeless nothings; and we could not normally exist there. But there are some weak points between our plane and the one next door; and sometimes things, well, break through. Over the millennia, enough atmosphere, and other components of our plane have seeped through in sufficient quantities, creating tiny bubbles in *theirs*. If conditions are just right, you can enter them."

He leaned back and continued puffing on the fat cigar. "My headquarters," he said, "which I call Haven, is a place like that. Except that by technological means I have sustained it and made it habitable. It is untouchable except through the opening nature made and I perpetuate. As no one enters or leaves except through me, The Bromgrev cannot get his agents in. Since only I can key the way in or out, they can't sneak past, either. But The Bromgrev keeps trying! Sooner or later, it will sink into my brother's coarse mind that the only member of his staff capable of penetrating Haven is The Bromgrev himself." A spark lit up Wade's eyes as he spoke, and his voice raised in pitch. "He'll come like a thief in the night—and in heavy disguise. He could be anybody—or anything—at all, any sentient beastie in the galaxy.

"You—and my other agents here—are my Early Warning System. All of you are former detectives, trained observers with particularly analytical minds. When he comes, it's your job to spot him, identify him, and then we will win this struggle."

"Terrific," Savage grunted sarcastically. "All I do is identify Superman, put him under arrest, and bring him to you, right? And all he does while I'm doing all this is come docilely along. No thanks! I've had a taste of one of you already!"

"He won't know that you know him," Wade said quietly. "He won't be able to take your body or your mind. I guarantee that. Making you a closed-loop organism, a self-repairing individual, was simple. But those days in the hospital, while you were unconscious, I did far more. I created mental blockages in your mind so impenetrable that nothing, no organism past or present except the whole of a God-race, could break through them. The Bromgrev uses telepathy skillfully—far better than I, from an operational standpoint. But my mind and powers are equal to his own—and your blocks are so strong that even I cannot penetrate them. I have been trying during this entire interview; and they are so firm that I can't undo them. To a telepath, you don't exist. The 'paths call you boys 'zombies'—you exist when the sense they depend on the most tells them you do not. They can get only the surface thoughts that you verbalize."

Savage sat still for a while, letting the implications sink in. A zombie, huh? Well, that's what he was: the walking dead. He tried to imagine what it must be like to be able to see anyone's innermost thoughts, to probe the depths of memory.

Except for a very few.

He suddenly felt confident again, private, secure. No more funny business. He was himself, a closed book to others, as always.

The germ of a plan was in Savage's mind even then, but it had not yet surfaced. He did not have enough facts, not enough to go on. Two problems surfaced immediately: How do you tell which of an infinite variety of organisms is the quarry? And how do you kill an invincible immortal?

"When do I start?" he asked.

"I'll show you your office now, if you like. Then get a hotel room downtown and take two or three days to find a place and get settled. I'll instruct Accounting to get you whatever you need in the way of funds. This will be your district: the southeastern United States. You'll work out of here. And you'll meet your share of characters before you're done."

6

THE JOB DID prove to be interesting at that. He worked, he found, for a nonprofit group called the Society for the Investigation of the Unexplained—a group that had some very real and quite ignorant members as well as some of Hunter's own people. As with many things, The Hunter had not created the group, but had merely joined it, endowed it, and then let it serve his purposes.

The society was concerned with the investigation of unnatural or apparently unnatural phenomena, from flying saucers to ghosts, poltergeists, rains of frogs, and anything else that science could not explain. It had performed some valuable services, and some interesting tasks were undertaken by reputable scientists on its behalf: a scientific expedition to Loch Ness, another to find Bigfoot, others hunting spectral shapes in the southern swamps. In most cases they came up empty-handed; but, in others, sound scientific and quite rational explanations—and some extremely nasty and clever hoaxes—were uncovered and released to the public. A lot of extremely talented and intelligent people worked, on and off, for the society.

The society also had, needless to say, a full compliment of nuts.

From Savage's point of view, his job was a simple and interesting one: to pick out of the reports, clippings, and news items any events that might be related to enemy activity—the landing of agents and supplies for Bromgrev men, for example. (That meant chasing a lot of flying saucer reports.) He also kept up with tales of demonic possession and zombie-like activities. Particularly with the latter two, it had been explained to him, since The Bromgrev had a highly effective and unique way of gaining converts.

In his wanderings through the galaxy, through many lives and in many bodies, The Bromgrev had discovered a large planet organized somewhat like a society of bees. Every organism—and there were billions of them—served a specific purpose, each acting like a single component of an organism. Through the years, on this world that apparently had been incredibly harsh, one group of beings had evolved with totally unshielded telepathy.

They developed a single mass mind which dominated the planet. When The Bromgrev discovered the place, the Mind tried to absorb him as well, but this time it met its match. The Bromgrev's mind was stronger, and instead of his becoming one with them, *they* became *him*. The Bromgrev was so powerful a telepath that, even after leaving, he continued to be with the Mind.

Should The Bromgrev come near you he could, at will, incorporate you into the Mind as well. This was a great discovery. It had given him an army that was always loyal, always obedient. But only The Bromgrev himself could incorporate you—the race of creatures he dominated were now too dispersed to be able to do it alone.

If such zombies showed up here, then The Bromgrev was here, too.

Years passed as Savage threw himself into the job. Far removed from the galactic conflict, he never even revisited the War Room, only a few hundred meters below his office. He *did* make Haven once, and had some obligatory training in spaceship guidance and control, as well as his first space flight, but that, too, was now long ago. He had not seen Wade since the first day—and that was fine with him: the creature that was Wade made him very uneasy.

During this period he had handled several hundred cases. In most, he'd struck out, or come up with convincing explanations. At least three had been clever crimes that he was well satisfied to have solved, or

helped to solve. He also became certain after his twen-
tieth such case that some ghosts did indeed exist—for
some reason these people had not joined the great synthesis. They remained, almost inevitably, quite insane
and occasionally dangerous. His countermeasures,
drawn from the computer banks and experts of the society, were sometimes effective, sometimes not.

But always Savage, and his counterparts worldwide,
remained mindful that the enemy was in fact about.
Twice now, he and several other agents had uncovered
small cells of Bromgrev agents, and blocked some of
their operations.

But The Bromgrev himself did not come. He was
busy elsewhere.

So Savage remained busy, building a casebook of
weird and fantastic cases—and he thoroughly enjoyed
himself.

Until the matter of the lost day.

Malloy, South Carolina, had little to distinguish itself
from the thousands of other small southern agricultural
towns spread throughout the southeastern United States.
It was, indeed, the sleepy, two-block village with diago-
nal parking on Main Street and the speed trap at the
beginning of town, right behind the tree-obscured END
55, BEGIN 15MPH sign. Its population of about 350 was
about 70 percent black and mostly in the peanut and cotton business, on one end or the other. But on the night
of August 16, when everyone went to bed, things became unique in Malloy.

They awoke at their usual times the next day and set
about their appointed tasks. It was, in fact, some time
before the discrepancy was noted—for the lone cop on
night duty and the two or three other night people were
unwilling to admit that they, too, had dozed. It was almost 2 P.M. before everyone in the town discovered one
minor fact.

It wasn't Wednesday, August 17. It was Thursday,
August 18.

The story got good play in the newpapers, but since
there seemed to be no harm, no ill effects—and, therefore, no follow-up—it died, after a day, to the news of a

more dramatic outside world. Those who heard of it generally dismissed it as a hoax, particularly since Malloy had been fighting unsuccessfully for charter government and needed to get noticed, at least by Columbia.

A quick plane flight and rental car put Savage in Malloy in about four hours. He had had a slow month, and had been going crazy with the boredom of the rather commonplace muggings, rapes, murders, terrorism, and petty wars of the evening news.

Malloy was exactly what he expected it to be: a musky smell, extremely hot and humid at that time of year, with flies and mosquitoes buzzing all around and a few cars parked in front of the post office and general store. There was even a sleeping bloodhound on the store's wooden porch.

The little bell over the door jingled as Savage entered. A couple of people were looking at some dry goods in one corner, and he noted with amusement their attempts not to stare at him. The proprietor, an elderly, balding man with a thin white mustache, appeared from a rear storeroom.

"Yessuh?" The storekeeper drawled, "What can we do fo' you?"

"Just directions, really," Savage replied. "I'm going to be here a day or two, and need some place to stay."

"That's the Calhoun, suh. Little hotel down the street on this side. It's the only place *in* town. Heah to buy crops?"

Savage shook his head. "No. I'm in a different line of work."

He reached inside his coat pocket and pulled out his wallet. His private detective's license showed clearly, and the storekeeper's eyebrows shot up.

"Detective, huh? All the way from Washington, too! What's the matta, got a runaway husband luhkin' 'round heah?"

"No," Savage chuckled. "I work for an agency that's very concerned when strange things happen. We like to be sure that these strange things aren't caused by familiar enemies."

The old man's face grew serious, and the duo over in dry goods tried ten times harder to pretend they weren't hanging on to every word. "The missin' day, huh? Somebody took it serious, aftah all."

"You mean it wasn't?" Savage shot back quickly.

"Oh, shuah as hell was. But the newspapahs—"

"Print what sells newspapers," Savage completed. "My employers don't have to sell newspapers."

The other nodded gravely, and it was clear that Savage had gotten the correct impression across. Soon the whole town would be talking about the "government" agent who took them seriously; and that would make things much easier in patriotic, rural South Carolina.

Savage decided he must press his advantage. "What about you, Mr.—uh?"

"Bakkus, Tom Bakkus," the storekeeper responded, automatically extending his hand.

"Paul Savage," the big man replied, and they shook.

"Well, Mr. Bakkus, I suppose you have some thoughts on the subject," Savage prompted.

Bakkus scratched his head. "I dunno," he replied thoughtfully. "Damned strange is all. Went tuh sleep 'bout eleven-thutty, as usual, right aftah the evenin' news on the TV. No dreams, no funny stuff. Woke up at six as usual, no problems, 'ceptin' it was Thuhsday, dammit!"

"Did your alarm clock wake you up?"

"Naw. It'd gone off as usual on Wednesday, I suppose. Nevah thought 'bout that. Nevah wakes me up, anyways—been gettin' up at six foah fifty yeahs. Dunno why I keep that ol' clock atall."

"What about the other people? Lots of people need alarm clocks—I know *I* do."

Bakkus frowned. "Nope. Oh, pro'bly the usual numbah of folks use 'em, but most just thought they ovahslept. Would *you* notice?"

"Probably not," Savage agreed. "But I'll check the people myself—particularly the job records—to see how many more people than usual were late on Thursday. Say, that's a thought. Does every kid in Malloy go to school in town?"

"No help theah," the older man replied. "It's August—vacation."

"And no visitors through town during the whole missing day?"

"Not a one they could find. Not really unusual—we'ah a bit off the beaten track heah, and it might be days and days befoah a strangah comes through."

Savage digested the information, turning it over and over in his mind. If the interviews proved out, it made a sinister picture.

Pick a town nobody's likely to disturb for a day. Pick a day even slower than normal. Then black everyone out for that period. Why? To keep them from seeing something? Possibly. But, if so, what would be worth the risk of national notoriety? To get something *through* town, perhaps? But it was a small area blacked out, and chances are you couldn't get something that mysterious both *in* and *out* of the place without somebody noticing.

It didn't make sense.

Savage spent the next three days canvassing the town and the nearby farms and got pretty much the same story. Yes, people had slept through their alarms; no, nobody thought it was unusual until they found out everybody had. By the end of three days, Savage was certain of only one thing: from the intensity of the witnesses, the blackout had occurred without a doubt.

Sinister enough. Particularly when he had talked to that out-of-town salesman who normally *did* come through Malloy on Wednesdays. When asked why he had missed that particular day, he'd explained, "I got tied up in a sales meeting all morning, then found my car wouldn't start. By the time I got AAA to tow me and fix the thing, it was seven in the evening. Since there was nothing critical, I skipped it."

Someone—or something—had stolen a day out of these people's lives. How it had been done Savage had no idea, and the mysterious force had left no clues to hang on to.

Or had it?

The Hunter organization could arrange a sales meeting delay, and tamper with the car. And an organization of Hunter's capabilities could easily black out a town, for they had done things far stranger. And—

For the first time, it also occurred to him that one other organization would have similar resources.

Had The Bromgrev landed? Was he—or "it"—one of the townspeople? If so, why do a thing so conspicuous? Why provoke an instant and predictable reaction from The Hunter's people?

Maybe "predictable" was the word.

It was well past three in the morning and Savage lay awake in the darkness of his hotel room. Except for the cricket symphony, there was an almost incredible silence.

What would be predictable?

That The Hunter would send someone to investigate. No. More.

That The Hunter would send *him*. Virginia through Georgia was his beat.

Savage crushed his cigarette in the ashtray and watched the glow slowly die in the darkness.

A soft knock came at his door. The sound, slight as it was, made him jump as if a firecracker had suddenly exploded. He reached over to the chair on which hung his shoulder holster and removed the .38 Police Special he always carried.

The knock was repeated.

Slowly he went over to the door and put his lips to the crack between door and door molding.

"Who is it?" he whispered softly.

"Someone who has gone to a lot of trouble to talk to you privately," came an equally whispered reply.

The voice was sharp, clear, every word perfectly formed in neutral American English, yet totally without color or emotion. Savage unlocked the door and stepped back, gun drawn. What was it about the Devil not being able to enter a place unless invited?

"Come in," he called nervously.

The knob twisted, then the door opened slowly, revealing a small and not very threatening figure in the gloom. The figure entered and closed the door behind him.

It was Bakkus.

No, it was something that looked like Bakkus—but it

had no humanity, no fire inside. It was an animated corpse.

"Please put the gun away, Mr. Savage," Bakkus said in that strange and unnatural intonation. "You can only shoot Mr. Bakkus, and he's an innocent and unknowing bystander in this affair, of no concern to either of us. It takes a great deal of power from my other dealings to communicate in this fashion, so I will be brief."

"You are The Bromgrev?" Savage asked breathlessly.

"No, merely one of his agents, as you are an agent of The Hunter. But I am on The Bromgrev's business."

"Just where—and what—are you, anyway?" Savage asked, not taking his pistol off the figure, who continued to stand motionless.

"I am in a ship quite a distance from your planet, using a device that amplifies my own rather powerful mental abilities a millionfold. That device—and our agents on Earth—caused the population of this little town to remain comatose for roughly thirty Earth hours, with little disturbance."

"All to get me here," Savage accused. "Why?"

"So you have deduced that? You are, indeed, as good as we have heard. As to the why of it, we mean to correct certain impressions you have received. We mean to give you all of the facts, the truth—unlike Hunter. And, at the end, we might ask for your help."

Savage's thick brows shot up. "*My* help? I belong to the opposition, remember. What makes you think I'll switch?"

"You have certain distinct personality traits we believe will make you a key person in coming events. You are, of course, not the only agent we have talked to—or will talk to. If you will permit me to give you my message, you might understand."

Savage still didn't lower the pistol, but he did flop back down on the bed. Bakkus made no attempt to move or sit. The creature controlling the body operated it as a robot.

Savage carefully lit another cigarette.

"Go ahead," he told the creature. "I'm listening."

"To begin with, The Hunter told you the true nature

of the war we are fighting. It is one of his characteristics that his lies are always cloaked in truths.

"For example, the evolution of the Synthesis is an integral part of natural law. An existing synthesis is necessary to maintain order in the galaxy. It's an order that is beyond your comprehension—or mine—but it is essential to the maintenance and development of all sentient life. But Hunter lied when he threatened you with that standard stage-play of his. Had you refused his offer, you would not have been submerged in insanity, but you would have found and slowly learned to use new powers as an individual—with the ability to synthesize at will with any other individuals, or the group as a whole, to become something even greater. You would have become a part of the management of your planet. You are now cheated of this."

"Well, I don't miss it," Savage responded dryly. "One doesn't miss what one has never had, wanted, or understood. What's all this to do with me?"

"Perspective," replied the creature using Bakkus. "You see, the last such race is gone—dead, finally, or, perhaps, gone on to even greater things. Nobody knows. But that race—the race of The Hunter and The Bromgrev—left far too soon. They were able to interpolate and determine that, left completely alone, the Next Race was far enough along to carry our galaxy through any rough spots. The problem, you see, was that one member of the old race enjoyed playing God too much. This was The Hunter's sector: Earth and the nearby planets. He'd played games with Earth, terrible games that could have cheated your people out of their chance—and it's only a chance—of attaining greatness. He introduced space travel at too early a stage. Such travel, before there is a temporal awareness and an acceptance of the Synthesis, can cause wide dispersion and the Synthesis will not be able to grow and evolve to its proper form."

"But we *have* space travel," Savage pointed out. "We've been on the moon and rockets—"

"Toys of no consequence," the creature responded. "It is the knowledge of how to bypass relativity that matters. The Hunter gave Earth the necessary equations to conquer space—and his people, the Kreb, caught him at it, as they had to. They caused a series of natural disasters that forced Earth's civilization virtually back to the caves, but saved its future. And they did something else: they expelled The Hunter from the Synthesis, and caused him to become what he is today—earthbound, material, and parasitic. The hatred he nurtures for this transcends all reason, and he will never allow any to reach Synthesis again. He is the apostle of chaos."

'You're saying The Hunter is the Devil—cast out of Heaven for playing God," Savage observed. "The Hunter says The Bromgrev is the Devil. So?"

"When the Kreb departed, they left a guardian, one of their own, to counteract the unforeseen and keep things in check until the Next Race develops. To do this, they reduced this agent to the same status as The Hunter, but not bound to this or any other planet. That is my master, The Bromgrev. Until now there was little need to do anything. Bound to this planet, Hunter was neutralized.

"But, about a hundred and fifty of your years ago, The Hunter discovered that the ancient destruction wrought upon Earth by the Kreb had left severe weaknesses in the space–time fabric; and, using one such, he was able to transcend the ancient curse that bound him here and to go out again to the stars. He built his headquarters here, and brought real space travel back to Earth from *outside*. Killed on Earth, he is doomed to remain here—body after body, life after life. But killed in Haven, he is able to overcome the ancient Kreb barriers and be reborn elsewhere. Once loose, his megalomania knows no bounds, his abilities for chaos are unchecked. To save the Next Race and all future races, The Bromgrev organized and began this war—to hold the key positions, to control the key sectors, to protect the Next Race until it could develop to a point where it can do to The Hunter what his own race was unwilling or unable to do."

"All very interesting, but not very important to me. Certainly it doesn't make much difference, from my point of view."

"There is a crystal world," the creature continued, as

if it had not been interrupted, "whose sentient life forms live for more than a million years; where time, and even thought, is that much slower relative to our own. Should hosts of The Hunter and The Bromgrev die at the same instant, in normal space, and if one *knew* of the impending death and the other did not, it would be possible for the one who *knew* to control the confused one who did not, to guide him to that crystal world, and there trap both in those near-immortal bodies. The war would end; the Next Race would develop normally and deal with them both, and millions of lives would be saved."

Savage was quick to catch the implications. "That means put the both of them together—and an executioner," he pointed out. "So The Bromgrev *is* coming here, after all. But you picked the wrong boy, Bakkus or whatever your name is. Once bought, I *stay* bought."

"Our agents reported the rather violent death of one Joseph Santori on a military installation. We made the assumption that you had killed him," the thing said.

"No comment," Savage replied with a smile. "How can you blackmail a dead man?"

"Blackmail has nothing to do with it," explained the agent of The Bromgrev. "Our people routinely check out new recruits to your side. We made the connection and decided, after much thought, that you were one of our best candidates. The key is revenge, Mr. Savage. You are a vengeful person. Your hate is deep inside, ready to explode. You killed Santori when he did not attempt to kill you except in defense. Rage, Mr. Savage. You killed a surrogate because your true murderer eluded you."

"McNally," Savage whispered. It was a tone that was almost inhuman.

"Ralph Thomas Bumgartner," replied the creature. "One of the best professional assassins around—and, like yourself, an immortal in the pay of The Hunter. You can *never* revenge yourself upon him, for neither of you could ever really damage the other. We could tell you where he is—but it would do you little good, you see."

"Tell me anyway," Savage commanded eagerly. *"I want to know."*

"Oh, I will . . . for it will verify my story. But you do not want him any more than you really wanted poor Santori. It is his employer you should seek—the one who arranged for you to die in a manner so bizarre that you would never truly suspect the premeditation of your murder. The one who had to know pretty closely the moment of your death so that you could be intercepted, in the proper emotional state, and subjected to the correct theatrics, so that you would do as was preordained by your murderer for you to do.

"I speak of your employer: Stephen Wade, The Hunter."

Savage sighed. "I'm ahead of you on that one," he told the creature. "I just didn't like to think about it."

"Bumgartner—McNally—has a cottage on an island village called Ocracoke in the ocean part of North Carolina, I am informed," the creature told him. "The description means nothing to me. Does it help you?"

"I know the place," Savage affirmed.

"It is near Haven, you see. Right now, Bumgartner is not at home. His team is on what you would call an exfiltration mission, roughly six hundred and fifty light-years distant from here. He will return in a few of your weeks."

"So what do you want me to do?" Savage asked.

"We will keep in touch," the creature replied. "I will now take Mr. Bakkus to his home and leave him. In the morning he will be unusually tired but otherwise unharmed; and he will, of course, know nothing of this."

"So I'll be seeing you?" Savage said, realizing it sounded inane.

"No, not me, but someone." Bakkus turned and walked out of the door. Just before leaving he/it turned back one last time. "Remember, not even Hunter himself knows this conversation took place."

And with that, it left.

Savage lay back on his pillow, still wide awake, thinking about the absurdities of this new life. That Bumgartner was McNally he had little doubt—and he would check, anyway. That Hunter recruited that way

was also probably true. But—if The Bromgrev recruited double agents, then which side had made him a
candidate for murder? The Hunter, because he wanted
another routine agent? Or The Bromgrev, who wanted a
traitor?

For the Devil was the Father of Lies, and the best lie
was always the truth told as one wanted it told. Who
was who? Who ran what? One wages a dirty war with
totalitarian methods. The other murders to get recruits.
In neither camp did the individual count for anything.
People were things to be used. It was, he thought, a
most uncharming philosophy.

The problem was, of course, that the Devil *had* lied
to him. But which was the Devil?

Whose game should he play? he asked himself. A
lifetime of experience had conditioned him to equate
each of two sides with either good or evil. It struck him
that those terms—any moral terms—simply did not ap-
ply.

In war, there is no good or evil.

Only interests.

STEP TWO

1

THE LIGHTS, THOSE ever-present, damnable lights on the Fraskan War Room board, had been blinking for an interminably long time. A tall, lean figure sat at the central console, gloomily studying the rapid series of printouts spewing forth.

He looked like an eight-foot skeleton over which a tiny, thin layer of blue-white skin had been stretched somehow. "Humanoid," Earthmen might have called him, but hardly "human"—although he was displaying some very human characteristics.

Aruman Vard, Agent-in-Charge of the Fraskan Sector home world, rose and paced nervously back and forth before the big board, disgusted with the information he been receiving but helpless to correct the situation.

Every once in a while, he would return to the command console and glance at the printouts and displays. The fear index, he noted, was almost perfect—for the enemy. The penetration ratio gave him very little time to do what he knew he must, as it was; yet he continued to put it off. One did not abandon one's life and homeland so freely.

He reached over and pushed a large button on the console. The war board picture flipped, and showed instead only the sector. Areas in friendly hands were in blue; those under enemy control were red. His own planet, Fraska itself, was a blinking red.

The board was mostly stable red, anyway. He looked closely at the tiny single light blinking, telling him his world was still free.

The light blinked red.

A telescreen on the far wall showed the spaceport, filled with ugly black keyhole-shaped landing craft. The announcer, almost in hysterics, kept repeating: ". . . *Rhambdan forces are now in the capital, and all citizens are warned to stay inside, where you are, until further notice. Military Command has announced that formal surrender will take place later this morning, all remaining ships of the line having broken contact and headed into deep space. I repeat again: stay indoors. Stay where you are until further—*"

Vard angrily reached over to a console and switched it off. That was that.

He sat down in the controller's chair, swiveled around to the transceiver, and punched in a ten-digit code.

"Open all channels!" he ordered crisply.

He did not wait for a reply or an acknowledgment, but began speaking as soon as the lights on the console told him that all connections had been completed.

"This is Group to all teams. I have a red light—repeat, red light. Enemy is in the city. *Dalthar! Dalthar!* Deploy immediately to primary objectives; use secondaries in numerical sequence only as local conditions indicate. We have lost and we must now do our duty. Every blow that you strike today is a blow to the enemy, and a step toward ultimate reclamation of our beloved motherland. I know not who you are, but I—"

He stopped, aware that he was trembling violently; the microphone was as a thing alive in his hand, writhing, bouncing uncontrollably. Finally he regained some of his composure, although his voice sounded thick and slurred to his ears.

"Luck be with you all," he managed, his voice cracking.

He switched off the communicator, sat back wearily in his chair, and contemplated the master board. Flipping a toggle switch he replaced the starfield with a projection of both sides of the globe, alive with thousands of tiny flashing lights representing at least as many anonymous Fraskans in organized cells all over the planet. He had never known any of them, he thought— and almost none knew him. One by one, the lights were winking out, representing duties done or attempted: sabotage, gumming up the mighty industrial works that were the enemy's objectives and prize, ruining the sweetness of victory.

Their homes and their jobs. Their lives.

Winking out.

Soon only a few were left: the nervous, the cowards, the unsuccessful, the traitors—and the captured.

For most of them, Vard knew, there would be no returning.

Suddenly very conscious of time, Vard juggled the dial combinations on the master transceiver for the last time.

"Group to Mystery. I have acknowledged and transmitted your red light. Will abandon post in a tenth-period or earlier. Prepare to transmit."

There was again no reply, but in a ship far out in space the words were heard by the cyborg signals unit on board.

A tiny transceiver implanted long ago in his brain suddenly began a sharp, high-pitched whine that was audible to no one but him. Vard knew he would have to live with that sound, live with it until he was picked up—or killed. If captured, the signal would rise until it struck a certain pitch, shattering his skull.

Taking a last look around the master control center, Vard went over to a small panel near the doorway. He opened it, revealing a small switch held in place by a complex electrical lock, and removed a tiny vibratory key from his belt. This was inserted in the lock, twisted first this way, then that.

Aruman Vard watched the lock give way and swing aside, revealing a clear path to the switch.

He pulled it.

Then he took the elevator to the surface and walked down a narrow corridor to the street level, past the sign marked ARUMAN VARD: IMPORT/EXPORT and into the almost deserted street. He moved briskly, not looking back.

When he was about two blocks away, the building began a slow dissolve, like heated plastic, all of it running together. By the time he was three blocks off, it was a huge puddle of boiling matter.

Living on an ancient world long devoid of its natural atmosphere, whose red sun gave off a dull glow but little heat, presented problems enough, just surviving there. But on this world of domed cities and underground honeycombs sustained by a highly sophisticated technology, the problem of escape was compounded almost beyond belief. Vard knew that The Hunter's boys did not expect him to make it, but he trusted them to keep faith with him as he had all these years with them.

Suicide or surrender were simply not in his makeup.

He headed for a small private garage a few blocks away. There, he knew, his escape vehicle had been maintained by robots awaiting its one use. Once there, he would feel far more secure. He damned himself for letting his emotions carry him to a possibly fatal delay. Now the Rhambdans were within the city; and getting out of the Dome, through the great locks, might be next to impossible.

A whine in his head told him that it had better not be.

There! The garage! Now, just place the identdisk on the plate, then raise the doorway by vocal command—

The door slid silently back. The garage was empty.

Vard felt panic rising within him. There was no way he could have made a mistake. The agents had acknowledged delivery! It just wasn't possible!

It was, however, fact. The car either had never been there or it had been stolen in some inexplicable way.

He wasted no more time.

The alleyway was still, but—were hidden eyes already viewing him? Were The Bromgrev's agents now preparing to pounce? What if he were a Known, and they were expecting him to lead them to others? What if—?

The alternative was to fight it out here—and die. Home was gone, his world was gone.

Aruman Vard walked swiftly down the silent alley.

"His car's not there," said a metallic feminine voice in the ship that was hiding off-planet. "Now he's making a hurried decision."

"Think he'll stand and fight?" Ralph Bumgartner asked in a tone that indicated he really couldn't care less.

"No, definitely not," replied the disembodied voice. "All Agents-in-Charge are chosen with a high survival index in mind. He'll go down fighting if caught, but he won't give up escape unless caught or dead."

"Very well. Keep me posted. Let me know immediately if he doesn't make it, and zap him at the first sign of trouble. We have several others to go, you know."

"Don't get worried," the voice reassured him. "Look on the bright side. If he makes it, he'll be one of the best agents we've got."

"If he gets out of this one, he's probably The Bromgrev," Bumgartner replied glumly as he slowly stirred his gin fizz.

2

Aruman Vard saw the bubblecar as he turned the second corner. It was empty, of course, and probably locked.

He went up to the little vehicle and tried the cockpit release. Yes, locked. Even in panic the Fraskans were an orderly people. They were, he reflected, a race almost apart from himself—a nation of domesticated animals, in which a throwback had no place.

He reached into his wallet pouch and brought out a key jammer, attaching it to the side lock. There was a humming sound, and the vehicle's top raised slightly.

Reaching over, he pushed the bubble up the rest of the way and climbed inside. His eyes fell to the identdisk on the dashboard.

Let's see, he thought. I'm Garon Hnub, a vasilis merchant from Kashar here on a business permit. That should be more than enough, unless I'm closely questioned.

He wished he knew what "vasilis" was.

Thanking the dead gods of his world for such a stroke of good fortune, he started the small engine and fed instructions into the auto's guidance system. The car moved smoothly forward.

Vard idly thumbed through the guidance card files in the center console, noting with pleasure that the bubble-car had not only a section of approved city routes but one, too, for the Great Waste Highway to Kashar. That made it much simpler. Vard marveled at his good fortune in finding a salesman's car—from out of town!—the first time out, although he *had* been in the commercial district. Things were going so smoothly that Vard halfway suspected a trap.

The car sped toward the Northeast Lock.

Almost immediately, behind him, came the unmistakable purple flashing of a police cruiser. His hearts sank as he felt the override of the cruiser take hold of his vehicle and glide him gently to a stop by the side of the road. The cruiser pulled up beside him and stopped, and its occupants became clearly visible.

They were not Fraskans.

One was a tall, orange creature, looking like a large, thin cone perched point upward on a mass of fleshy tentacles. Spaced evenly around its midsection were seven stalked eyes, three of which were studying him. The other occupant resembled a small, green monkey. While the orange thing seemed to glide up and out of the cruiser, as if on a cushion of air, the little green creature scampered out the other side. Both approached Vard, who remained seated in his car for want of anything better to do.

These, then, were Conquerors: mercenaries and allies from greedy worlds who had flocked to the Rhambdan call for war; former fifth columnists on occupied worlds; and suchlike. Opportunists, in for a share of the wealth that was what they believed the winners' prize would be. If either was telepathic—

The tiny whine in Vard's head seemed to grow ominously loud.

"Good day, citizen!" boomed a deep voice in Universal.

Vard started slightly; he knew somehow that it came from the orange cone, although no mouth or other orifice was visible.

"Thought criminal!" shrilled the green monkey in a high-pitched voice.

Vard's hand was already on his pistol.

"Pay no heed to my friend here, honest citizen," the orange cone put in hastily. "In a fight on Bluxada he was just finishing the statement 'Some of these creatures are thought criminals,' when one of those unworthies proved it by cracking his head open. Since then, they're the only two words he's been able to say. Not much of a conversationalist now, I admit, but still a good partner."

"Thought criminal," agreed the little monkey, a tear glistening in one eye.

Vard relaxed his grip on the pistol. Stupid, overconfident, arrogant ones. He doubted that they had ever been in a battle, or could face an enemy. They could be handled.

"Now, then, kind sir," continued the cone, "you are a rarity in the city this day."

"Thought *criminal*," agreed its partner.

"You have," said the cone, "been speeding where few have dared to crawl. This makes us wonder about you, understandably."

"Oh, noble sirs," Vard replied, trying to sound as anguished and scared as he could, "I am but a poor merchant, caught here and seemingly stranded many *careps* distant from my home in Kashar, away from my mates and many offspring. I want only to get back to my family group, to be with them during this troubled time! I have been unable to call them, and they fear me dead, I am certain."

The orange cone remained impassive; the little green monkey scratched its nose.

"Well, Twixl," the cone said suddenly, "what do you think of him?"

"Thought criminal," answered Twixl idly, much more concerned with fondling his own tail.

"Well, not really," the cone replied, "but I do think our Fraskan friend warrants some sort of inspection." The cone drew closer to Vard. "I'm afraid, dear citizen, that we must bring in all who violate the curfew. However, since you are doubtless who you say you are, and in the interest of promoting the new spirit of brotherhood between our people and yours, we will probably be able to fly you to Kashar as soon as you are cleared."

Vard nodded, resigned to his course of action. As obviously stupid as these creatures were, that very dullness gave them a literal attitude toward their orders. They could be bought, probably, in a different situation, but never bent.

"If you will just follow us to the local station, we will process you quickly and see about getting you home," the cone concluded, already gliding back toward the patrol car. Twixl nodded and turned also.

Stupid.

Vard fired into the mass of the orange cone first. A piercing scream rang out, followed by a loud *pop,* and suddenly the air was filled with little pieces of orange sludge raining down like confetti.

Twixl had not waited to be next. The moment the weapon flashed, the small creature had, in one motion, drawn its own weapon and dropped into a roll to the street, quickly getting under the armored police cruiser. On the third roll he fired at Vard, narrowly missing the Fraskan as Vard jumped from the bubblecar to protection behind it. He was beginning to have second thoughts about Twixl. The little creature was too cool, too professional in its reactions. Before its accident or whatever, Twixl had not been a mere patrolman.

A second discharge came at Vard, quickly followed by a third. He realized that Twixl was eating away at crucial parts of the bubblecar, turning the Plasticine vehicle molten, causing splashes of the hot material to fly behind the car itself. Twixl had realized that, due to the extreme cold in which they had evolved such heat could melt Fraskans as well.

"Thought criminal!" yelled the little patrolman, and for the first time he seemed to mean what he said. His voice was full of panic, yet his aim was coolly deliberate and very close.

Very close.

Vard awoke to the fact that the angle of fire was changing. He had been so busy dodging the lethal bits of melted plastic that he'd lost the advantage. Twixl, it was clear, was trying to work his way to the police cruiser door. Once inside, the creature could command the weaponry built into the car to disintegrate the entire city block, if need be. Vard made his move.

Lunging out into the street, he kept low and ran zig-zaggedly for the cruiser, all the while keeping up a steady fire. As he did, Twixl gained the far door of the vehicle. But, just as the Conqueror reached out for the handle, he slipped in the orange goo that was the remains of his partner. Vard lunged at him, ramming him against the side of the door.

As Twixl was hit, the pistol flew from his grip and clattered to the pavement. Both had been stunned at the encounter, but Vard's gun was still in his hand. Twixl, lying facedown on the street, scrambled toward his weapon. He had almost reached it, when he saw out of the corner of his eye that Vard was raising his pistol.

Twixl froze, and turned slowly toward the Fraskan, arms outstretched, a defeated look on his face.

"Thought criminal?" he asked peevishly.

"Quite right," Vard replied, and pulled back on the firing stud.

Twixl seemed to be lifted up by the beam, charred, and then reduced to a pile of dark ash.

Vard leaned against the police cruiser, catching his breath, then walked back to his stolen bubblecar and studied it. Twixl had made a mess of the whole thing. It was obvious that the car would never move again.

He reached in and removed the guidance cards from the console box, which had remained untouched in the fight. For the first time he noticed the buildings and the street. Undoubtedly, hundreds of eyes had witnessed the battle, yet they remained hidden; it would probably be sometime before the shooting was officially reported or discovered.

Vard walked back to the cruiser and got in. The vehicle would be a problem—he had only driven one manually twice before. But the controls were similar and well labeled. It might take a little getting used to, but he could manage.

Activating the power, he closed the side ports. The cruiser glided out of the parking area, weaving and bobbing a little, as Vard got the feel of steering the large vehicle. In a few seconds, he accelerated.

No one challenged the police cruiser as it glided, a bit tipsily, along the deserted city byways. Meanwhile, Vard searched the cluttered control panel for the police radio, and, after a little experimentation, found it.

". . . *Police cruiser assumed to be heading out of the city. All lock guard stations are warned to be on the lookout for any breach. Until further notice, we are closing lock stations to all but official traffic* . . ." The voice rambled on.

So they were definitely aware of him already. They would love to take him alive, assimilate him, perhaps, into the Rhambdan Mind. How far would they go to get an Agent-in-Charge? Mass assimilation? The Rhambdans didn't like assimilations at all, because there was a finite limit to the Mind's effective control when it was so widely dispersed—though no one had ever defined that limit. Could assimilation neutralize that whine in his head?

Thinking about it, it really didn't make much difference: dead is dead.

The North Gate, one of the seven major airlocks controlling entrance and exit to the city, swung into view ahead of him. As it did, Vard saw that he not only had to contend with getting through the lock somehow, but also with a massive traffic jam of Fraskan bubblecars massed there.

The lock was as traffic-ridden as the capital city was devoid of it. Citizens of other cities, trapped by the sudden capitulation, were frantically seeking a way home. Vard thanked all the gods that the controls in the police car were plainly marked. He punched the button marked CLEAR and hoped that it was the traffic control he wanted. Spotting three other cruisers parked at the lock station, he headed for them, the bubblecars in the jam moving quickly and obediently out of the way like a parting of the waters—much to the consternation and frustration of their owners, some of whom were not in them at the time and a few of whom were run over by the automatic action and now lay screaming in the street. Well, so much for good relations with the conquered, Vard thought cynically.

As he pulled up to the lock tower, he saw that the Rhambdans were preparing to clear the area on their own. They had brought in one of the Kah'diz.

The creature and its host stood atop the platform in front of the lock control station, looking at the fantastic mess below. The host body, Vard saw with revulsion, was a Fraskan. On his back perched the Kah'diz, a purplish, somewhat indistinct mass like matted hair, each strand of which was imbedded in the victim's neck.

The Kah'diz were vampiric; they had no way to manufacture their own blood, and could adapt to almost any creature's metabolism. They saw, heard, felt, spoke through the host body—and that body was simply that: a body, manipulated by the thing like a puppet. Sentience died when the Kah'diz took you.

The Kah'diz, for reasons unknown to anyone, had developed the strange talent of becoming empathic broadcasters; they could induce almost any sort of emotional reaction in any other creature. They could make you love them, or fear them, or any of ten thousand other, more subtle reactions. They played on emotions like an organist mastering the greatest of concert organs, seemingly for sport but actually to fulfill a need not well understood by potential hosts. And a Kah'diz would wear out a body in a fairly short time.

Long frustrated in expanding and developing their own civilization because of the lack of suitable host bodies, they reproduced quickly, though; and the development of modern medicine on their world had left them with a mushrooming population. They had, therefore, been among the first to leap on the Rhambdan bandwagon. Rhambda, badly in need of allies and confident of its own power, accepted.

The value of the Kah'diz to the Rhambdans was illustrated by this situation. Occupation was their work and their own personal goal; and for it they were well suited, as Watch Officer Baathiax, the Kah'diz at the North Lock, knew. Although the Fraskans were decadent, and normally absurdly easy to control, this gathering had all the earmarks of a riot. Emotions, the Kah'diz reflected, are curious, fickle things.

The creature knew it could never control this mob alone; its whole race couldn't do it. But the empathic amplifiers aboard its ship would magnify its own natural powers a billionfold.

A dead hand reached down and lifted the communications microphone. "Baathiax here. The situation is critical at North Lock. How many of our ships are now in port?"

A rustling sound on the other end was audible as the communications officer checked.

"Nine," came the reply.

"Very good—for the moment, anyway. What must be done here is clear. I have a control rod with me, but no external power source. Get some of my people to each airlock station, then have the standby crews in each of the ships feed the power from the generators into the rods. Most of these creatures couldn't get out of this mess if they wanted to, so it will have to be handled carefully."

"All other locks already have at least one of your people on hand," replied the communications officer. "All have rods except at Northwest, and we'll have one out there by the time the standby crews can get the generators working. I'll signal you when we're ready here."

Baathiax mumbled assent, and switched off. As it did, it heard the muffled whine of a police cruiser and saw a sleek, black vehicle clearing its way through the muddled traffic.

The Shrine of the Black Roots protect me from petty bureaucracy! it swore to itself. Any more befuddled, stupid policemen, agents, and fellow-travelers in the lock control center and there would be no room to raise an arm without knocking out ten people!

Baathiax started to fume that such a thing would not happen with Kah'diz in total control, but after all these years the creature was just too cynical not to let the feeling pass. A bureaucrat was a bureaucrat was a bureaucrat in any and all ways, shapes, and forms; and it was an immutable law of the galaxy that in any operation there would, for every competent agent, be ten clotheads to foul things up. Baathiax felt doubly lucky to be a line officer; in the field, such beings died.

Baathiax shook off the pessimistic introspection. Such problems were part of the job, Baathiax reflected sadly. There was always that dream of every Kah'diz of being alone on a world of hosts, feeding peacefully until finally dying in a mass orgy of emotional pleasure. But such a paradise was more than a little unrealistic for a second officer.

The Kah'diz returned its gaze to the police cruiser. Why, the driver was a Fraskan! Curious. What was a Fraskan doing in a cruiser at this stage of the game?

The new occupant of the crowded lock tower stepped from the elevator and walked straight toward the Kah'diz. Baathiax sent a playful urge that the newcomer be overcome with humor. The Fraskan stopped, looked momentarily puzzled, and then started laughing maniacally. Peals of laughter issued from the platform, and the Fraskan tried to brace himself to keep from doubling up. Baathiax watched him with cold indifference.

After a few minutes, the Kah'diz released the subject. The others on the platform had viewed this strange behavior with alarm; and a couple, fearing a madman was loose among them, had drawn their weapons. Baathiax waved a host hand to stop them. *Genuine* laughter, it thought, would be a real treat, but marionettes were childish.

Aruman Vard stopped laughing abruptly. His body convulsed, he retched and gagged repeatedly, until he regained control of himself. Although nervous and scared by the unexpected attack, his wits held together. He could afford to be this monster's toy for a little while: all Kah'diz were too arrogant to believe that they

could be conned, and none allowed a telepath within
easy range. If he could survive this sadist, he might just
pull it off.

The other Conquerors on the platform, realizing what
had happened, were shooting nervous glances at Baathiax, and most seemed to find urgent reasons to be
needed elsewhere. The platform quickly cleared. An
objective of both Baathiax and Vard had been attained.

"Noble sir," gasped Vard, "if you will but permit me
to speak."

The Kah'diz remained impassive.

"I am Colonel Hadusan, of the Fraskan Liberation
Army," he lied. "I have been ordered to offer my services as needed, then proceed with a mission."

So that was it, Baathiax thought disgustedly. A fifth
columnist. A traitor come up from his dirty hold to ex-
hibit the dirt proudly in victory. Such men were dangerous—their loyalty lay only to themselves. But what was
this idiot doing *here?*

"I do not require you," the Kah'diz told him coldly.
"What do you wish of me?"

"My mission, sir," Vard explained carefully. "A very
dangerous traitor, one Aruman Vard, escaped the lock
just before it closed. He has been hiding out in a bubblecar and we have just discovered his approximate location on the Great Waste Highway. However, many
Fraskans are trapped out there, and only another Fraskan could tell which was which. I have been ordered to
go to the mountain exiles and pick him up before he slips
the net.'

The Fraskan sounded logical enough. They all
looked alike to Baathiax. And, considering the under-
current of fear the native had been radiating, what he
said must be the truth. The Fraskans were just too slavish and decadent to keep their composure through the
kind of treatment this one was being given.

The Kah'diz's reasoning was as logical as Vard's
story—and equally false. It simply did not occur to the
creature that a good agent of the opposition would be a
carefully trained and fully programmed psychotic.

The transceiver buzzed.

"The generators are on, and up to full power," the

voice of the communications officer reported. "All stations are manned and ready."

"All right," replied Baathiax. "I'll clear up this mess right now."

With that, the creature removed from a small, skin-lined case attached to its belt a thin, gleaming silver rod, about a meter long. With its host's hands, it reached up and attached a wire from the rod to one of its own tentacles, which it had disengaged from the host's neck. A thin drop of golden-colored Fraskan blood dropped onto the host's shoulder.

The wire was actually a tiny tube, Vard saw, and the hair-thin tentacle slipped into it. The "wire" uncoiled from inside the rod, giving enough slack so that the rod could be held in front of the Kah'diz. Vard heard a faint hum of power, and a sickly purple glow seemed to overtake the rod, clinging like an eerie mist.

Baathiax turned to Vard and the few others still on the platform. "You will feel certain things," it warned them, "but it won't be the power that the ones forward and below will receive. The field is quite directional. You should have the willpower to reject anything you might get as feedback. If not, get as quickly as possible to the other side of the platform, opposite the beam. The effect will be minimal there."

Baathiax suppressed a quick urge to shoot his fellow-Conquerors a jolt of suicidal tendencies with a flight motif—considering it was forty meters to the ground and none of them had wings. But, there was diplomacy. Baathiax returned quickly to the business at hand.

Vard, the closest, was the first to feel it: a vague lethargy, a feeling of wearied quietude, a will to forget whatever one had in mind and return to the comfort and safety of the previous day's lodgings. Nothing much was very important, it seemed. He felt as if he was in a dream-like fog, unaware of his location or purpose. With great difficulty he shook it off, but he stepped back and away from the emotion-master. If this was a case of mild feedback, what must it be like out there in the jam?

Vard now felt the mood slowly changing. And he saw that few in the crowd below had moved.

Slowly but surely, Vard found himself getting horny;
the craving for sex grew slowly stronger within him.
This time, however, he realized what was happening
and was able to keep something of a detached mind.
But he was aware that the peaceful, lethargic feeling
was still with him, as well. The Kah'diz strategy was
now apparent: the combination of the relaxing, quasi-
narcotic "high" and the powerful sexual stimulation created a single-minded behavioral attitude on the part of
the people below.

Vard could see that the crowd below was beginning
to react. People were seeking out members of the opposite sexes—and, in a few cases, the same sex—and con-
gregating in sexual groups of four.

Now Vard felt a third urge superimposed on the first
two: the urge for privacy, to get away, to walk to a
place of concealment, of safety, of solitude. The great
mass below was slowly breaking up, moving off, away,
in almost all directions.

Vard stopped and shook himself as he realized that
he, and most of the others on the platform, had been
walking around the platform area in circles. Many of
the others, looking dreamily into a fog of their mental
creation, continued to do so.

The quadrisexual groupings of the walkers below was
unmistakable. There would be some orgies, and perhaps
some new family groupings, before this day was out!

Still some remained, of course—those with strong
family ties on which the induced reactions and desires
only reinforced their will to go home. But these numbered in the hundreds now, hundreds among the thousands of deserted cars; they could be handled directly
by the authorities.

Baathiax gave them a powerful urge to obey authority, a will to follow any command given them. Since the
only real authority figure around was represented by its
own figure on the platform, Baathiax picked up a public address microphone and began speaking, stepping up
urgings to obedience as it talked. Vard had gone all the
way to the far end of the platform and stopped up his
ears. He wanted to be around after the finish.

"Fraskans," crooned the dead voice of the Kah'diz

host, "return to the city. Your families and loved ones are being cared for. They have been informed of your safety, and the government guarantees that safety. You are to be good citizens of the new government, and return to the place of your last night's lodgings, remaining there until further notice. The government, of course, will reimburse you for any expenses. In this way can you best help us—and you want to help us, don't you?"

The crowd felt it really did want to help the government. It would do anything for the government. It would die for the government.

"Go, now," Baathiax exhorted them, and, obedient as trained animals, they went. Within five minutes the entry–exit port below was the largest used car lot on Fraska, but without a single customer. Even a number of Conquerors, Vard noted with some amusement, were in the process of obediently walking away.

Baathiax turned to the few remaining Conquerors on and near the platform.

"Do you think," it asked acidly, "that clearing the rubble below would be beneath your powers, means, or dignity?"

Having no taste for an additional treatment of the creature's power rod, which still glowed softly in its hand, the few remaining Conquerors practically fell over each other in their rush to get to work.

Baathiax relaxed and disconnected the rod, then idly flipped on the transceiver.

"Baathiax here. North Lock cleared and operational in twenty or thirty minutes, maybe sooner if we can get a few wreckers in here."

"Ah, no wreckers available right now, sir, but do your best. It's really bad at West," came the reply.

"All right," the Kah'diz replied, "we've done our part."

It switched off the radio. Suddenly it heard a noise behind it, and whirled. Why, that Fraskan was still here! With more respect, Baathiax motioned Vard closer.

"I congratulate you on your self-control," it told him. "Such a strong will will be a true asset to the new empire. Now, what was it that you wanted?"

Vard bowed slightly.

"My only wish, noble sir, is to serve the new empire. I must leave the city to identify the suspect Vard in the mountains."

"Oh, yes, yes," Baathiax muttered with annoyance. "I shall open the lock."

Vard emerged from the elevator and chose the cruiser nearest the lock. He was feeling pretty pleased with himself. Starting the car, he moved slowly and confidently into the lock area. None of the wrecking crew took any notice.

Baathiax closed the *"A"* lock compartment behind the cruiser and began pumping the atmosphere back into the Dome. As soon as the atmospheric pressure dropped below proper levels, the cruiser's internal air and pressurization kicked in, much to Vard's relief. Until then, he had not thought to check and see if it even *had* such devices.

There was a *pop* in his ears and then the cruiser's atmospheric controls blasted in. Soon it was a comfortable 25° Kelvin.

The *"B"* lock opened noiselessly in front of him, and Vard moved the cruiser forward as soon as he had enough clearance.

He was out of the city.

Vard glanced down at the outside temperature gauge. It was hot enough here to melt oxygen!

The cruiser sped onward through the twilight-lit desert stretching out before it, seemingly to infinity.

The little whine in his head changed, became more of a direction finder. He turned the car in the direction of the strongest signal, confident that the ship had not deserted him and that he was away free.

Hours later, he was in the middle of the desert, heading for a small lifeboat sent down on auto to pick him up. He pulled up next to the small airlock.

It was fortunate that his race could withstand a vacuum and warmer-than-normal temperatures for short periods, for he had no spacesuit or other protection. Shielding his eyes from the red sun's dull rays, and taking a breath, he depressurized the cruiser and opened the door, bolting as fast as he could into the lifeboat airlock.

The boat's lock closed behind him and he could feel air and temperature being introduced and brought up to Fraskan normal. After what seemed to be about two minutes longer than he could hold his breath, a buzzer sounded. He exhaled, then took in great amounts of air.

Opening the second lock, he went over to the pilot's control couch, strapping himself in but not touching the control helmet. This would be an automatic operation. Quickly, without any sensation felt inside the little craft, it was speeding out into space.

"You will have to live in the lifeboat until we reach Valiakea," an alien, metallic voice told him. "The conditions inside our ship would kill you instantly. We have several more pickups; then we will all go to Valiakea for Adaption Procedures necessary for Haven. The proper food for you and some reading matter are supplied. Should you want or need anything we can supply, simply speak up. I shall be monitoring you."

"Thank you, nothing now but some sleep, I think," he answered, and relaxed fully for the first time since the long day had begun.

Adaption. He hadn't considered that angle. Funny, he thought, no matter how cosmopolitan, old, and experienced you are, you still tend to think of everything in terms of your own normal existence. And yet the universe was a collection of the diverse.

Physically, anyway.

He did not like the idea of Adaption. It seemed to cut him off completely from his own people and homeland, as miserable as those now were.

He was thinking these thoughts as he drifted off into a dream-filled but lengthy sleep.

3

IT WAS NEARING dusk, and a gentle, warm wind was blowing the fields below in wave-like patterns, carrying the scent of new-mown grasses toward the loess caves. In the distance, the rich blue sky was giving way to hues of orange, and magenta reflected off the clouds, creating a wondrous artist's palette of beauty. The inhabitant of one of the caves barely noticed the sight, but the scent from the fields was driving her almost mad with hunger.

As the last rays of the setting sun vanished in the east, she came carefully out of her refuge, looking warily around her with caution born of weeks of being a fugitive.

Standing just outside the cave, sniffing the wind for more fearsome scents—perhaps of sentient beings—she presented a sight that would have been strange to any alien to this quiet, agrarian world. She stood about 150 centimeters high, a squat humanoid body begun with a squared head looking something like a blue gorilla's but with short-cropped silver hair now dirty and disheveled after weeks of hiding. Her head rested on a thick wrestler's neck and a tough, muscled torso covered with very fine, thin, bluish hair. Her arms were thick and bulging with sinew; she could easily lift twice her own weight. Two large blue-black breasts, firm and well proportioned, were left uncovered by the blue hair, which—close to the waist—became much more coarse, long and curly, going down to and covering even the tops of her feet, which despite rudimentary toes, were hard and more like hooves. Her stance, due to the unusual nature of the feet, gave her the appearance of being on tiptoe; and she seemed about to become unbalanced and fall.

Nostrils flared as she tested the wind and found it empty of anything but nature's own aroma.

Satisfied, she turned and made her way circuitously

down the slopes, trying to leave no telltale tracks in the soft earth. Her short, bushy tail was kept straight as she moved with amazing speed down the now familiar pathways. Although she looked awkward and ungraceful at rest, she was capable of sprints of up to sixty kilometers per hour.

Reaching the fields below, she started pulling up some of the grain and grasses and shoving them into her mouth. Her people were herbivores and usually prepared all manner of exquisite and highly seasoned dishes from the plants they favored. But simple fare would have to do this time: hunger overcame civilized custom. Having had nothing since the previous evening, she gorged herself on what she could get.

The stars were out in full glory by the time she had finished, and she lay back in the grassy field looking up at them. So distant, so devoid of hope. She thought back in time, as she did almost constantly—of the good times, the happy times, the times of hopes not crushed by despair. The times before "they" came.

Her name was Gayal.

Her race was, like Aruman Vard's, an ancient one. Unlike Vard's, it had never gone beyond orbital space. Her planet, Delial, which meant "Mother," was the sole planet of its sun; it had no moon, and the next-nearest star was over seven light-years distant—too huge a jump when it had to be your first time.

Her culture was dull by some standards, but it suited her people just fine. Their botanical sciences were second to none in the galaxy, but an era of feudal wars had killed off the excess population that threatened Delial just as effective birth control had been developed. As a result, her people were remarkably long-lived but comparatively few in number, and the population was almost totally stable. There was little government on a national or world scale, merely a few coordinators of things like trade that the local regions could not do for themselves. Delial had no large cities; the population was almost wholly agrarian, and it clustered about the thousands of small towns that were the centers of trade and commerce. Long ago, orbital flight had led to huge space stations circling the globe. It was there that the heavy manufacturing was done, almost entirely by machine, and ferried to well-placed spaceports.

Because an average of ten females were born for every male, a polygamous society had been the norm since civilization evolved on the planet.

Gayal's herd-husband had been an old man named Fala, to whom she had been wedded while still an infant. Fala was teacher, guide, and overseer of the large plantation where they lived. From him she had learned to read and write, and to attain the skills needed to work and run the huge farm along with her sisters. Gayal had been an excellent student, and Fala had sent for some of the best scholars to come and tutor her. History and theology had particularly fascinated her, and the pride and sense of accomplishment she felt when her first book of philosophical essays was published was almost as great as her bearing a son to the herd.

She remembered one stern, pessimistic scholar-teacher, whose soul was empty and devoid of sensitivity to the beauty around and in the life of the world Gayal loved. They had been discussing the gods, and immortality of the soul, and had quickly gotten into a heated argument.

"There is nothing beyond this life," she could hear the teacher's voice saying, distantly, ghost-like in the rippling across the darkened fields. "We go out like a candle."

"I must disagree," she recalled her own youthful voice protesting. "All around us is a world of life interacting with life, in position around the sun at precisely the correct orbit for us to survive. Out there in space are the stars, with other such planets; and beyond them, the galaxy itself—one of many, all functioning according to precise natural laws like an orderly machine. Surely this proves the existence of the gods."

The old teacher had shaken her head sadly, and replied as one would to a retarded child. "Galaxies crash, suns explode, civilizations rise and fall. The nar-bug is eaten by the fikkil, who is in turn eaten by the dros; and good people worldwide are visited with undeserved affliction.

"No, do not look for civilizing influences," the old one continued, and she had taken the young Gayal's arm and brought her over to a window. The sky was ablaze with stars, exactly like this night. "When all is said and done, you will find no paradise out there— only a jungle of stars."

The teacher, Gayal reflected, must have felt very smug and self-righteous when the invaders came, in their great black ships, settling down and burning acres of grain and grass.

She had heard the news on the television and on her wall had seen tapes of the great ships landing and disgorging their weirdly alien troops. There had been no army to oppose them, no ships in which to flee . . .

A new order had been established planetwide: henceforth, they were to provide food first for the conquering hordes. What was left over was for themselves, *if* they worked particularly hard and *if* they increased production as well.

Fala had called her in, shortly after. He looked particularly old and very, very tired.

"Gayal, my favorite of all," he began, his voice cracking with emotion, "it is time to show you some things that must be shown, and to do what must be done."

"You have heard, then, of the invaders?" she asked innocently.

"I have known of them since only a few years after I was born," he told her. "I have feared this day, though I knew it would come. An army travels on its stomach, always, and The Bromgrev has a huge army."

She looked puzzled. "Who or what is a Bromgrev?" she asked—and he told her: of the Kreb, of the Union of Souls, of the great battle for the minds and hearts of the galaxy that was then being waged.

"I was taken early, when I was but three or four, to an alien world far from here. How *I* was chosen, or why, I know not—although it was with the approval of the Agent-in-Charge here before me, who was then old and dying, lucky him!

"I was raised both on- and off-planet by the agent and by the greater organization of beings that he served.

A great installation lies below our feet, with charts of the battle and the great starfield. It has kept me in contact with them for many years, and I have friends of strange races, many of whom I have never seen. Even so, none foresaw our conquest this quickly—though we could do little with simple handguns against such a powerful horde. Now they are here and my job is complex."

"What sort of job, my husband?" she asked, curious and apprehensive.

"My organization is activated. It will, by its actions, attempt to deny, at least for a time, that which the enemy seeks. Our beloved world is to be placed in ruins by my own hand."

His voice gave completely, and he dissolved for a time in tears. Finally, he composed himself.

"There are key missions that I have not been able to verify which must be carried out," he explained, "and we have a very little time to do them. I must see that they are done, personally, if there is no other way. The least of them is dangerous enough. Thus, someone must be here to do *my* job."

He had shown Gayal the wondrous communications equipment, and the rudiments of operating it. He had told her what to say and how to say it; how to interpret the sabotage reports that would come in and how to report these to the unseen agency far off in space. Had she been any less of an intellectual, it would have been too much to grasp; as it was, her head still reeled with it.

The final shock was the little surgeon with tiny, shifty eyes who had planted something, painlessly and invisibly, in her head.

"When you have lost contact with me and my principal people, you are to destroy this place as I have shown you and use the signal to get picked up, in order to flee the planet."

"But," she had protested, "what about you? I would rather stay, as you would, and fight these monsters."

Sadness had tinged his voice as he replied. "I will stay because I expect to die. If I somehow live, I will join you, I promise. But you *must* survive—for I have made certain that within your brain are the moral and intellectual foundations of our race. One day, these monsters will be defeated. Live for it! Work for it! And then you must come back and make our people free again!"

He had taken her head in his hands, and together they had coupled for the last time. In the morning, he was gone.

Gayal had done as instructed, and from the reports she learned just how utter the destruction was. Bacteria had been released by Delialians that killed the grain crops in most areas; by signals, they destroyed their orbiting factories. Retaliation had been swift—although the Conquerors' first attempt, public hangings, did not work: the Delialians had neck muscles too strong to allow them to be choked by rope. The enemy therefore settled on public torture of old men and children—particularly children. The planet caved in.

After nine days, reports from Fala ceased and all attempts to raise him failed.

Slowly, too, a horrible pattern of conquest developed. Kah'diz were dropped in the key regions and made the "adjustments" in the locals. The emotion-masters could turn hatred into love, horror into worship; they methodically started work on key towns and plantations across the planet. And there appeared to be an endless supply of them for the job. Their task was the most difficult thing in warfare: pacification of captured indigenous populations. Slowly, very slowly, but quite efficiently, the Kah'diz turned the bulk of the population from heartsick resisters into willing and loving slaves.

Word came one day that it would soon be the turn of Gayal's plantation for the treatment, word sent at grave risk by as yet "unaltered" relations

The Kah'diz had entered haughtily, mounted on the back of a Delialian, and demanded to see the man in charge. One of Gayal's sisters—all the females in a herd were called "sisters"—had explained that he had gone away and had not been seen or heard from since.

The Kah'diz had nodded, and demanded an inventory of stock, farm reserves, tools—and people.

Gayal and her sisters had talked of killing the creature, but then decided that this would only bring more—and perhaps death and ruin for them and their children. They agreed to go along with the Kah'diz, but do as little as possible for the conquerors.

Then the true horror had begun.

She and her nine sisters had been sitting around talking of the heartbreak and bleak future that must surely await them, when the intercom buzzed.

"Send in Maral," the Kah'diz's dead voice commanded.

Maral, the plantation's voice, and overseer of the business end of the operation, was not surprised; she had gotten used to being summoned whenever the Kah'diz was unhappy over something—which was always.

She left in her usual defiant spirit, ready to do battle with what she called the "one and a half-wit" in the front office. She was gone over two hours, and they began to worry. They had just decided to see what had happened when Maral walked back into the room. A tiny smile was on her lips and her eyes had a faraway, dreamy look.

They crowded around her, dying to hear the new story of what the creature had demanded and what she'd told him.

"The Master commanded that we increase production and tilled acreage, and I assured him that we would all do our duty," she replied matter-of-factly.

There was a stunned silence. Finally, Freyal, the youngest, spoke.

"You're not serious, are you? We swore not to help—"

"You are a thought criminal!" Maral snapped, cutting her off. "The Master warned me of this, but he assured me that he could cure such thoughts. I certainly hope so!"

And with that she stormed out of the room.

The sisters were all talking at once, most of them in stunned disbelief, when, suddenly they noticed that the Kah'diz stood in the doorway.

"You see how easy it is?" it said casually. The creature was obviously enjoying their shock and horror, almost bathing in it. "If you're thinking of leaving," the Kah'diz warned them after a long pause, "I would advise against it. I have people around to see that no one leaves—and you cannot even be certain of your lifelong friends anymore. Besides, there is nowhere to run. Accept the new order, and work better than before. I shall be finished here in two days, anyway."

With that, it turned and left.

There had been no mistaking that last: within two days, the entire plantation would be run by loyal slaves willing to work themselves to death to please their conquerors.

Later that night, Gayal had slipped away to the hidden passage in the stone wall of the main hall. No one saw or heard her, as it was the *outside* that was guarded.

She stepped into the elevator and the wall in front became solid once again. For the final time she went to the War Room, and for the final time she made her report to the anonymous, alien voices.

"This location is in enemy hands. Those horrible parasites are enslaving everyone here. If I do not get out now, it will be too late."

"Get away," came a tinny reply. "Seek some place to stay that is safe for a few days. We're very busy, but we'll get someone there as quickly as possible."

"My sisters and children—"

"Only you. We trust Fala's judgment. Also, more than one of you will be too many to remain hidden until we can get there, and a child would be impossible to hide for days on end. Go. Pull the switch and get out by the emergency exit. This is the last transmission."

"But how will you find me?" she asked.

"We will," came the voice for the last time, and the line went dead.

The little whine had begun instantly in her head . . .

Gayal had been living in caves with only that whine for company for almost ten days.

She got up now, reluctantly, from her grassy mat and headed back to the cave. As she neared it, she sniffed the air for unfamiliar scents. There was no scent in the air at all.

She stopped dead in her tracks. There is never no scent in the air at all.

They were waiting for her to return to the cave. Looking hard through the darkness, she thought she could detect movement.

Slowly she edged back down the slope and, when at a safe distance, started running for the little patch of forest just on the other side of the fields from the hills.

She had just made the first trees when she heard noises on the hill behind her—four clear shots, *pop, pop, pop, pop,* then silence. She stopped and stared at the trail, clearly visible from her position.

After a short interval, a creature appeared, walking slowly on the trail, from time to time consulting a little device which glowed. In its right hand was a large rifle of a design she had never seen.

Abruptly the creature halted, and seemed to be looking around. She saw that it wore goggles.

A night viewer!

She froze.

"It's all right, Gayal," the creature called in her own language. "I am here to pick you up. The four who sought to capture you are dead." It patted its rifle.

Gayal was puzzled and frightened. How could she know if this weird creature was friend or enemy?

"I'm locating you by the device in your head and the device in my hand. You are—let's see—behind the fourth tree and slightly to the right of me. Since I know where you are, you might as well trust me."

Gayal had never felt such fear, but the creature was right. She was saved—or dead. She arose from her hiding place and came toward it.

Ralph Bumgartner smiled and slung the rifle over his shoulder. Four dead, another soul saved. All in a day's work.

4

THE LAST RESCUE was the easiest for Bumgartner and his cyborg pilot.

"We have the lifeboat in sight," the cyborg's voice told him as Gayal entered from the aft compartment.

The trip had not been wasted on her; she had been handling language tapes and had progressed very well in several of the "essential" languages needed to get along in The Hunter's polyglot world of refugees, and she'd been making use of the ship's master library to acquaint herself with the conflict into which she was so newly propelled. Bumgartner kept the atmosphere in the ship deliberately rich in oxygen for her sake, toning it down day by day so she could get used to the Terran atmosphere.

"What's the story on this one?" she asked him in Universal, the trading language used by most of the galaxy's races when communicating with those not of their kind.

Bumgartner shrugged. "Nothing much. Koldon's world hasn't been touched directly by the war, and probably won't be. They're a race of nasty telepaths with the ability to jam some of The Bromgrev's most useful mental frequencies, and they can't be conned by the Kah'diz or have a successful attitude change. Also, their planet isn't very valuable—a neutral clearing house for interplanetary business, run by Koldon's race of middlemen. Take them out—and The Bromgrev would have to take them out—and it would foul up trade and communication, not to mention finances, on such a drastic scale that it would hurt The Bromgrev as bad as us."

"They are salesmen, then?"

"And bankers. Strictly mercenary, loyal only to money."

Gayal was appalled by the vision of such cold, robotic, greedy creatures. "So what do we want with one of *them?*" she asked.

"Oh, Koldon's on our side. He was a commodities broker—would buy and sell anything, really, for a price. When The Bromgrev took over Rhambda, he acquired three billion willing servants. You remember that, don't you?"

"Yes," she replied gravely. "A whole world of unblocked telepaths. The mass mind."

"Right. Well, The Bromgrev had three billion little Bromgrevs, but because they had lacked competition for so long it was an extremely primitive world, too. To put those soldiers into action required technology: starships, weaponry, and the like. To get them, The Bromgrev went to Koldon."

"Then this—this Koldon is responsible for the war!" she exclaimed. "He should be killed, not rescued!"

"Well, perhaps, but Koldon didn't know who or what he was really dealing with. It seemed legit on the surface—and if *he* hadn't made the deal, somebody else would have. At any rate, Koldon has suffered his guilty conscience over the deal ever since the first shots were fired. He feels as you do—that the war is his fault. He's been working with us ever since."

"But, if that's so, what's he doing being picked up?"

"Well, after several years of being a double agent, somebody caught on. They decoyed him onto a liner, where he thought—or was led to think—some highly sensitive information on Bromgrev fleet movements would be passed to him. They caught him; but he's a rather imposing sort of fellow and he broke free, got to a lifeboat, and cast off. Now his cover's blown, so we have to pick him up."

"Lifeboat alongside," reported the metallic feminine voice of the cyborg. "Prepare to link." A pause was followed by a mild bump. "Lock linked."

Bumgartner and Gayal went back to the lock area to receive the latest refugee. Gayal watched and waited as the pressure gauges showed the air transfer. The red light turned green, and the ship's lock door opened.

Gayal wasn't quite certain what she expected, but she

could not shake the image of a mechanical man of some kind, all facts and figures. Or perhaps a wizened, serious gnome accustomed to dreary offices and accounting books. Koldon was not so easily stereotyped.

"I thought you'd never get here," came a voice— No, not a voice, really. It seemed to boom, full of life and emotion, yet *no sound had been uttered*. The words formed inside her head.

"Your fat belly could stand to lose some lard," Bumgartner shot back good-naturedly.

The creature he addressed was almost three meters tall. It had to bend to get through the port. Gayal had seen nothing remotely like it in her life, but to Bumgartner the creature could have been a reddish-blond grizzly bear with a skeletal structure better suited to walking upright. It's eyes were huge, a bright blue, and very human; while its long, thick forelegs ended in stubby, fur-covered hands with coal-black palms—three fingers and an oversized thumb that was almost as long as the hand itself. Gayal also noted that he was incredibly fat; it hung in droopy layers all over him.

The newcomer spotted her.

"Ah! What's this? A Delialian? And a female at that!"

"What's so odd about that?" she snapped angrily. She didn't care for the continuously humorous note of the newcomer's thought projections.

Telepathic Koldon caught this immediately and grew serious.

"I know what your world must have gone through. I'm terribly sorry. I feel—well—somewhat responsible . . ."

"And so you should!" She almost shot the words at him.

He showed it, and his "voice" took on a tone that was incredible for its depth and range of sadness and hurt. She felt suddenly sorry for the big creature.

"I—I don't know what to say," he went on. "There has been too much tragedy already, and this is, I fear, only the beginning of it. But you must learn to accept those who are on your side, you know, no matter what you think of them personally. We live, work, breathe for the same cause." He jabbed a stubby index finger at her. "But never lose that moral tone! It's what separates *us* from *them*."

The great bear-creature went over and plopped down on a cot. It was far too short for him, and he finally lay straddling the end of the cot with his great hind legs as it sagged and creaked.

"I trained Fala, you know," he said quietly.

Gayal turned as if shot. "What do you know of Fala?" she asked sharply.

"When this network was set up long, long ago, I trained him. He was just a boy then. An orphan, alone, a castoff among his own kind."

"But why?" she asked, remembering the strong, sensual man she had known for so many years.

"He was born weak—a runt, with little to ensure survival. Too much inbreeding, I think. He was a bleeder, and had a humped back. They threw him out to die in the fields."

"That's not so!" Gayal protested. "He was neither of those things!"

"Oh, but he was," Koldon replied. "Our field agent discovered him and took him in, realizing that in that rotten body was a keen intellect, if properly developed. We took him to where we're going now—to a world called Valiakea, in the Aruni Cluster. They're master biologists—had to be. Things are so unstable on that planet that they change shape and metabolism ten times an hour just to stay alive.

"They fixed him up. I don't know how, they just *do*, that's all. You'll see. Made Fala into the best-proportioned, most athletic Delialian ever. He and I lived together for almost five years, off and on, and I got to know him *very* thoroughly."

Gayal nodded. "I think I understand."

Koldon raised himself up a little. "No, you do not. I am a telepath—a very good telepath. No one—except The Bromgrev himself—can be false with me, for I know their innermost thoughts and feelings, I dream their dreams. Oh, God, the dreams!" He sank back down. "Leave me be for now," he snapped suddenly.

She started to say more, but thought better of it, realizing that this was not the time. She continued to stand near him for a while, however. Then she saw that he was asleep, his massive chest rising and falling rhythmically. She sought out Bumgartner, who was sipping a drink while reading some reports.

"This Koldon is a very sad person," she said.

Bumgartner barely looked up as he grunted and replied, "Everybody's got a problem, and for him it's the weight of the universe. *You* didn't help any, you know."

Gayal felt very guilty. "I know . . ." she replied hesitantly. "I—I didn't realize at the time—"

"Neither did he," Ralph Bumgartner interjected, and went back to his reports.

The ship sped on to Valiakea.

"Successful trip, Ralph?" Koldon asked over his dinner—which was massive.

"Not really," replied the Terran, nibbling a sandwich. "We got you two, and the Fraskan in the baggage hold, but we lost two. One we had to zap and the other got trapped in his own headquarters before he could destruct and wound up taking the whole gang with him."

"Anybody I'd know?"

"Don't think so. Pyayya of La'ahin, pretty green and prone to mistakes—needed a few more years to season. And an unpronounceable blob of jelly from Flalkan's Star The Bromgrev's agents made before they even took the place."

Koldon grunted audibly. "Things aren't going so well for the good guys, are they?"

Bumgartner chuckled. "There *are* no good guys, Koldon. You know that. Only those who do what they want to do, and their victims."

"The side really doesn't matter to you, does it?" Koldon prodded.

The Terran smiled broadly. "You know the only side that counts is *my* side, you old grizzly. The army of my country trained me to kill people. After a while, I found I liked it—it was the greatest game of all. The trainers really thought so, too, deep down, no matter what patriotic platitudes they spouted. If they didn't, they'd have been in a different line of work.

"Me, I progressed until I was too big to do the stuff myself. I graduated, you might say. I arranged revolutions, started civil wars, whatever my country asked me to do in the name of freedom and democracy."

"How'd you ever get mixed up in *this* mess?" Koldon asked him. "Seems to me that you were headed for fifty anonymous medals and a heart attack."

Bumgartner shook his head. "There are universal constants in behavior, Koldon. Intelligence develops on worlds where organisms need it to survive—that's the law. You, me, Gayal, and Old Frozen back there, all of us are as different as night and day on the outside. But in here"—he tapped his head—"we're all the same, really. It's the real definition of what *my* people call 'human.'"

"So?"

"We fight, we strive, we survive. And in the struggle there're always people like me. We're born for it, bred to it. We're always in demand to go out and herd the cattle. It's what The Hunter looks for in his agents. Why I'm here. And why the others are here."

"And I'm included in that crop?" Koldon asked, bemused.

"Sure. You fight for conscience—whatever that is. Gayal fights to free her homeland, as does this fellow Vard. Me, I'm just more honest—I *like* it."

"We're in station off Valiakea," the cyborg's voice interjected. "Their control would like to speak to you."

Bumgartner sighed, and went over to the forward console. Koldon remained seated on the floor, finishing off the last of his monstrous meal.

The Terran flipped the transceiver switch. "Ship with load of three, as arranged. Appointment code R-821."

"Thank you, R-821," came a calm, toneless voice. "What do you have for us to do?"

"Got a Fraskan that must be acclimated to C-10 oxygen/CO_2 norms, a Delialian and a Quoark for gravitational adjustments of muscle tone to $+2$ norms and some mild atmospheric tolerance adjustments."

"I see," answered the voice. "We'll outfit a ship and be up to you. Give us a half-hour. In the meantime, no one is to eat anything and tell that Quoark that we'll pump his stomach."

Koldon dropped his plate. "Dammitall!" he swore. "I think those bastards presume too much!"

Bumgartner chuckled and switched off. "It'll be good for you, you know. Haven's a lot heavier G than you're used to."

"I've been there before," the Quoark reminded him brusquely, "and it's never troubled me before."

"Suit yourself," Bumgartner shrugged. "I'll call Old Frozen."

He flipped a switch and called Vard, explaining what would happen. Vard acknowledged the call but didn't seem too thrilled by the idea, even though this would mean the physical company of others that he'd been denied.

Gayal entered. "Is this the Adaption process coming up?" she asked.

The Terran nodded. "Yeah. It's fairly quick and absolutely painless. I've had to undergo treatment here a couple of times, and there's nothing to worry about. The only thing that'll happen is that you'll feel more comfortable."

"This place we're going to—are there other Delialians there?" she asked, a bit hesitantly.

"No. You know there aren't," Koldon replied. "And if you're willing, it might be better for you . . ."

Bumgartner, who could not read minds, looked puzzled. "What's this all about?" he demanded.

Gayal started to speak, then thought better of it and turned sheepishly to Koldon.

"Psychology," Koldon explained. "Delialians are herd types, Ralph, not loners like us. You know, we generally let everybody retain their forms because of the identity sense?" Bumgartner nodded affirmatively. "Well, it's a little different here," Koldon continued. "Gayal is *afraid* of being a pariah, a freak. She'd rather fit in."

"Well, I don't know . . ." the Terran said, scratching his chin. "The Valiakeans can make you into anything at all—four legs, two, tail, anything at all." He stopped, and coughed apologetically, realizing that Gayal already *had* a tail. He looked up in the air. "Hey, doll, what do *you* think of all this?"

"Leave it to me," the cyborg's voice replied. "Alien but familiar. The Valiakean ship's just pulling alongside and I think I can feed in the necessaries."

"Okay, doll, do it," Bumgartner ordered. Then he looked directly at Gayal. "But on your own head be it," he warned her. "Whatever you come out is *it* for the duration."

Gayal nodded seriously. "I'm willing. They *can* change me back if—when—I return home, can't they?"

"Yeah, or any other time you're out here. Okay, let's do it. What about you, Koldon?"

The Quoark snorted. "You know this is a perfectly normal shape, the only proper one for civilized people. Besides, if things go sour at Haven, I'm set for life at the San Diego Zoo."

The airlock door opened and a creature stepped in. It looked like a hairless, half-formed humanoid, devoid of identifiable organs of sex, and totally naked.

"Are the subjects ready?" the Valiakean asked.

Bumgartner nodded, and gestured for Koldon to go with the strange creature.

Gayal stayed, hesitant. "So that's a Valiakean. Looks like a nothing."

"Pretty much," the Terran agreed. "That's just the best form for limited use in this environment. If we should suddenly lose temperature and pressure or start having a neon atmosphere at absolute Zero, that critter would just instantly change form to the proper requirements. Their world's such a horror and a hell that they're all really just blobs of protoplasmic jelly, able to adapt to any environment—and they *have* almost every environment almost every day down there. We wouldn't last ten seconds."

"Sounds useful. Why don't we just become like them for the duration?"

"It would be," Bumgartner admitted, "but they just won't do it. It would louse up their business. Now, get going! This is costing!"

She went.

The Valiakean came back and looked around. "There was a third? You?"

"No, a Fraskan. Had to keep him in the lifeboat because he couldn't survive here."

The Valiakean nodded. "Very well. We shall open a lock and a tube for Fraskan norms. I'll get him."

Gayal entered a chamber glowing with a greenish light. A stool stood in the center, with a notch for the tail so that she could sit down—something uncommon to her race, which even slept standing up.

"Sit on the stool," instructed a Valiakean voice that sounded like the other Valiakean voices she had heard. "We will need some pictures."

She sat, feeling very uncomfortable, and heard a series of whining noises, then nothing. A Valiakean entered, holding some photographic plates. It looked enough like the other to have been the same creature.

As it started to examine her, much like any doctor, Gayal noticed some strange phenomena. Tracking a muscular series with the aid of the photos, its right hand grew long enough to go around her left shoulder while the right one stayed short. She glanced at the photos— and didn't see much of anything. She'd expected at least X-rays. Then she looked at the creature's eyes. They no longer looked like hers, but were more prismatic, multifaceted. She had the opinion that the creature could see right through her.

Finally, the Valiakean went over to the wall, a pulsating bright green plane that seemed to have no outlet, and pressed a part of it. A chamber, something like a coffin, materialized from the wall and slid into the larger room.

"Get in, please, on your side," the Valiakean instructed.

It was almost a perfect fit, she saw as she climbed inside.

"You will be unconscious for a short period while the alterations are made," the Valiakean told her, sounding like a tailor. "Do not be alarmed. This will start— *now!*"

Everything went blank for Gayal.

Elsewhere in the Valiakean ship the other two experienced the same thing.

Koldon was the first back, having needed the least work.

While they were out, Bumgartner had readjusted the entire ship to Earth norms. Koldon, now adapted to the changes, felt no real differences, but did feel a bit more comfortable and at home.

"That's *much* better," he said—aloud!

The Terran jumped. "You spoke!" Bumgartner almost accused the other.

"Sure. Easier for radios, intercoms, and the like, where mostly nontelepathic people are. I thought of it *after* I was in, but I assumed the expense account would stand it."

Bumgartner shook his head in dismay. "All these changes . . . ! Man, I'll have to justify the whole batch!"

Koldon shrugged. "Got the food locker sorted out?" he asked. "Those bastards really *did* clean out my stomach!"

In about fifteen minutes Koldon was gorging himself once again, his appetite unaffected by the changes, when Gayal reappeared in the ship. The bear-creature stopped his eating and Bumgartner rose out of his seat.

"*I don't believe it!*" they both said in unison.

"Is there something wrong?" Gayal asked, concerned.

"No, no, no, nothing at all. A perfect compromise," Bumgartner assured her. "Perfect."

The cyborg had been presented with a problem and had solved it. Simply stated, it was to retain as much of the Delialian as was possible to remain comfortable and normal-seeming, while making her more acceptable to the far more Earth-human types she would be around.

Long black hair tumbled over very Earth-human shoulders. Her face looked Oriental, somewhat Mongoloid, and was a beauty by Earth standards. Her breasts had been Earth-humanized and perfectly proportioned. Yet a very slight bluish cast remained in the skin. It gave an exotic, almost erotic effect. From the waist down, starting just below the navel, her more equine features remained, although trimmer and more proportioned, giving her more the appearance of a faun. They saw that the tail had been trimmed back, softened, and reshaped, so that she could sit on it.

"Put a long dress on, down to the floor, and she could walk in New York City—even though that complexion would drive everybody nuts," Bumgartner said at last. "Perfect," he muttered, and shook his head in wonderment.

"I—I look more like your people, don't I?" she asked him.

"Well, yes, I guess—and no, too. Good enough to drive some guys wild, from the waist up," he acknowledged.

Koldon said nothing but was generally satisfied, even though he knew the apprehension in Gayal's mind. It would fade. It was different for most of the races: *they* had families, or compatriots, or the like similar to themselves back in Haven. Gayal didn't, and the more human, or human-mythological approach, was the best available compromise. It was still alien, but it would make *her* feel much more comfortable.

Vard was the last through. He had been barely changed, physically—he still looked like a very tall walking skeleton over which a thin, transparent skin had been stretched. Any normal Earth-human seeing him would be convinced that the dead *do* rise from the grave. But this, too, was all right, since Vard had felt alienated even at his *internal* acclimation and would have suffered worse with a more severe change. In a pinch, Vard, too, could pass on normal Earth—if it was dark, and if the observers were not too close. That probably wouldn't be necessary for any of them, Bumgartner knew, but it was helpful just in case.

The Fraskan studied his alien companions awhile, then went over to the cot which Koldon had almost crushed and lay down. He, too, did not fit on it, although he was as thin as Koldon was fat.

"I intend to sleep for a time," Vard said imperiously. "Please wake me for anything important."

The other three stared at him and at each other, and shrugged. So much for the need for companionship.

Bumgartner arranged for payment of accounts with the Valiakeans via Quoark, and the two ships broke off. The Haven ship moved out into space.

Ralph Bumgartner made his way back to the aft cabins and stopped at Gayal's. She was reading something from the ship's library tapes, and it looked like physics. "Heavy reading," he commented, indicating the reading screen.

She smiled, and flipped the viewer off.

"I was studying something on how these ships operate," she told him. "It is quite confusing, really. All of the science I ever learned said that nothing could exceed the speed of light, yet we travel vast distances in very short times."

"Oh, it's not impossible to grasp. It involves tiny particles called tachyons, particles that move always faster than light and do unpredictable things. These things have a pretty weird set of characteristics when you put them into a 'spin' or half-'spin.' "

"But—this book says that they are so tiny they cannot be seen. How can such things power us at all?"

He grinned, and sat down on the little ledge on the wall. "Well, it's a pretty big engine below us, much larger than the living area of the ship. The thing's basically a figure eight—sorry, a toroidal shape," he corrected, remembering that eights were not 8's in all languages. "The front of the ship is a scoop; it sucks up any materials, large and small, that we run into while traveling in space. And despite what you've heard about space being a vacuum, there's a lot of junk—gases, tiny particles of matter, and the like—out here. This matter is scooped in and fed to the toroidal plasma 'bottle' and past high-flux density coils. There's a reaccelerating field for maintaining linear exhaust through the nozzle assembly much like the electron field manipulation in a cathode-ray tube."

"Like television!" she put in.

"Exactly!" he agreed. "The vibration—the pulsing—you feel through the ship is the result of the collapse and regeneration of the fields that keep the engine going and protect us from the effects of this kind of travel."

"This action generates tachyons?" she asked. "And starts them spinning?"

"Right! Tachyons can spin in one of two directions, and cause some of the strange effects I mentioned in the field—and we're in the field, too. The pilot, or cybernetic monitor, has different uses for the tachyons, depending on whether they spin positively or negatively. When only the separated, positive tachyons are used, we attain what we call 'A' impulse—slower than light, but very fast. This is the local drive we use for getting in and out of systems and suchlike—a conventional drive. The progression using these 'plus' tachyons can get us from almost dead slow to close to the speed of light. For in-system work, not more than a couple thousand kilometers per second, we call the ranges A-1, A-2, and the like. Each increases the speed geometrically."

"But, at interstellar distances and velocities this would put everything and everyone within the ship into a slower time rate than the rest of the galaxy," she pointed out. "We would arrive centuries, even longer, after we'd left—only to find those born our contemporaries long dead."

"That would be true," he responded, "if we had to live with positive-spin tachyons only. Without the incredible speed and accuracy of the cybernetic controls, we couldn't use a tachyon space drive at all. If *you* tried to run an engine like this, it would explode, because tachyons are also generated that spin negatively and *they* are anti-matter—they annihilate positive matter. Their field and that of the plus-rotating tachyons interact, releasing tremendous energy, and cause the basic drive.

"But because of the separation possibilities, we can choose which field will envelop us. The positive field gives us 'A,' or 'normal space'; the negative field gives us 'D,' or 'anti-space.' We get the same accelerative effects as the positive spin, but we are operating in a negative universe—and in negative time."

"So our ship is really a time machine," Gayal said, awed.

"More or less," he agreed. "But the amount of matter available to the scoop controls the time differential we get. In general, it's sufficient to offset the difference in relativity, and get us where we're going on pretty much the same time scale as the rest of the galaxy. If we pushed it and didn't travel too far, we might gain a couple of seconds on subjective time—that's the theory behind fighter engagements, ship-to-ship. You'll learn a lot more about that shortly."

"But dealing with this 'anti-matter'—isn't it dangerous? Couldn't we be canceled out?"

"There's danger in every kind of power source," he answered offhandedly. "The atomic power used on your world is equally so. But we have a lot more safeguards on board. In addition to the pilot, we have nine separate safety devices that would shut down the engines or produce compensating factors to offset any problems. You'd have to introduce something into the nozzle throat that was much denser than lead but without great mass—and lots of it. Even then, the safety systems would avoid a blowup simply by shutting us down to a halt until we could clean it out. No, it's probably the safest engine ever devised. I've never heard of a ship being lost due to engine malfunction, and, if we didn't run into enough matter to power it, we could even cannibalize enough of the ship to get to a better place."

"It's all so new . . ." she gushed enthusiastically.

"Well," Bumgartner shrugged, "they've already got tachyon theory on my world, and we're pretty backward by most people's standards."

"Your world?" she repeated in a puzzled tone. "But I thought your world would already have all this."

"No. It's a primitive world, really. A very young one. Most of my world has no idea that all this even exists— or that you, your world, The Hunter, Haven, or The Bromgrev exist. Most of them would label this type of travel impossible. Barbarians make good fighters, however, being so close to the animal themselves. Quite a number of our best barbarians have been recruited to help out, and the fact that most of my people believe this impossible helps us enormously to do our work."

He switched over to the head of her bed. She put her head in his lap.

"Do you find me more pleasing now than before?" she asked suddenly.

"Very much so," he replied softly.

"Are we—" She hesitated. "Are we sexually compatible?"

He grinned. "Not really. Your genes are Delialian, mine Terran; and we've never found the answer to that one."

"No, no! Not *that* way!"

"Oh, I *see*." And he did see. "Well, we're both from bi-sexual races, and we're opposites."

"I thought as much. Would you like to show me the barbarian's way, Ralph Bumgartner?"

He was ahead of her.

"I hate to disturb you, lover boy," the cyborg's voice burst in a half-hour or so later, "but I just thought I'd tell you both to take your time."

Bumgartner groaned, and rolled over onto the floor. He'd screwed a hundred alien life forms for the hell of it, but he had never been through an experience quite like this one.

"Wow!" he exclaimed, and exhaled. Regaining his composure, he asked shakily, "What's it all about, doll?"

"This is hard to believe," came the reply, "but we've been ordered to stand to and not come in-system."

"Huh? Why?"

"According to the report I just got, a Rhambdan fleet is starting to materialize between Neptune and Pluto. It looks like a full-scale attack force. The Bromgrev is going to try and take us."

STEP THREE

1

ALARMS RING. MEN, women, others—of many races and shapes—all drop what they are doing and run to their ships. Had they been on Earth, it would have been called a "scramble"—get to your ships and get into action formation as quickly as possible. They had trained for it, practiced for it, until the actions were as reflex as the eye reacting to a change in the light.

There were approximately fifteen thousand ships of varying sizes and classes, mostly housed in bases hollowed out of asteroids and outpost planetary moons. Titan and Pluto alone accounted for about half, the latter being the only planet used for such things.

It takes time to group for an attack, and all defense is based on that fact. The Bromgrev's fleets' materializing almost in the midst of The Hunter's was a complete surprise, and they did not materialize in any apparent order. Had the aggressor's hand been tipped in any way, a waiting, much smaller group of defense ships could have eliminated the fleets easily, before they could orient themselves. Such was the value of spies in interstellar warfare, and such was the value of the Rhambdan mass mind that major decisions almost never leaked.

After the lead ships of the attacking force appeared, they quickly vanished once again into null, or zero stasis, accomplished when the rotation of the tachyons in their drive achieved parity of spin. Subjective time literally ceased to exist for the ship and the beings on it.

Zero stasis made them almost impossible to locate, and gave them maximum protection, since the moment temporal stasis was achieved the ships were nearly impossible to locate—and their guns would be trained and manned. But it was a two-way street: the attackers could not know what was happening on the true, or A-1 time line of the battle, either; and communication was impossible between their ships.

Stasis time was used to make final checks and to head for rendezvous on automatics at D-1. Most battles were won or lost on the strength of planning and the precision of crew training: the trick was to arrive in a pattern so varied that the grouping points could not be predicted by the defenders' computers. Otherwise, the defense would have you.

Joining the defense fleet within minutes were several large supplemental units that could be contacted and called in quickly. The attacker, then, had to hit fast and win decisively, since the tachyon drive played games with time and new units could show up within seconds of the defenders' distress signal—because of the greater mass available to the drive scoop near a stellar mass.

The Bromgrev's intelligence was extremely good, but there were simply too many different races and too many generals to consult, and, too, defensive patterns became obvious after careful study. The Bromgrev was his own planning staff, and could feed attack information even to the ships of his allies without their own commanders knowing where they were headed.

Once in position, his ships would rendezvous at predetermined points and move in on the target. The defenders would have to halt the attack, turn it, or force losses too great to continue. True, spatial warfare being what it was, a large number of ships could attain the objective—but they could not hold it unless they scattered or destroyed the defending forces. Thus, ship-to-ship warfare was the rule, fought well outside the objective.

The pilot was like all his fellows: a specialist, highly trained and fully aware of the capabilities of his ship and the objectives of the enemy. Like all of them, he

had never really believed that there would be a battle—
not here, anyway, and certainly not now. He did not have
time to think of strategy, brilliant maneuvers, or fast master strokes. When the buzzers sounded, he dropped everything and ran to the ship. The pilot was seated in the
command couch within forty seconds of the alarm. Check-
ing his board, he noted that the gunnery crew was already
in place and the automated systems were functioning
normally.

Gunnery consisted of two other individuals with
whom he shared his quarters. A move had been made
to make the ships entirely automated, but it had never
worked; somehow the programmers never quite imagined all conceivable situations.

At +00.06, a systems check showed everything
green and the pilot moved his command couch which
resembled a common lounge chair with foot rest, to the
halfway position—best for maintaining circulation.
Reaching to his right, he removed a helmet from its
holder and placed it on his head as the gunners did the
same. From the rear of the pilot's helmet trailed a series
of thick cables which disappeared into the floor behind
his couch.

The pilot placed his arms and legs in straps and
pulled an X-shaped belt series loosely over his midsection. If anything hit the ship, it would be essential that
his body stay in place.

At +00.09, the pilot leaned back, relaxed, and
flipped in order a series of eight toggle switches on a
small console to his right.

Then he shut his eyes.

The starfield opened around him, seen as no one but
a ship's crew ever saw it.

His mind melded with the ship's master computer,
combining the incredible programming of a thousand
military geniuses with his own brain, linking the ship's
controls—all controls—to his own mental whims.

He *was* the ship.

Within sixty seconds of the buzzer's sounding, he had
closed the locks, energized the piles, and was speeding
out of the hole in the floating rock that was their station
and home.

The gunners had slightly different views. They saw their own hemispheres in perfect depth and detail. As the pilot became the ship, they became one with the guns, which shot concentrated beams of energy able to rip huge holes in other ships, energy drawn from the surpluses produced in their ship's drive. But each was also a qualified pilot; should anything at all happen to the pilot, the ship would instantly switch to the one of them least dangerously preoccupied with the enemy. This was rare, though: normally, one hit and you were out.

The pilot felt like God, with a total view of the heavens and fantastic depth of field. The sense of being alone, one with the universe and in total command, swept him every time, and did this, in fact, to all the pilots. Some became so intoxicated that they could no longer bear to return to their normal selves. These the Valiakeans had "adapted" to the ships themselves: the cyborgs. Their number was steadily increasing.

The enemy was ahead. He could see them as energized dots, covering the sky like the center of a galaxy. And yet he was able to distinguish each and every ship, know instantly its size and relative distance. He slowed from D-1 to A-1, normal time, and the cloud of the enemy grew too dense to believe.

There must be a quarter of a million of them, he thought. All stops had been pulled out on this one, all right.

By the time defensive formations had been attained at +00.14, the defenders' ships numbered about a hundred thousand—not enough, but good enough for a start; they could depend on the steady arrival of reinforcements as superfast messenger ships carried the news to the far fleets. These would proceed here at D-4, an anti-time rate that would get the closest of them here before they left, and where deceleration could place whole friendly forces instantly in the midst of the enemy at any moment.

Defense was linked, overall, to a series of regional flagships for each battle theatre; these, in turn, were linked to the master flagship on which the overall battle commander—The Hunter, if it was possible to get him—would call the shots. The coordination could never have been done by brain alone, for simply to transmit messages the flagships and their units had to be on the same level at the same time.

All commands and comments were at the speed of thought.

"Commit on right flank," came the order from Flag 144.

The pilot and his backup units went into action.

The objective, of course, was to identify and knock out the opposition's flagships; when that happened, his formations lost the close contact needed for coordinated action, and, in the seconds before alternate communication lines could be established, the enemy group could be eliminated. This was also true of the ships of the Rhambdan mass-mind; incorrectly time-phased with each other, each *was* The Bromgrev but momentarily on its own, out of touch with the mass-mind itself.

The pilot identified the flagship and started in, his formation of fifty ships in a rough cross. Flagships were generally built to look like fighters—small and unassuming—to decrease their vulnerability, but they were never hard to spot, as they were always the most protected ship in the formation. In the first few feints they could be easily pegged—but not easily taken out.

The cross fanned out, seeking a way around the fighter horde that advanced. The gunners opened up; the pilot put them in a slow spin at A-1. Shots rang out—invisible, silent but deadly beams from almost all of the ships on both sides at once. The attackers took the widespread formation with guns aimed out and on constant fire; the defenders depended on short, accurate bursts.

A Rhambdan ship flew across the beam of the pilot's vessel, causing him to pull up and sending the ship into a fast reverse spin.

"Two on the right, six o'clock," came the flagship's warning, but the gunners had already pegged them and were hammering away.

One of the enemy suddenly turned into a pinpoint of light, then vanished. The other crossed to the pilot's rear and did a roll, bringing his ship up on the pilot's tail. Maneuvering for the best shots, the pilot almost rammed the wreckage of the enemy ship they had destroyed.

"Three more on. Dive! Dive! Re-up minus, repeat, minus," the flagship ordered.

"Dive!" the pilot called to warn the gunners, and went to D-1, in the minus temporal level. "Down to 3 and back up fast," he warned them, then executed the acceleration at the mark. He reversed at the halfway, pulled back to his original position, and immediately phased back into A-1.

Ahead he saw the fighter chasing his own ship and he was now behind the chaser. As his own A-1 ship phased into D for the maneuver he had already accomplished, the gunners took the chase fighter out.

All over the millions of miles between Neptune and Pluto the battles went on, fleet to fleet, squadron to squadron, ship to ship, in levels of sub-light subjective time and at the four basic levels of faster-than-light, or D time.

But normal time progressed with the battle; and the more normal time that passed, the more numerous the defenders became. They came from all over the galaxy, at null-speeds, as fast as the messenger ships could get there, phase in, broadcast the alarm, and phase out for the next destination. An attack on Haven brought them all.

The pilot, in his own battle sector, had done well, sustaining no injury while taking seven of the enemy. His squadron's luck had been equally good: of the fifty that started, thirty-seven were still operational.

The fighters had been drawn out or destroyed in the enemy squadron he had been facing, and new reinforcements had brought him back up to strength. The flagship, still covered with fighters, was nonetheless exposed here and there, phasing in and out of stasis to confuse the attacking shots without losing contact for long with its defenders. One moment it was there, the next not.

The pilot's flagship deployed some of the newcomers along the entire D-line front while keeping the original ships at sub-light. Enemy protective fighter screen actions became multilevel as well, thinning them out.

The defenders had made a breach almost in the center of the attack line, and The Bromgrev had called in a lot of reserves to plug it. This left only the rapidly thinning screen ahead, with no reinforcements. They had to nail the flagship of the enemy squadron before the center plug was achieved and the right flank could be relieved. A breakthrough here would mean a total fragmentation of forces—and a link with Haven forces on the other side of the offensive line.

The pilot decided to go in.

"Dive! Dive!" he warned the gunners, who mentally switched phase as the ship did, going to D-1, then back up through the center of the line at A-1, almost on top of the enemy flagship.

There was a rumble and a tremor as one of the enemy beams struck a glancing blow on his ship, but, for a split second, the gaps in the fighter screen exposed the enemy flagship. The gunners struck and the flagship winked out.

Almost as soon as it happened, the rest of the squadron rallied and moved in on the disorganized enemy fighters, mopping them up.

The pilot saw one ship of the defeated force phase into D, and received permission to chase. It was headed in-system.

The pilot located it at D-1 and started to close, but could not get in close enough for a good shot. Suddenly the object of the pursuit went to null, stopping dead almost literally in both time and space and causing the pilot to overshoot.

Cursing himself for his carelessness, he halted and backtracked, but the fugitive slipped through the defense zone at D-2, then came back up on the pilot's tail, firing steadily.

He rolled, and managed to come up just under the enemy ship. The gunners fired and seemed to strike the enemy—but did not destroy it. It vanished into A.

The pilot brought his own ship up to A and finally spotted the ship, wobbling crazily but still headed in-system. He noted the trajectory but did not give chase.

The enemy ship, disabled, sputtering on its last legs, would be captured in Earth's gravity well and pulled down before he could phase to get to it. Let the ground men take it.

Moving back to the battle, the pilot could see the field emptying. The Bromgrev had lost too many ships in too short a time to penetrate and hold; the defenders were mopping up, but it was over. Back in contact with Flag, the pilot was told to break and return. The ship was no longer needed.

He broke and headed back for Base in the asteroids. As he completed the course setting, he could feel his power ebbing, his strength diminishing. The starfield was closing in on him.

"No! No!" he protested. "I can't go back! I can't . . ."

The man on the couch awoke. For a few minutes he just lay there; then, slowly, his head throbbing with pain, he disconnected the helmet and straps. He heard audible groans over the ship's intercoms. The gunners, too, were coming out of it.

Shaking his head to clear it, he raised the couch to a sitting position and fed the coordinates for the remainder of the flight back to Base.

It was always this way: that feeling of freedom, of strength, of power, when he was the ship—and the sense of puniness, of being an insect bound to the flesh, and one of billions, when he came out of it.

Flag had sounded Recall, and it reached the one very tiny area of the ship's computers that he couldn't reach: the automatic equipment that pulled them out of their union with their machinery even though they did not want it.

They never wanted it.

He felt a pain in his left shoulder and, rubbing it, saw that the shock of the glancing blow had caused him to be cut by the straps. Another aggravation of the flesh.

He glanced over at the two chronographs on either side of the control console, one labeled SUBJECTIVE and the other OBJECTIVE.

The subjective control read 04.51.

Almost five hours of battle. It had been a rough one. The objective clock read 00.13.

In normal time, the whole thing had been fought in thirteen minutes.

"Hey! Var!" hailed the voice of the right gunner.

"Yeah, Gro? What's the problem?"

"Who won?"

2

THE SHIP CAME in low over the horizon, like some ghostly, misshapen balloon floating wobbily down as the helium slowly escaped and it glowed a sickly blue much stronger than moonlight.

Everyone in town who was out that night saw it. A meteor, most said, and families rushed out into backyards to get a better view.

Jennifer Barron heard the commotion outside her apartment and made her way over to the French windows and out onto the balcony. The warm, humid air enveloped her like a moist rug, and the mosquitoes took the exit as a signal to attack. She heard her neighbor muttering exclamations under his breath.

"What's going on, John?" she called over to him.

"A meteor, Jenny. Biggest damned thing I've ever seen! It's bigger and brighter than the moon! Wow! *Look at that!*"

"Describe it to me, John," she asked. "What's it like?"

For the first time, through his excitement, John remembered that Jennifer was totally blind.

He coughed apologetically. "It's really kinda huge, Jenny—larger than this apartment house. Sorta glowing, kinda floating down. It's gonna hit pretty soon. Funny, though . . ."

"What is?" she asked, trying to picture the unprecedented.

"It's coming in so damned *slow*. Every meteor I've ever seen has come in like fireworks."

She remained on the balcony, feeling the excitement and hearing the comments and sensing the awe, but she could not escape the dark thoughts. In a few minutes it'll be all over, she told herself. And I'll go back in again and be alone.

In the dark.

But she was wrong. For her, it was the beginning.

For Alice Mary McBride, age nineteen, it was the end.

She threaded her way up the mountain in her little yellow sports car at over 60 miles per hour, hypnotized by the speed and the sound the car made on the curves. She was high and she knew it. She felt as if the car were going about an inch an hour, and she kicked the accelerator down even harder, urging the little car forward, faster, faster.

There. The big curve. How fast can I take it?

As she made the curve, wheels squealing, she came in sight of the object, coming straight in toward her. For a moment she thought that the pot had been even better stuff than she'd believed, but she suddenly realized that the thing was real—and getting larger every second. As she had been hypnotized by the driving before, now the object held her attention. She could think of nothing else, the marijuana high creating a one-track mind of fixed but limited purpose. The road aimed her straight at the thing, now reflected in Lake Moses a thousand feet below.

There was a curve ahead.

It was never determined whether the object hit Lake Moses—throwing up a huge wave that splattered areas hundreds of feet from the water's edge—before, after, or at the same time as Alice Mary McBride.

The old man, standing on the front porch of his house about eight hundred feet farther up the mountain watching the weird object like everyone else in the town far below, saw the car go through the railing, spin, and plunge into the lake below. There were two bubbling areas in the lake after they both hit: one about in the middle of the lake; the other, much smaller and briefer, toward the mountain side.

"Oh my God! Mary! Mary!" he screamed, and started running down the mountain road although his truck was handy.

Cutting through the switchbacks on old vertical trails, it still took him almost twenty minutes to reach the lake below, tired, huffing and puffing. He didn't stop, the adrenaline forcing him onward. He jumped into the water and started swimming to where the car had gone under. The lake was deep in the center, but only eight or ten feet near the mountainside.

It wouldn't have mattered.

Joseph McBride was going after his daughter.

It had taken only three hours to reach Mycroft, Virginia, from Washington, and Paul Carleton Savage didn't feel very tired. Although it was almost 4 A.M. when he pulled in, he could see the red lights of the State Police cars up on the mountainside near the break in the barrier and others down at the lake's edge. Pausing for one of the three traffic lights in the little town, he reached into the glove compartment and brought out three wallets. Glancing into them, he found the one he wanted and put it in his right breast pocket before the light changed.

He headed out to the base of the lake.

A roadblock stopped him about a hundred yards from the place where the State Police cars and ambulance were situated.

"Sorry, sir," said a trooper in the hard hill dialect of western Virginia. "Nobody 'lowed past this point."

Savage smiled and reached for the wallet and gave it to the trooper without comment.

Under the emblem of the Department of Defense was his picture and vital statistics; around the seal it said, "Defense Intelligence Agency." The trooper was impressed.

"Okay, sir, you can go through. Nothin' much happenin', anyway."

"I can start right here," Savage told him. "What happened? All we got was a report that a meteor, or UFO of some kind, crashed in the lake."

"That's about it, sir," responded the trooper. "Ever-

'body saw it—weird thing, pretty big, kinda *floated* in from the east, there." He pointed. "Local girl got panicked drivin' up there, and went in with the thing. The lake's the local reservoir—natural, but pretty deep in the middle. We got a coupla guys up from the Department of Highways with some divin' gear they use to check out drainage and the like in the lake, and they're tryin' to get the girl out now. The car was a softtop. You know, one of them little foreign sports cars, convertible. She landed upside down, so it may take some time to get the body out."

Savage nodded. "Okay. Thanks, officer," he said, and slowly moved the car up to the small crowd of police and rescue people ahead.

One officious-looking middle-aged individual spotted him and came over to where he had just gotten out of the car. Savage mentally bet himself that it was the mayor.

"Hello, sir," Savage hailed, and pulled the ID out again. "Savage, DoD. Any progress?"

"Tom Horgan, Mayor of Mycroft," the man said, and offered a pudgy hand which Savage shook.

Horgan barely glanced at the ID; like most people, he never questioned anyone who spoke with obvious conviction and authority. First rule of being a private detective: be a convincing liar.

"I'm out to check on your mysterious new resident," Savage explained. "DoD takes a dim view of uninvited guests dropping in like that."

The mayor chuckled, then became suddenly grave.

"You heard about our tragedy," he said more than asked.

Savage nodded. "Yeah, too bad. Who was she?"

"Girl named Alice McBride—only, only her old man called her that. Everybody else called her Kip, name she picked sometime and liked. A wild one—booze, drugs, and all that. But, still, a good looker—and nineteen."

"Um, yeah," Savage murmured dryly. He craned his neck and viewed the spot from which she had plunged. "You'd never even know there was a road up there from here," he commented. "What the hell was she

doing driving up there around midnight? Lovers' Lane?
She was alone, wasn't she?"

"Naw, nothin' like that. She lived up there with her
pop—you can't see the house quite from this angle. Ex
Army man. His wife died giving birth to the girl, and he
retired from the Army and moved here. Bought the old
place and fixed it up pretty good. Drives the fuel oil
truck here in winter; right now, he's the ice cream
man."

One of the divers surfaced and swam in toward
shore. The second's head appeared shortly after, about
forty feet out; then he, too, started in. Everyone rushed
over to where the two were emerging from the water.
The first diver was shaking his head from side to side.

"No way," he told them. "The goddam thing's upside
down in about fourteen feet. We'll need a block and
tackle rigged on a couple of rowboats to get it over. The
doors are jammed shut."

"We'll get her out," the second diver assured them,
"but it'll be tomorrow afternoon before we can get the
stuff we need up here and ready. Won't make no difference, though—'cept I'd like to get that car out of there
before the oil and shit fouls up the whole reservoir."

"What about the other thing that went in?" Savage
called out. "See anything of it?"

"Naw," the first diver answered. "It's too far out, and
water's too dark. Maybe we'll see it when everything's
completely settled in there and we got some light."

"Okay, men, nothing to do until tomorrow!" the
mayor called out. "The troopers'll keep watch on
things. Why don't we all get some sleep? It's gonna be a
long day tomorrow."

Murmurs of assent could be heard, and men started
for their cars and trucks. The two divers unloaded their
tanks and masks in the back of a yellow state truck and
prepared to go as well.

Savage walked back to his car, started it, and drove
back toward town. Short of the town itself, he pulled
over to the side and pressed a stud under the right side
of the dash. A small radio unit dropped down into
place. Switching it on, he picked up the telephone-style
handset.

"Savage to D.C. Night Watch," he called.

"Night Watch," responded a bored woman's voice. "What you got, Savage?"

"Looks like trouble, Eleana. This was no meteor, baby. It's almost certainly a ship, probably a small fighter."

"Yeah, that's what we think," she responded. "One of the ships was hit and managed to fall toward Earth. Looks as if it had enough power to slow its fall. Too bad."

"Oh, sure, too bad," he mimicked acidly. "So what the hell am *I* supposed to do?"

"Any sign of survivors?"

"None that I've seen. Why?"

"It was one of *theirs,*" she explained patiently, "and somebody was alive enough to bring that thing in. It's got its own atmosphere, and it's still pressurized. Chances are that at least one of them's still in there, alive and trying to figure a way out."

"Oh, boy!" Savage muttered, sounding less than thrilled by the prospect. "Something tells me I'm about to earn my keep."

"You better believe it," the Night Watch replied. "You know we have some pretty weird and nasty life forms, but what's on *their* side makes ours look like Sunday School class. And if it's a Rhambdan you've got, the whole mind and intellect of The Bromgrev is in there."

"So what do you want me to do about it?"

"Stall 'em. Keep anybody from going in until we can get a good Team out there. And, if there's a breakout, use your own judgment—but make sure you kill anything that comes out of there, *fast!*"

"They've already *been* down," he told her. "A girl got panicked and jumped her car into the damned lake and she's still in there. They haven't gotten her body out yet."

"Um. Did they see anything?"

"No, nothing. But they're going down tomorrow afternoon to haul the car out, and they're sure to see something that big with daylight and clear water. How soon can you get a Team here?"

"Tomorrow morning. What cover do you want?"

"Better make them Defense Intelligence Agency," he told her. "That's what I'm supposed to be, and if they have to blow the thing up it'll make more sense. But by tomorrow afternoon it's got to be done—or the shit's hit the fan."

"Okay. Will do. Get yourself a room and catch a few hours' sleep. As soon as you get the room, let me know where, and then call it a night. I assume they're guarding the site?"

"Yeah, State Police."

"Good enough. If anything blows, you'll hear about it. Watch clear."

"Savage clear," he responded, and put the phone back in its cradle. It slowly rose back up into the dash.

Getting a few hours' sleep wasn't a bad idea, but it seemed odd. Not watch the area . . . ? On second thought, what *could* he do if some alien monster came up? Hush it up? Hardly. And if the troopers couldn't kill it, then neither could he, without the Team's weaponry.

The sign said MERRITT MOTEL AND APARTMENTS, and a faded red neon "Vacancy" sign was lit underneath, the second "a" burnt out. He pulled in and saw that the office was still lit. Considering all the excitement and the near-perfect view of the lake that the place presented, this was not unexpected.

A slight, elderly woman was talking to a man about her age—seventyish, Savage guessed. They stopped as he entered. People usually did: the huge, brutish-looking man with the metal claw for a right hand was a showstopper even in cosmopolitan New York.

"Yes, sir, may I help you?" she asked pleasantly, but her eyes kept drifting to the claw.

"I need a room. I saw your vacancy sign—"

"Oh, yes," she responded, giving him one of the usual white cards to fill out. "Thirty a night. It's the in-season, you know. Only reason we're not full up tonight is because it's a Monday. Always slow on Mondays."

"Uh-huh," Savage mumbled. "I may be here a couple of days."

"Oh, that's all right," she assured him. "Checkout's eleven any day. Let us know as early as you can when you decide to leave, won't you?"

Savage assured her that he would and, getting his key and directions, he drove down to the room.

The place was fairly new, he saw, with neat balconies all around.

The room was actually a studio apartment—a large room with full furniture and a kitchenette. The place had obviously been built more with apartments in mind than a motel, but when it hadn't been completely rented they had supplemented.

Going over to the French windows, he saw that they led to the small railed balcony with two metal chairs. Off in the distance he could see the flashing lights of the troopers at the lake. Not a bad base, he congratulated himself, as if the choice had been deliberate.

Setting his portable alarm clock for 8 A.M., he stripped and plopped on the bed.

He awoke to the sound of somebody fumbling around with his door.

Quickly but quietly, he jumped up and pulled his .38. The clock said 7:15.

The sound went away, but he heard someone going down the hall. Putting the pistol on the bed, he went to the door and opened it chain-wide.

A woman wearing sunglasses and carrying a bamboo cane was at the next door, feeling it. He instantly realized what had happened. She was blind and feeling the numerals to find hers. The sound had been the cane hitting the door as she'd reached up.

She heard Savage open the door, obviously, since she turned in his direction.

"I'm—I'm so sorry," she said apologetically. "Did I wake you?"

"Yes," he replied, "but that's all right. Time I was up and about, anyway."

He studied her for a moment. She was short—about five-two or -three—and very chubby, with thick legs and pudgy fingers. But she had long auburn hair draped around her shoulders, a pleasant, almost cheery-looking face, and a pretty large set of boobs that were obviously braless under the dark overlarge T-shirt she was wearing. Dressed right, and with a little makeup, she could still be a decent-looking woman; absent a fair number of pounds, she'd be downright cute.

"I—I just had to change apartments after three years, when my air conditioner broke down," she explained in a voice that was soft and low and very pleasing. Her somewhat halting manner of speech showed her to be a person who didn't talk to many people. "I'm, well, not used to where the apartment is now— how many steps and the like. You get into a habit, and it's hard to break."

"That's okay," he assured her. "I'm only a temporary guest, with work to do. But—say, had breakfast yet?" She looked hesitant for a moment. "I'm a stranger here and there's no coffee shop in this place. If you'll tell me a decent place to eat, I'll treat you."

She paused a moment more; then her face broke into a why-the-hell-not? smile and she said, "All right. No, I haven't had breakfast—and I—I don't get out very much. Tell you what: I'll buy. It's the least I can do for waking you up."

"You're on," he chuckled, and suddenly realized that he was nude—not even the claw was on. "Just let me get dressed."

"I'm in 207—no, 213," she corrected herself, and laughed nervously. "See what I mean?"

"Okay. Be with you in five minutes," he told her, and shut the door.

He dressed quickly, the hardest and longest thing being rigging the claw to respond to his muscle movement. Funny, he thought. Two cripples meet in a hall. What an ideal couple, he chuckled at the thought. She was probably the first girl he had ever met who wouldn't be repulsed by his appearance.

Before going to get her, he glanced out the window and saw several Army vehicles of varying sizes parked around the lake. He felt reassured. The Team was already on the job, and all he had to do was watch. Plenty of time for breakfast.

He went down the hall and rapped on 213. "Ready for breakfast?" he called out.

In a moment, she opened the door. The apartment was almost a duplicate of his own, but the furniture showed signs of that owned, lived-in look. It was also pretty messy—unkempt in much the way she seemed, herself. As if she just didn't give a damn.

He had known some other blind people, but almost to a one they'd been fanatically neat and led near-normal lives. This girl obviously did not. He wondered what her story was.

She walked over to the door with confidence: the furniture had obviously been arranged as in the old apartment, in the manner of the blind, so that she knew the placement of every single thing. She carried no purse, but a wallet was tucked in the rear pocket of her jeans.

"I had to put some sandals on," she explained. "They don't allow bare feet in the diner."

She went out and he closed the door after her.

As they walked down the hall, Savage resisted the temptation to help her. This was *her* territory, and he knew that the sure path to alienation was to remind her of her handicap. He had resented too many people trying to handle things for him.

"What were you doing up so early?" he asked conversationally.

She laughed shyly.

"Promise not to tell anyone?" she whispered.

"Promise," he replied with mock solemnity.

"There's a sundeck up on the roof that's not unlocked until 8. I have a key to the door and I go up there, lock myself on top, and sunbathe in the nude. The early morning sun feels great. The old people who run the place know it, but they take pity on a poor blind girl's one pleasure, and run interference."

"Hmmm . . . As a member of the Future Rapists of America, I'll file that away."

She laughed—a very amiable laugh, he thought.

"Just try it. I'm the best blind karate student in the county!"

"Say, will we need a car to get to this diner?"

"Yes, it'd be better than walking seven blocks," she replied. "But you'll have to guide me to and help me in the car."

This he did easily, and soon, following her directions, they pulled up to THE DINER.

He thought of it all in capital letters because it looked like a million diners he'd seen—silver, long and thin, sort of like a wheelless railroad car. He helped her in and they took seats in a booth near the door. The diner wasn't all that crowded—by 8:30, the regulars were on their way to work and any others were out gawking at the operations by the lake. He ordered sausage and eggs for the two of them.

"Well, sir," she said playfully, "what with this being our first date and me buying, I think we ought to be properly introduced."

"Paul Carleton Savage," he answered. "And you?"

"Jennifer Barron."

She put out her right hand. He hesitated for a second, then shook it awkwardly with his left.

"How come the odd handshake?" she asked as the waitress poured coffee.

Savage hesitated. Here it was. Well, it was only strike one. She couldn't see the rest of him.

"I—well, I have a handicap," he told her.

"Well, that gives us something in common . . ." she replied uncertainly. "What's yours?"

"Put out your right hand again— Careful of the coffee!"

She did, and he put the claw into it. She took it, felt it carefully, shaping its line and form. Her face was serious and intense.

"A mechanical hand?"

"Yep. Call me Lefty."

"How'd you lose it—if I can ask."

"Vietnam," he replied. "It was shot off."

A slight shiver went through her at the thought, but it passed quickly.

"In case you haven't noticed," she said after a moment, "I have a handicap, too. Nothing so glamorous."

"Well, I told you about mine. Tell me about yours."

"Nothing to tell, really," she replied. "I was born blind."

She reached up and took off her dark sunglasses. Her eyes were snow white. She had no pupils. She put the glasses back on.

"*That* usually turns everybody's stomach," she said sourly.

The eggs came as if on cue.

"So does the hand," he replied. "Looks like we were made for each other!"

She laughed, and started in on the sausage.

The eyes had been a mild shock, but, as his claw had with her, they quickly became irrelevant.

"The only thing repulsive," he told her, "is the amount of ketchup you're pouring on perfectly good scrambled eggs."

She laughed. "Savage," she said. "That's a good English name, like Barron."

"Actually, I have no idea of my ancestry. I'm an orphan."

"Then where'd the name come from?"

"Well, let's just say I'm not really handsome," he explained gingerly. "Never was. Too much hair, and a build more like an ape than anything. I was a *really* ugly baby. I think my parents thought I was retarded or something. At any rate, one of the wits at the orphanage thought I kind of looked like a caveman he'd seen pictures of in an anthropology book, and Savage I became. Paul was just a good name for a boy in a Lutheran orphanage, and I added the middle name, Carleton, myself because it sounded classy."

He woofed down the meal and started on his second cup of coffee, starting to feel fully awake for the first time. "What about you?"

"No real story," she replied casually. "I was born here. Daddy was a real estate agent and did a pretty good business, upper-middle-class and all that. I was the only child. I think my parents blamed themselves for my blindness; anyway, they lavished all their attention on me—special tutors, braille class, Seeing Eye dog, the whole bit. But I was really sort of a prisoner in the house. It was my world. I knew it absolutely.

"The tutors helped me get state certification, and I graduated from high school sort of without ever being in a school. I could have gone—but Mama wasn't willing to let me out of her sight, it seemed."

"Where are your parents now?" he asked.

"Dead. Car crash coming home from a New Year's party, 'bout two years ago. I might've gone, but there were only older people there and I didn't like to socialize much—all this 'Please, dear, let me do this for you' and 'Oh, you poor, poor girl' bullcrap. I stayed home—and inherited about a hundred and fifty thousand. I hadn't known Daddy was worth nearly that much. I sold the house for another sixty, and banked it, then moved into the apartment. It was all I needed: I have few expenses, the money draws good interest, and I can probably last the rest of my life on the money."

Savage decided on a calculated risk. The torrent of words that poured from her demonstrated her extreme loneliness, and told the whole story. Isolated from the mainstream of society—even blind society—by overprotective parents, and told she was crippled and treated that way all her life, she had not known how to communicate. Dropped suddenly into real life, she had no experience to cope with it. She'd retreated into the small world of her apartment, and stayed. People wanted to help, of course, but their obvious motive—pity—only increased her own self-pity. She dressed sloppily because she didn't have anyone to dress for. She kept a sloppy house because she had lost hope. When she was feeling *particularly* lonely, she ate.

Savage chose his words carefully. "Did you ever," he asked softly, "wish you'd gone to that party?"

She froze, sitting straight up for an instant; then she seemed to melt. Tears welled up behind the glasses and streamed down her cheeks.

"I—I'm sorry I said that," he apologized. "I shouldn't have."

"No, no, that's all right," she said. "You're right. Yes, I've wished it. I—I've even thought of correcting the mistake."

"What the hell for?" he chastised her. "There's no reason for it. You're not unattractive, and, being *born* blind, you're less handicapped than somebody who *goes* blind. There are lots of productive things you could do. Jobs. Get out!"

"For what?" she asked bitterly. "For who? Why? So I can exchange one prison for another?"

"Maybe for me . . ." he said softly.

"For you . . . ?" She gave a bitter, humorless laugh. "Who are you, Paul Carleton Savage? A traveler? A man of great experience? Somebody who got here last night and will be gone tomorrow morning."

Savage sat thinking for a few seconds. How strange, he thought. How really strange. Come in on a dirty case, and in the space of an hour in the morning get caught up with somebody. She was right, after all. If the Team cleaned things up, he would be gone. Somehow, he felt very guilty about all this. Abruptly, he decided he would take a vacation—they were pretty flexible around D.C. headquarters, anyway—when this job was done. Here. Stay a while. See it through. He'd made a commitment somehow.

"I'll be here for a while, Jennifer," he told her. "Let's see what develops."

She smiled a wan smile, but she didn't believe him. Even so, this was the first time *anything* had happened. It was like the excitement last night, she thought. Enjoy it while it lasts . . .

"Let's go," he said, picking up the check.

"How much is it?" she asked him.

"Never mind. My treat."

"Oh, no!" she shot back. "Remember—this is *my* date."

He shrugged. "Three twelve."

She brought out the wallet and counted out three ones and took a quarter from the change purse. "You leave the tip," she said.

As Savage got in the car, he heard the buzzer alarm inside.

Jennifer heard it, too. "What's that?" she asked.

"Car phone," he replied, and touched the stud. "Hang on a minute while I answer this."

She sat quietly as he picked up the receiver. "Savage here."

"Savage! My God, been trying to reach you for some time!" came a gruff male voice.

"Breakfast with a pretty lady," he answered, and Jenny smiled.

"Well, time to get to work. We can't get the Team assembled there until four or so this afternoon. You'll have to delay the dive until then."

Savage felt a knot tighten in his stomach. "You mean that's not the Team out there now?"

"Hell, no! What gives?"

"Hate to tell you this, but the Army is out there—and it's not what we planned at all."

"Oh, shit!" exclaimed the watch. "You mean the *real* one?"

3

As SAVAGE DROVE out to the lakeside, Jennifer was silent for a while. Finally, she asked, "Just what sort of work *do* you do?"

"I investigate. That big visitor you had last night is my baby—the reason I'm here. It's my job to check out all sort of weird happenings around this area of the country."

"For whom? I mean, for what do you work?"

"Well, a combination of agencies, really," he said carefully.

"Government?"

"Some," he admitted, "and some private foundations as well. Whoops! Here comes the roadblock. Army men this time. Hope you don't mind the delay."

"That's all right," she said quietly. "I have nothing else to do."

The sentry was not as trusting as the trooper had been; Savage's DIA credentials were meticulously scrutinized. However, when the man was satisfied, he motioned Savage on through and told him to park next to a troop carrier about a hundred feet farther on.

"Wait here," Savage told Jennifer, and got out.

In a few minutes, he had spotted the obvious supervisor, a chicken colonel, who, Savage saw from his nameplate, was named Marovec.

"Morning, Colonel," Savage called pleasantly.

"Who the hell are you?" snarled Marovec, some exasperation in his voice. Ever since coming in at about 6 A.M., he had been besieged with town officials, public works men, and a few reporters.

"Savage, DIA, Pentagon," he replied crisply. "I didn't get any word that regulars were being sent up."

"You wouldn't," Marovec replied in a more subdued tone. "Didn't know it myself until a few hours ago. I got the order to move down—have a little installation up in the hills there—and wait for an Air Force specialty team."

"Any idea why?"

"Not really," he admitted. "I think NORAD tracked this thing down and didn't like something about the way it came in."

"Flying saucers?" Savage asked derisively.

"Naw. None of that goddam silly stuff. Could be a lost Russian item or something, though. I'm told that what bugged hell out of them was the slow descent and the fact that it changed course for no apparent reason, like it wanted to hit just where it did. Anyway, we want to see what's there."

"So do I, Colonel, so do I. What's going to happen now?"

"Well, we wait for the flyboys to come in. Should be good—never saw flyboys in scuba gear before. All we need now is the Navy."

"Well, look, I've got a local in the car. Let me drop her off and I'll come on back."

"No hurry," the lieutenant colonel replied. "They're flying in some people fom Vandenberg and"—he looked at his watch—"they just now left. It's almost ten now. I don't figure they could get to Mycroft, get their stuff, and get out to this site before three or four. Good thing it's summer—plenty of working light."

"Okay," Savage replied. "I'll complete my interviews with the locals in town and meet you about three, then."

"Should be time enough. Probably just a big rock, anyway, buried so deep they'll never get it out."

"I don't think so, Colonel," Savage objected. "Look out there at the center of the lake. See that dark blotch? I think that's it."

"Could be," Marovec admitted. "We'll see."

As Savage walked back to the car, he saw that Jennifer had gotten out and was leaning against the door, letting the warm breeze off the lake hit her in the face. He stopped to stare at her for a moment.

Funny, he thought to himself. Here I meet her only this morning and, in the middle of the biggest job of my life, I can't think of much else *but* her. This sort of thing happens to other people, not to me, he told himself. But the strong emotional feeling, somewhat ill-defined and very alien, just wouldn't go away. He found himself liking—even admiring—the unkempt, informal look; her deficiencies, so obvious earlier, seemed to turn into assets or become suddenly irrelevant.

Walking back up to her, he put his left hand in hers. She smiled. "So how'd it go?"

"Nothing much doing until the big boys get here this afternoon," he told her. "Let's go back."

He helped her into the car and started back to the Merritt. As he drove, he punched the stud and picked up the transceiver once again.

"Duty Watch," responded the same gruff male voice he had talked to earlier.

"Savage again," he reported. "The big boys are coming in from Vandenberg at three. Can you vouch for me through DIA and get me in on the show?"

"Already done after your first call. Looks like a rough one, Savage. Particularly if there's still something alive in there."

"Don't see how we can put the lid on it now," Savage agreed. "The best we can do is cover the examination when they get the thing out. That won't be easy—a couple of days and some heavy equipment."

"Okay. Stay there and do what you can. Above all, *keep us informed*. We have Della Rosa already on that

Air Force team and Peterson's there with his Washington *Post* cover. We're ready to drop in the Team and to hell with it if things get really messy."

"Right. Back at three or earlier, if things develop," Savage told him. "Clear for now."

"Clear," responded the watch officer.

"That really *was* a spaceship that crashed in there, wasn't it?" Jenny asked suddenly.

Savage was startled. "Huh? What makes you think the flying saucers are among us all of a sudden?"

"When you're blind," she explained, "you train your other senses to a fine point. I heard both ends of the conversation."

Savage turned into the parking lot and parked the car. He sat for a along moment, thinking about what to say.

"Yes," he said finally. "We think it was. And it could be extremely dangerous."

He got out of the car and opened her door, helping her out. As he closed her side and they started for the door to the inside hall, Savage heard a series of electrical bells.

"What the hell is that?" he asked.

"The ice cream truck," she replied. "It usually makes two runs through the area, right about now and later this evening."

"But I thought the guy who ran the truck was the father of the girl who was killed," he said in a puzzled tone.

Jennifer, too, looked suddenly strange. "He *is,* come to think of it."

Savage took her by the hand and they walked around to the front of the apartment complex. The truck, one of the snub-nosed, box-shaped trucks that specialized in soft ice cream, was just pulling out, its bells jangling. A half-dozen or so kids were standing in the lot, watching it go. Most were holding ice cream cones or bars, which were dripping messily in the hot sun, but none seemed to be eating. Instead, they all watched the truck roll down the road and out of view, dreamy sort of half-smiles on their faces.

That was what was wrong. That and the fact that

kids almost never mill around *after* a truck leaves. They rush to buy the stuff, then run back to eat, get messy, and return to play. Savage described the scene to Jennifer.

They approached one of the kids, a boy of eight or nine just standing there, a double-dip chocolate cone oozing down.

"Hi!" Savage greeted the boy cheerfully. "Was that Mr. McBride?"

"Yeah," the boy answered sullenly, sounding like his mouth was full of mush.

"Is that you, Tommy?" Jennifer put in, recognizing the voice.

"Yeah, Jenny," he replied with the same mushy indifference.

"How did Mr. McBride look and act, Tommy?" Savage asked him.

The boy shrugged. " 'Bout the same, I guess. Didn't notice, 'cause of Charley."

"Who's Charley, Tommy?" Jennifer prodded.

"He's our friend," the boy responded dreamily.

"Is Charley a dog or something?" Savage asked.

"Naw. He's—well, sort of a little purple haystack, y'know."

And, with that, Tommy seemed to lose interest and wondered off with the other kids.

Savage frowned. "Ever hear of anything like that before?" he asked Jennifer.

"No," she admitted. "Not that. But kids have such great imaginations, and McBride was always good with them. He always pretended he had an invisible friend in the freezer who handed him the ice cream bars. They love it."

Savage shrugged, and they returned to the doorway, but something in the back of his mind told him that things weren't kosher. McBride out the day after his daughter was killed, her body still in the lake. And the kids' reactions . . .

He put it out of his mind for now as they approached Jennifer's door.

"Come on in for a few minutes, Paul," she invited as

she unlocked it. "You said you had some time. And excuse the looks of the place."

He entered without a word and watched as she kicked off her sandals and plopped on the bed. He just sort of stood there for a second, cursing himself, unsure of what to do next. He knew what he wanted to do, but there were inhibitions long ingrained in him which whispered that, no matter what he did, it would be the wrong move and blow it. Calm and as implacable as ever on the outside, he was a raging torrent on the inside.

"Come on over and sit on the bed," she said, and he did, putting his left arm around her.

"Have you had a lot of girls, Paul?" she asked. "World traveler, detective, and all that—you must have."

"No," he answered her softly. "Nobody. I grew up as much a social prisoner as you, Jenny. The ugly one, Mr. Ape Man, and all that. I never really had much of an adolescence. I stayed away from social contacts—the ridicule was too much. Finally, when one girl did show some interest in me—I was eighteen—I blew everything by not knowing what to do. I—I couldn't be human. The armor grew up with me and it proved too thick."

"You haven't had any problems with me," she pointed out.

He leaned over and kissed her, long and hard.

"Did you know I'm twenty-five years old and still a virgin?" she whispered.

She lifted off the T-shirt and slipped out of the jeans, kicking them to the floor. He, too, stripped down, removing also his hand harness, and climbed into bed with her.

"That should be an easy condition to fix," he replied, his heart pounding.

She reached out. "Oh, God, it's a big thing," she whispered.

He had never done it left-handedly, and hadn't done it at all in a long, long while.

Time passed, but they didn't notice it; two extremely lonely people, armor down, had found something that transcended such things as the outside world. After, they just lay for a time, not talking, simply touching, knowing for the first time in their lives the involvement that one human being can have for another.

Finally, Jennifer reached over to a clock on a bedside table, its faceplate removed so that she could feel the hands.

"It's ten to two," she said. "Hungry?"

"No, not really," he replied. "I should be, but I'm not. And I have to go to work soon. And if things turn out the way I hope, it's better that I don't."

"What do you mean?" she asked, concerned. "Are you going to do something—dangerous?"

"I'm going to dive into that lake, I think—and see that thing close up."

"Don't—don't get killed," she pleaded with him, a tremor in her voice.

For the first time, the true irony of that comment struck him. He kissed her again, lightly.

"Believe me, honey," he said enigmatically, "there's absolutely no way for that to happen."

Almost inaudible in the apartment, there came the soft sound of electrical bells, moving away.

4

THE HELICOPTERS STARTED landing at about 3:30, making the area around the lake look like a military invasion.

Savage had dressed and said good-bye to Jenny. She'd wanted to come along, concerned for his safety, but he was very firm: if anything came out of that thing, he wanted her as far away as possible.

The route back down to the lake took him past the diner and along a suburbia-looking little section of town he had not noticed before. This time, he saw the crowd of milling children around the ice cream truck up on a corner about half a block from Mycroft's main drag.

He drove on to the lake.

Two Air Force sergeants were already suiting up for the dive as he approached. A nervous-looking major was pacing in front of one of the copters. Savage identified himself to the man.

"Oh, yeah," the major said. "I got something on you. What do you want to do here?"

"If you've got a spare scuba tank, I'd like to go down with the men."

"Well, we got spares, all right," the major replied slowly, "but . . ." His gaze fell to Savage's claw.

"Oh, the thing's rustproof, shockproof, waterproof and antimagnetic," Savage assured him. "Causes me a little balance problem but nothing serious. I've dived in worse than this with—and without—it."

The major threw up his hands. "Okay, then, on your own head be it. We both work for the same boss."

Savage decided to wear only trunks and the basic scuba gear; he didn't want to chance the rubberized suit fouling up his hand mechanism. In a few minutes, they were all ready. The two divers stared at the claw-and-strap arrangement, but made no comment.

"Got any weapons with you?" Savage asked them.

The nearer diver, a young man not more than twenty, raised his eyebrows. "Why? They dump sharks in this pool?"

"No," Savage laughed. "But we have no idea what the thing is. We know, though, that it appeared to be *guided* by something. Who knows what. A Russian? A Martian . . . ?"

"We didn't bring any weapons, mister," replied the diver, "but if anybody's in there, they'll have to come out up here. Let's not worry about it. Ready to go?"

"Ready," Savage assured them.

They walked into the water.

It was extremely clear, the only fouling element their own wakes and air bubbles as they made their way out. After a short time, the lead diver gestured, and they went down.

A small, smashed yellow sports car, upside down, was up ahead. They stopped to look it over. One of the divers attached a line to the car and, using a small canister, inflated a large orange balloon that floated quickly to the surface. The car could now be located by a rig on top and brought up. But this was not their main objective, and they pushed on.

It loomed ahead of them: a large black blob settled in the mud.

As they drew up to it, they saw that the exterior looked like a painted surface, or car finish, that had undergone tremendous heat. Little chips came away easily when brushed. Clearly, from its symmetry, it was not a natural object. Someone—or something—had definitely built it.

Savage felt his stomach tightening becoming worse. It was the missing enemy ship, no doubt about it.

A diver took out a small pick and chipped away at it. Some of the burn-chips flew off, but he got nowhere with the bulk. Savage and the other diver took off in opposite directions to circle the craft.

About a third of the way around, he found the open hatch.

Savage waited for the other diver. He had no stomach for going in there alone.

Savage gestured to the other man as he approached, then slowly made his way inside the hatch, which, large enough for a small man, he nevertheless had problems squeezing through. Although an airlock, the inner door was also open and underwater. He made his way through to it—

And broke the surface. The ship was still dry inside: an air pocket had formed due to its twenty-degree lean and the almost bottom location of the hatch.

He had been in The Hunter's ships, and saw that the design here did not differ much, but was more cramped. There were two command chairs forward, and two facing the rear.

Three of them had occupants.

The second diver broke the surface and looked around, awed. As he started to remove his breathing tube, Savage motioned for him not to. No telling what kind of stuff these things breathed.

The third and last diver came through moments later.

The two stared, amazed at first, but soon began to film the interior.

Savage walked over to the closest command chair—a gunner's—and examined the inhabitant.

It was dead, fortunately. A scaly green lizard, slime oozing from its body in death, eyes open wide. Savage did not recognize the race—but he *had* been briefed about the other occupant of the chair. Implanted on the lizard's back, oozing the same ichor, was a small object like a purplish mass of matted hair.

The other two occupants of the craft were identical— all dead, all with equally dead Kah'diz on their backs.

The fourth chair was empty.

This was a puzzle, anyway. Why would a fighter have a crew of four? Two could handle it easily; three was the normal complement for insurance. But with a Kah'diz ship, well, who knew what sort of design those parasites might come up with? Or why?

The two divers seemed hypnotized, but they knew what they had.

A spaceship. A real, honest-to-God spaceship.

Savage motioned them back through the lock. Air time was getting low, and he wanted to get the report out of the way.

He saw that the last diver to enter had marked the thing's dimensions outside with four more balloons, and they all started swimming back to the bank.

"What did you see?" shouted a little bald man in a gray tweed.

"You're not gonna believe this one . . ." called out one of the divers.

Savage made his report along with the other two, to the growing excitement of the scientists and the growing alarm of the military. He wanted to wrap it up as quickly as possible and report. The divers' films would be pored over for what was *in* the pictures. The empty chair and the open lock told the *really* important story.

He was too late. Something was already loose.

"No sign of *anything* . . . ?" the watch officer asked incredulously. "Not even the host's body? After all, the place *was* patrolled, and a four-foot green lizard is pretty conspicuous."

"Nothing," Savage replied. "Looks like whatever it was skipped as soon as the mud settled, long before the gendarmes arrived."

"Well, I checked with Data Services and they tell me that, from the description of the other three, the lizard had to be almost as bad—couldn't have lasted long."

"Yeah. But if so, where's the body?"

"More importantly, where's the Kah'diz?" said the watch officer. "Those things are incredibly adaptable. It could be on a dog—anything large enough to sustain it for a time."

"What about locomotion?" Savage asked. "If the host body died, how much time would it have?"

"Not much. Ten, fifteen minutes, no more. It would drain as much of the blood from the dead body as possible, then sort of roll itself into a ball and try and claim the first host possible. It can't roll very fast or very far—but, remember, they have this empathic power. If it got close enough to somebody, say, then that somebody would actually *help* the thing dig into its neck. The Kah'diz would then slowly expel the old blood externally, and alter its biochemistry for the new host. It has to be adaptable: it's so vulnerable and helpless on its own. Beats me how it swam to shore, though."

Savage thought for a few moments. Then, slowly, he asked, "If you'd never seen a Kah'diz before, would you describe it as, say, a 'little purple haystack'?"

"Well . . . no," the watch answered, "*I* wouldn't. But it could be described like that. All I know is what I've seen in the pictures. You saw three of them on the ship. Why do you ask?"

"I think, later, I'm going to see a man about ice cream," Savage said absently, almost to himself. Then: "Who else is out here?"

"Well, Petersen from the D.C. office, good man with a gun; and Della Rosa, out of California, a technical man who's in with the Air Force team. He's giving us pretty good reports. They sent a couple more divers down after you left, and he tells us they're going to try to lift the thing."

"Lift it! With what?"

"One or two of the Big Bertha helicopters they use for transporting huge tonnages. Two of them will be in from Meade by tonight."

"Tonight! That means they're going to try it tomorrow morning!"

"You betcha. Be there. Best we figure we can do is let them get it out; then we'll try and destroy it before they start tearing it apart."

"Okay, let the other two stick with that end. I'm going to find our alien," Savage replied, and cleared.

He knew he should try and find that ice cream truck, but he wanted to get back to Jenny first. Despite the gravity of the situation, she remained uppermost in his mind. He cursed himself for it, for letting it interfere with his job, but he couldn't help it.

It's a hell of a shock discovering that you're human, he thought.

She was waiting for Savage when he arrived, and she threw her arms around him. "I was so worried about you," she almost sobbed. "What did you find?"

Savage told her of the dive and of the strange creatures.

"And you think one of them's escaped?" she asked.

"Yes," he answered honestly. "And, unfortunately, I know what it is." He told her about the Kah'diz.

"But—but *how* do you know about this thing?" she asked quizzically.

Savage sat down and ran his fingers along the coffee table. Finally he said, "Because I work for the people who shot it down."

She was quiet for a minute, digesting all of this. To her credit, it was not too much for her, but it was like being in a dream—the whole day was like being in a dream, like being trapped in some kind of Grade B movie script. A sudden love after years of loneliness; a ship from space, monsters of some kind on the prowl.

And, she was quite aware, the United States government wasn't going around shooting down flying saucers.

"Are you human, Paul?" she asked. "Are you for real, at all?"

"I'm for real, beautiful," he replied gently, and kissed her. "That's the only thing in this cockeyed mess you can count on absolutely."

They sat silently for a while. Jennifer had a million questions, of course, but asked none. It just didn't seem the right time.

Eventually Savage broke the silence. "It's getting dark and I haven't had anything to eat since breakfast. Want to get something?"

"I can fix something here." She brightened. "I'm not really a bad cook."

"No," he answered. "You bought, this morning. My turn, now."

He felt much better after dinner, and the menu at the little restaurant she'd suggested was unimaginative but extremely well prepared. He went over to the pay phone next to the cashier and thumbed through the small phone book covering the Mycroft area.

McBride, Jos F, 1444 Pinevw.

"Want to take a little ride?" he asked her when he returned to the table.

He knew he should have left her in town, but the thought of being away from Jenny seemed more and more repugnant to him. There seemed little danger, anyway. It was just a hunch . . .

The ice cream truck was parked in the driveway, making the house easy to spot. The place was dark except for a single dim light in the front room. Telling Jenny to wait in the car, he went to the door and rang the bell.

There was no response.

He pushed in the bell again, insistently keeping the electric switch in contact. Inside, he saw a formless mass come up to the door.

"What d'ya want?" a nasty-sounding voice snapped at him.

"Mr. McBride . . . ? Paul Savage here. I'm an investigator. I'd like to talk to you for a minute."

"Go away!" barked the voice from inside. "I don't want to see anybody! The cops were up here about Alice Mary this morning, and I don't think I have to talk to you or anybody else about anything!"

"Mr. McBride, I—" Savage began, but the old man cut him off.

"Get the hell out of here, damn it, or I'll get my gun! I have enough grief now. You can only add to it!"

With that, the figure—never clearly seen through the thick lace curtains on the door—walked away. Savage peered in, trying to see more, but it was too dark.

McBride was right, of course. If it *was* McBride. He had to admit to himself that this was the way *he* would react in similar circumstances. The Kah'diz were not telepaths, and such normal reactions would be difficult to fake this early in the game.

But why had he taken the truck on the normal run?

"It still doesn't fit," he told Jenny as they drove back down the mountain road. "Whoops! Hold it!"

He braked the car to a stop.

"What is it?" she asked apprehensively.

"A trail, I think—leading down the mountain . . . Yep, it goes all the way down to the lake. Not used much, by the look of it."

Savage got out and inspected the path, seeing that the soft earth had been only recently disturbed after a long time. A little way down he saw where someone, apparently running, had fallen and mashed two or three of the small bushes almost flat. He walked back to the car and started up.

"I'm convinced McBride is our man," he told her, explaining the evidence of the trail. "I think he was watching the ship crash just like everybody, and saw his daughter go in, too. He ran down, panicked, and jumped into the water trying to get to her. He didn't. But he met the lizard and its master just out from the ship. It fits."

"But why take the ice cream truck out today?" she mused. "You'd think with all the investigations going on, it'd want to stay hidden."

"Orientation, maybe," Savage theorized. "After all, the creature wanted to see what sort of place it was stuck in. And, I think, the *kids* have something to do with it . . ."

Jennifer looked startled. "The kids? What—?"

"I dunno. Maybe the Night Watch can give me some answers."

He called in, and told them of his progress to that point.

"Well," the watch replied, "they're supposedly really self-confident, cocky bastards, so they'd have nerve enough. And they get 'high' off other people's emotions—like a drug or something. Nobody more emotional than kids."

"Well, may be. But the thing must know it's on The Hunter's home world. It's not natural for it to tip its hand like this."

"Maybe it is," the watch replied. "After all, it's only six or seven hundred miles from Haven. If it's going to survive, it needs allies. Tell me, was the power in the ship still on?"

Savage thought for a moment. "Yeah," he answered. "Come to think of it, all the lights were on."

"That's what the creature is, then. I think you're all in real danger."

Savage's face was grim. "What do you mean?"

"I mean that the little bastards generally can't work their emotional games on many people at a time, and only on a few for any sustained period. They've got to get a willing host. But they've got amplifiers in some of their ships that work through a gadget they carry with them, and with it they can change love to hate, laughter to tears, fierce opposition to slavish devotion. I've got a report on the Fraskan takeover about five linked ships' generators controlling mobs up to ten thousand at a crack in six different places simultaneously. What's the population of Mycroft?"

Savage turned to Jenny. "How many people around here, Jenny?"

She thought for a second, then replied uncertainly, "I *think* it's about twenty thousand, give or take."

"Call it twenty thou," Savage told the watch.

"That's what the fourth seat is, Savage," the watch replied. "The engineer's seat, for the gadgetry. And that's the engineer you've got running around—and he's plugged in with the power on. If you don't move fast,

you're gonna have twenty thousand slaves surrounding
you—and you might be one of them."

Savage swallowed hard, then looked over at Jenny.
She was sitting very still, staring straight ahead, but he
knew she had heard the conversation. She was trembling slightly. For the first time in recent years, Paul
Savage was scared, and not just for himself. He began
to realize why people in his profession should not have
any really deep emotional attachments.

Another, even more horrible thought came to him.

"Hey, Night Watch," he called. "Could that water
have an inhibiting effect on those generators this thing's
depending on?"

"I dunno. I'll have to check with somebody good in
that kind of physics and let you know."

"Well, let's assume it does. That could explain everything: the Kah'diz out testing its powers today, sure,
and finding out our ranges and limits through the most
emotionally vulnerable, the children. But without that
ship out of the water it can't get the full power it needs.
Remember, three of us, at least, were down in that ship
today and there was no noticeable effect."

"So?"

Both the watch and Jenny listened anxiously.

"Sure. The military got here first because The Bromgrev's boys on Earth pulled the strings to beat us to the
punch. Now, the military will do all the work for them,
and the moment that thing's up in the open air—
whammo! He's got everybody."

A silence followed at the other end. Then suddenly a
new voice broke in.

"Savage," came Stephen Wade's voice, "this is The
Hunter. I think you're right. Truth is, the Kah'diz can't
hold twenty thousand with only one generator, but he
can hold two or three thousand—and that's more than
enough. That military unit that came down first—it's in
charge of the presidential retreat in case of nuclear attack. The place is sophisticated, almost impregnable,
and practically never visited. What a perfect headquarters!"

"So what do you want me to do?" Savage asked the
boss of the whole organization.

"Kill *it* first," The Hunter ordered. "Get it tonight. Take Petersen and Della Rosa with you. Any ideas where it is?"

"One," Savage replied, and described the ice cream man theory.

"Okay, act on it. Assume you're right—it sounds right. Think of the girl."

Both Savage and Jennifer jumped at the comment.

"How'd you know about the girl?"

"Good God, man! What do I pay my agents to do? Falsify reports?"

"Can you get her clear before all hell breaks loose?" Savage asked.

"No!" Jenny said firmly. "I won't go!"

"Possibly," Wade replied, "if you do it right now. Give her to Della Rosa out at the lake site. Now *move!*"

The channel was clear.

Savage looked at her. "What do you mean, 'No'?"

"I won't," she repeated. "Hell, I'm scared to death right now, I admit, but I'm not going to leave you. You can't force me."

They got out of the car and started walking back to her apartment. He stopped her on the stair landing and grabbed her firmly.

"You've *got* to, Jenny," he pleaded. "Look—I know what this thing is. I've been trained to fight it. But *you* haven't. You're vulnerable to it."

"No, stop, listen!" she shot out angrily. "All my life I've been imprisoned. First in a big house, then in a tiny apartment. All my life I've been running away from the world out there. *I'm not going to run anymore, Paul.*"

He sighed. "Okay, wait here and I'll be back as soon as I can," he said resignedly.

"No, Paul. Let me come with you," she urged. "It'll be dark up there—very dark. I'm used to the dark."

He was about to absolutely veto this when they heard a crash and a tinkling of glass outside. He made his way slowly and cautiously back down the stairs. Jennifer followed.

He could see from the doorway what had happened.

Somebody had just lobbed a rock through his windshield.

Drawing his pistol he ordered Jenny to stay inside the door; then he opened it and stepped into the parking lot, pistol drawn.

It was night, a cloudy, ugly night. Flashes of lightning showed in the distance, and the heavy, humid air felt and smelled as if a storm would break any minute

For a moment he saw nothing. Then came a betrayal of movement, first from just behind the car, then around him, in the dark.

It was the children of the neighborhood.

You're an enemy of Charley," accused a piping voice of a kid of six or seven, sex indeterminate in the dark.

"You're a bad man," another asserted.

A rock flew out of the darkness and almost hit Savage. He ducked back inside and practically pulled Jenny down the first floor hall toward the building entrance to the office, explaining what had happened along the way.

"How horrible!" she said, and shuddered. "And that's what will happen to everybody?"

Savage nodded, forgetting for a moment she couldn't see the gesture. "And that's only mildly augmented—or unaugmented—power. Imagine boosting it a thousand-fold. A millionfold!"

"I'm still coming with you," she insisted.

"You better believe you are!" he said firmly. "You're safer with me than alone. Not only do *we* have people here, so does the enemy. You're identified with me—and trapped. They would want you here, I think, as a hold on me."

He used the pay phone and called Petersen's mobile. He told the other agent the problem, and Petersen said to hold tight, he would be out quickly.

Looking around at the windows, Savage could see six faces, hatred glowing in their eyes, peering in at him. But they would do nothing, he felt confident, as long as he stayed inside. "Charley" or whatever it was changed the way you looked or felt about something—not the whole you. Those kids owed their loyalty to the creature up on the mountainside, but they were still kids—and reacted like kids.

The old couple were apparently in their own quarters or somewhere else in the building. Savage and Jennifer were alone.

"Paul," she said suddenly.

"Yes, Jenny?"

"Marry me, Paul."

He kissed her, and managed a chuckle. "You better believe it, beautiful. As soon as this night's over." He pressed her hand firmly.

"No," she replied. "*Now.* Right now, Paul. Before we—face what we have to face."

"Well, I'm sorry, miss," he replied jokingly, "but I don't happen to have a judge handy. And the blood tests aren't in yet."

"You don't need those things, Paul," she whispered. "I'm serious. Will you do it?"

He realized she *was* serious, and he understood.

A loud clap of thunder rang out, and the rain started down in buckets. The kids outside scattered.

He turned and faced her.

"I, Paul Carleton Savage, take this woman to be my lawful wedded wife, to have and to hold, in sickness and in health, until death do us part," he intoned solemnly.

"I, Jennifer Ann Barron, take this man to be my lawful wedded husband, to have and to hold, in sickness and in health, until death do us part," she responded.

They embraced and kissed.

"Well, Mrs. Savage, when do we have our honeymoon?" he asked her.

"*Ms.* Savage, if you please," she replied, and laughed. "I gotta protect myself and keep you in check."

"I promise you this, Jenny," he said seriously. "Never have I taken a more serious or solemn oath. I swear it."

She smiled and was silent.

At that moment, the lights of Petersen's car showed out in front. Savage quickly checked to see that it *was* Petersen and that the kids had fled the driving rain. In the car he saw the other agent, the little bald-headed man he had seen earlier. Grabbing Jenny's hand, he and she dashed through the rain to the car. Both were soaked as they piled into the back seat.

Petersen nodded, and started off. "This is Della Rosa," he said, introducing the little man. "I thought we should all be in on this."

"This is Jenny," Savage responded, "my wife."

Both their eyebrows shot up but they said nothing. Jenny smiled, and tried to wring the water out of her matted hair.

Savage leaned over to her and whispered, "You know, that rain made that T-shirt a real clinger. You look like a shameless harlot with your assets stuck out front."

She laughed. "Be quiet and just remember my karate," she warned.

Savage turned to the men in the front seat. "I brought her because she wasn't safe back there, and with all of us working on this there wasn't anyplace else."

"Probably won't make any difference," Petersen commented dryly. "If we don't get him tonight, we're all up the creek, anyway."

They traveled on up the road, careful in the driving rain. Savage briefed the others on the way, sparing nothing. They passed the warning flasher where Alice Mary McBride had jumped the road and continued on to the house.

By the time they reached it, the rain had almost passed, although they could see lightning off in the distance. It felt much cooler.

Petersen drove on past McBride's and stopped a hundred yards farther down the road, on a curve out of line of sight with the house. Making a three-point turn, he switched off the car lights, and eased slowly back down on the shoulder.

It was pitch dark and no lights showed in the house. They heard no sound except the ever-present crickets celebrating the end of the rain.

Della Rosa reached down and took out a belt on which hung a half-dozen hand grenades. "Picked them up this evening," he whispered. "Easiest way to get the thing, if we can spot it."

They took two each. "Give me one," Jenny urged.

"Why?" Della Rosa asked. "You're staying in the car."

"No, in that darkness I'm better than you," she shot back firmly. "I can hear better. Besides, if he's *not* in the house, I'm a sitting duck here. I'd feel better with you."

"Okay," Savage told her, "but keep hold of me. I'll keep the pineapples, but if you hear anything tell me what and where—fast."

They all got quietly out of the car. Savage and Della Rosa took off their coats, revealing their shoulder holsters. Petersen strapped his own on over his flowered sports shirt. They all removed their shoes and socks.

Della Rosa went off through some underbrush to cover the back. Petersen checked out the ice cream truck. It was empty. Slowly the three edged toward the front of the house. Quietly, gun drawn, Petersen slipped a skeleton key into the lock and turned it with an almost inaudible click.

The door opened inward at a touch.

A hall led directly back to the kitchen. They could see that Della Rosa had made the back porch, but had not been able to enter.

Petersen tiptoed upstairs while Savage and Jenny went into the pitch-dark living room.

"It's too dark to see anything in here," he barely whispered in her ear.

"Let me take the lead," she said, so faint he could hardly hear her. "I've been in strange rooms before."

She had hold of his left hand and gingerly started making her way forward with the caution of the blind. She reached down and pulled her left pants leg up, then proceeded, using her left foot and arm as gentle probes. Savage's eyes could not adjust to the bad light, for heavy drapes obscured all the windows. I'm in her world now, he thought.

They made their way, slowly but surely, around into the small dining room and around to the hall again, this time in the kitchen, where Savage could see a little.

Petersen was already there, and gave a shrug. "I'm going back and call in," he whispered. "Looks like the only way will be to blast that craft before it can come up." He made his way back to the front door and stepped outside.

"We're too late," Savage said in a low normal tone.

"Quiet!" Jennifer hissed. "Listen!"

All he could hear was the extremely loud cricket chorus.

"What?" he demanded. "I don't hear anything."

"Below us! The basement!"

Savage cursed himself for a fool. He spotted the basement door, slightly ajar, just under the stairwell, and brought Jenny over to it. She felt it gingerly. He gave her one of the grenades and put her finger into one of its rings. She nodded that she understood.

This was some kind of woman! he thought. Thanks to his single real hand, he could handle a pistol or a grenade, but not both.

Edging open the door cautiously, he saw a shaft of light down below. Jenny felt the edge of the step and descended with him. They found a small landing, or platform, where the stairs turned right; and, as they stepped on it, it creaked noisily.

The sounds downstairs ceased for a moment, then a low whine began. Savage saw a shadow flicker on the cement walls of the basement, and heard someone walking toward them. Jennifer heard it almost before he did, and froze.

"Well, Mr. Savage!" Joseph McBride's voice boomed out, echoing through the cellar. "I guess I couldn't avoid it."

A beam of searing hatred—that was the only way to describe it—hit them both, and Jenny gasped.

"Ah, the girl, too!" McBride's voice exulted. "That makes it just perfect. Some entertainment to pass the lonely hours till morning!"

Savage and Jenny both felt it come upon them: they felt their love for each other grow larger and larger within themselves until their sexual drives were driven into a sudden frenzy of lust, pushing all other thought from their minds. Standing on the landing, they became animals in heat, forgetting everything but each other, the overpowering emotional blitz sweeping them both into madness. They virtually clawed at each other in an animalistic orgy, all reason gone.

The figure of McBride, smiling broadly, now appeared at the bottom of the stairs, a shotgun casually under one arm. A purplish mass sat in the curve of his neck.

The Kah'diz was well satisfied with itself. It could maintain this all night, and if—or, rather, when—they tumbled down the stairs that would still present no problem. The waves from the two on the landing poured forth, bathing the creature in ecstasy.

At a thumping sound, Savage's pistol tumbled and slid down the stairs and landed at the Kah'diz's feet. It kicked the weapon idly away.

"Savage!" Petersen's voice rang from the floor above. "Savage! Where are you? It's got a portable force-field generator! We can't get through!"

The creature bathed itself in the ocean of rapture, worrying little about the other two—knowing that, in the morning, when the ship was lifted and the control was effective, it could dispense with such trifles.

Savage and Jennifer had practically torn each other's clothing to bits in their animalistic attack, it noted with amusement, and the girl was bleeding from some superficial wounds.

All night. It could keep this up all night! The Kah'diz reveled in the knowledge of what it was like to be a god.

Then, abruptly, another object bounced down the stairs, hitting the fourth step, then the sixth, then the ninth, then rolling onto the floor almost up to the feet of the Kah'diz, who glanced at it idly. But suddenly the creature realized what it was.

In her desire to do it right, Jenny had removed the pin from the grenade and had been holding the handle shut tightly in her grip. Now the handle was out.

The Kah'diz felt momentary panic seize it. The force-field generator that kept the others out would keep the blast very localized. Eight seconds seemed like an eternity as it tried to seek shelter in some part of the basement.

In a hundred households across the peaceful, sleeping valley below, a hundred or more children suddenly awoke, screaming.

STEP FOUR

1

SHE WAS CARRIED along in a gentle fog, floating in air like a bird. She had no visions—there had never been anything to envision—but there were noises, some harsh, some sweet and high, like alien bells.

Slowly, very slowly, the sounds became voices.

"Yeah, that was some smart girl," the lower voice was saying. "She pulled the pin so even if shot or whatever—and what a 'whatever'!—she'd drop it and gravity would do the rest."

"And one not-so-clever Kah'diz," added the higher voice. "If the creature had done anything else to her, it wouldn't have worked."

"Right," the first voice agreed. "Love into hate or that kind of thing wouldn't have served the purpose. Only by amplifying as much as possible what was already there could it get the feedback it needed."

"Bet it was something!" the higher voice enthused, a bit envious.

"Indescribable," replied the other. "I think I tore her up more than the grenade did. It's a miracle she's alive."

"What would have happened if the grenade hadn't gone off?" mused the high voice.

"Well, that force-field generator was pretty good, but it was only a portable from 'Charley's' crash kit, really intended for fending off wild animals and the like. Della Rosa had already called for heavy artillery, and they'd have been able to penetrate, I think, in time. I hope so. But that was closer than I'd like."

"Did they find the body of the fourth lizard?"

"Yeah," the low voice chuckled. "Guess where."

"Oh, not in the—"

"Yep. Preserved good as new in the ice cream truck's freezer compartment. Not a mark on it."

Jennifer moaned. "Paul . . . !" she cried out.

"It's all right, honey," soothed the low voice. "I'm here." He reached over and patted her hand.

Her whole body ached fiercely, but she was conscious—and alive—and Paul was here.

"What . . . happened?" she managed.

Savage summarized the events up to the moment, concluding, "The moment it died, its hold on everybody— us included—stopped abruptly, although it looks as if the kids got some kind of death feedback. The blast knocked both of us out, and Petersen got in and hauled us away."

He let go of her hand and she cried out, tried to sit up, to reach out for him. He calmed her down by murmuring softly to her, "I'm here, love. I'm here."

"Don't let go, Paul, please don't let go," she pleaded, and he gripped her hand tighter.

"An aftereffect of the emotional overload," the high voice explained. "She'll get over it in time."

"Who's that with you, Paul?" Jenny asked.

"Just a doctor. You're in, well, a hospital."

"I don't care where I am, as long as it's with you," she breathed.

"You're stuck, Savage," the doctor smirked. "For a while, you'll be God to her. She'll be like an obedient puppy—loving, absolutely willing to please, insistent on constant love and attention. You're lucky —you ought to see some of the *really* messed-up ones we get. If you're gonna be crazy for a while, that's the way to do it."

"How long did you say this would go on?" Savage asked in an anguished tone, his hand already paining him from her grip.

The doctor shrugged. "Varies with the individual. A

few hours—days. Not more than a month at the outside."

Savage groaned.

Paul Savage entered the small office without knocking. It was the first time he had ever been in Stephen
Wade's Haven headquarters office, although he'd been
in Haven itself several times.

If the office was any indication, Wade was a pig.

It was not a large room, as things go, but it had an
enormous assortment of business machines, from a
typewriter to a total communications system that would
connect Wade with any part of his domain, Earthbound
or otherwise. Books lined the place—not only covering
every wall, but on top of file cabinets, desk, even piled
up on the fancy stereo system. Mountains of paper covered the floor, and Savage had to thread a narrow passage to one of the chairs.

Wade sat in a large, green highbacked swivel office
chair that could scarcely move because of the junk
around it.

"Take a chair, Paul," he invited, not looking up from
some reports he appeared to be sifting through.

Savage unpiled some papers and books from a
wicker-type chair and sat down. After a couple of minutes, Wade lit one of his fancy cigars and turned to him.

"Aren't you afraid the place will catch fire?" Savage
asked nervously.

Wade shrugged and said, "In Haven, all things are
possible. I think you know at least part of the reason I
sent for you."

Savage nodded. "I'm off the investigative payroll."

"Yes. Unless you're willing to leave Jenny here at all
times and go back to the normal routine, you're of no
good to us on the outside. So I've put Bumgartner on
your territory and you'll take his place here."

"Bumgartner!" Savage's bushy eyebrows rose. "So
destiny strikes again."

Wade looked somewhat sheepish. "You *know* that
you two have met before?"

"You hired a *detective,* didn't you?"

"I guess I did," Wade laughed. "Maybe one day we'll

put the two of you together in a room and let you kill each other until you get bored with it. And, in our defense, I might say that we didn't invent that patrol—just took advantage of it—and if it hadn't been for Ralph's little gadgets you never saw, the VC would have found you and killed you all, anyway. Enough of that, though. I have more serious work here—a bum situation. It smells, and I need help."

"Everything connected with this operation so far has smelled of something or other," Savage retorted. "Why should *you* be different?"

Wade's face grew serious. "I've had 114 agents get dug up, exposed, or run out of town in the last few weeks," he said. "A total of only 92 made it, to get picked up."

"So? Is that an unusually low number?"

"No, it's an impossibly high one. Far too high to be mere chance. Almost a record."

"So what's the problem?" Savage asked. "I'd think you'd be happy to get them out. They represent a substantial investment in training and experience, and we can always use them."

"True," Wade agreed, "but—well, let's take these in my hand, here—which came from Bumgartner's pickup.

"Item: One Aruman Vard, a Fraskan—which is meaningless to you. But the record says that Vard delayed unpardonably in getting his operation shut down, then made his way single-handed out of a domed city *already secured by the enemy.* Or this one:

"Gayal, one of the wives of our resident agent. Absolutely no training. Now, while our resident agent goes off and gets his fool head blown apart Gayal runs the whole communications net on two days' training, yet sticks around until a Kah'diz with a nice silver rod starts converting the family to loyal citizens of the empire. Then, in the middle of the night, she sneaks out of a house filled with relatives and the enemy, radios her pickup, gets away after blowing up the installation, and hides out in the hills for three weeks, evading an intensive search until she's finally made by them at the very moment Bumgartner arrives to conveniently shoot a batch of them and spirit her away. Think about it. Or, this one:

"Koldon, a double agent who's always been reliable even if he *was* the bastard who originally outfitted Rhambda, gets taken for a sucker—one of the finest telepaths in history!—and lured onto a ship just teeming with the enemy. Despite this, he knocks off a few of them, steals a lifeboat—which is no easy matter—and escapes close enough to one of our worlds that his distress signal reaches us almost immediately but somehow is never picked up by the enemy. He spends nine days in the lifeboat, yet Bumgartner makes him in ten minutes. See what I mean?"

"You think they're ringers," Savage put in.

Wade shook his head no. "No, they're not *all* ringers. I think *one* of those 92 is a ringer. I know all of them were helped to escape, to 91's good fortune. It's number 92 that I'm worried about."

"Camouflage," Savage replied, seeing the point. "Too many suspects to really get down to cases on, and The Bromgrev's in and lost in the crowd."

"Exactly!" Wade pointed his finger at Savage. "And one final note. That very daring attack on us was well planned. It came damned close to breaking the line. It caught us flat-footed, and it was as well directed as you can get. If The Bromgrev didn't have to keep all those reserves back on the occupied worlds, he could have taken us. But *since* that battle, not a single offensive, not a tiny grouping, not even a feint. They're avoiding battles whenever possible."

"Like they're in a holding pattern?"

"Right! If The Bromgrev's in Haven, he's out of contact with the Rhambdan mass-mind. That puts a strain on The Mind just to keep things together. In fact, the Rhambdans themselves have drawn back, leaving the conquered systems entirely to allied troops."

"I suppose it wouldn't have done any good to kill or quarantine new arrivals?"

"None at all," Wade replied. "The Bromgrev would just become someone else—and make the work even harder. Look what it's taken just to narrow things down to this number!"

Savage shifted in his chair and reached for a cigarette. Wade passed him an ashtray.

"So where do I fit in?" Savage asked.

"I call myself The Hunter. That implies an offense, an aggressive seeking-out of the quarry. So far, I've spent all my time *de*fensively—and I'm losing! On the other hand, The Bromgrev's conquests are agonizingly slow. He's obviously decided that the best thing to do to speed things up is to take me out. That's why I'm sure he's here, waiting for some chance at me. I'm sure of it!" Wade banged his fist on the desk. "And I have to get him first! To do so, I long ago developed a plan which so far is working out. But it can go against me at any moment."

Wade explained things as they had progressed to date, to Savage. And cleared up a lot of minor mysteries.

"And now, the big one," Wade concluded. "I have divided the new arrivals into teams, three to five to an agent. The guise will be routine indoctrination and training, which will be complete. *You'll* undergo it with *your* people. Along the way, we'll sow some traps and see if my wayward brother falls into them."

"And if not?" Savage objected. "You've blown up the cleverness of this character to diabolic proportions. What if there are *no* mistakes?"

"Then you'll have to make certain that nothing happens to me," Wade told him crisply. "Right now, The Bromgrev's uncomfortable—he's one of a finite number in a finite space—and that space is of my choosing. I intend to start counterattacking across the length and breadth of his territory. The Bromgrev will be vitally needed elsewhere before too long—at least vitally needed outside of Haven for more than the short times everybody will be out. He'll have to make a series of moves whether he wants to or not."

"But," Savage objected, "what good will it do if one of us *does* peg The Bromgrev? Imprisonment is impossible, control out of the question."

"I thought you understood . . ." Wade replied softly. "I intend to murder him."

Savage shot straight up in his chair. "But that's impossible! You yourself said as much! How do you murder an invincible immortal?"

Wade smiled. "You'll know that, *when* and *if* necessary. In the meantime, those three I told you about are your assignment." He passed the trio of files to Savage.

Savage glanced quickly over them, then put them aside for later reading. "Well, that leaves only one horrible little problem in your whole master plan," he said sourly.

"What's that?" Wade asked.

"Suppose *none* of them are The Bromgrev . . . ?"

He had fixed a small apartment in the personnel quarters for Jenny and himself, and arranged the furnishings to be almost identical to those in her old apartment. All that remained of that terrible night, weeks before, was a remembrance of a bad time, much like a vivid nightmare which nonetheless is allotted a smaller and smaller space in the mind as time goes on. She never dwelt on it, preferring to think of the more positive aspects of that day that so changed her life.

They were lying in bed together when the intercom buzzer rang.

Savage reached over and pushed the operational bar down. "Yeah?" he snapped.

"Duty watch, sir," came an officious voice. "Your team is to report to the Small Briefing Room for orientation today at ten hundred hours."

Savage glanced at the wall clock, which read 0915. "Okay," he responded, "I'll be there. Have you notified the others?"

"Yes, all is ready," the reply came back.

"Right, thanks," Savage told the watch, and clicked it off.

"They pick the damnedest times," Jenny snapped.

"I've got to do my job," Savage said philosophically. "Want to come along? The orientation talk will answer a lot of questions about Haven."

"Hmph!" she snorted. "Forty minutes. And the only thing I have to wear is one of those stiff uniforms."

"Come naked if you want, wench!" he teased. "Be a shameless harlot! After all, lots of the life forms around here are alien, and a lot of folks—human and not—go around in the buff. Nobody'd give you a second glance."

She hit him.

They entered the Small Briefing Room—really large enough for a dozen or so—and Savage saw that the others were there. He recognized them from the file photos. He seated Jenny in a chair and strode over to them.

The three aliens all saw that his companion was blind by the way she moved and was led into these unfamiliar surroundings.

Savage introduced himself to each in turn, then to Jenny; and Koldon and Gayal allowed Jenny to "feel" them—what she called "getting a good look at people." Vard remained polite but aloof.

Savage beckoned them to be seated again, and sat down himself by his wife. "Pick up the earphones clipped on the right side of the desk," he instructed her. "Wade will speak in Universal, which you don't know. The gadget you've got there will translate. We'll have to get you plugged into Universal in the next few days— it's *the* language here."

"I was always pretty good in French," she quipped. "Par-lays vows Frankias, and all that."

"You learn this one by machine. It's a nightmare. And it's good."

Wade would speak through the wallscreen, to minimize contact between himself and the teams. He did not want a chance meeting with The Bromgrev. He could see everyone on multiple monitors in front of him, however.

As they waited, Jenny whispered, "I really *am* going to be a nature buff from now on! If that Gayal can let hers all hang out, so can I!"

Savage laughed and hit her on the rump, then leaned over and kissed her.

She bit him.

The screen came to life. Wade stood at a podium, a small screen in back of him. He looked, for all the world, like a TV network newscaster about to give the six o'clock news, Savage thought.

"Glad to see you're all here," Wade began pleasantly.

"I'm going to start with some fundamentals many of you know. But this is supposed to be a leavening process, so those people who get bored please bear with me.

"First of all," Wade went on, "you are all now in Haven, as we call it." A diagram of the Solar System, with an arrow pointing to Earth, appeared behind him. "Haven is reached by first reaching Earth, the third planet of a pretty young system out in the third spiral of the galaxy. It is not, however, actually *on* the planet, but is, rather, contiguous with it."

The picture shifted to a view of the United States with a good portion of the Southeast and Atlantic Ocean to out beyond Bermuda bracketed. The map changed again, featuring only the spotlighted area.

"I've been on this world for some time," Wade continued, "and I became aware that certain places on it were really extraordinary. There were about a dozen such, where strange tides, weird weather patterns, and the like occurred—the one shown here, near an island the natives call Bermuda, is a good example. For centuries, this place has puzzled the natives: the weather was freakish, currents reversed themselves or ran in circles, and there were records of ships and such being lost here with no sign. Because of its fairly geometrical shape, it's called the Bermuda Triangle."

The area was duly marked off on the map.

"When I heard of it, I was fascinated," Wade went on, "and so, about sixty or seventy years ago, Earth time, I took a boat into the region. I suddenly found myself in a strange storm, and there was a roaring maelstrom—a whirlpool of air. Suddenly the lights went out, and I found myself in an enormous bubble of air and water suspended in . . . well, total blackness is the best, if inadequate, way to describe it. All sorts of things were floating around: ships, chunks of rock, even some stuff dating back to the prehistory of the planet. All dead, of course, as the temperature was killing, once you got away from the contact point with our planet here. Absolute Zero by the time you reached the rim—with even the air frozen solid."

"Then why didn't it kill you?" came a skeptical question obviously from one of the newcomers.

Wade's features registered surprise.

"Why, it did, of course. As you all know— But, well, obviously you *don't* all know. All right, some *real* fundamentals coming up."

Wade put his head in his hand for a minute, thinking. Then his head jerked back up.

"I am a Kreb," he said at last. "One of the last two of my race. Combined, our race was, in every corner of the galaxy, God, controlling the spin of planets and the birth and death of suns. All of your races are the products of our handiwork."

Wade heard the sound of murmuring, and some comments did not get translated. He ignored them, and continued.

"My race was suppose to last until the Next Race evolved into our state; then we would pass on—to where or what, no one, myself included, is really certain. But—something happened. My people simply advanced too fast; they began passing into that next stage involuntarily. Finally, only a few of us were left, including The Bromgrev—as he now calls himself. We didn't have or need names. The Bromgrev, to put it simply, believed in more direct involvement than did the rest of us. He saw the races of the galaxy as small children, who needed to be led—and who needed a tangible god to worship and obey. The Bromgrev, of course, would be that god.

"To stop this, my remaining brothers . . . well, *devolved* him—into a parasitic creature capable of going from body to body but never merging with the superior races. To keep The Bromgrev from nonetheless causing great harm before the Next Race could develop, I volunteered to undergo the same treatment. It has not been necessary to act against him—until now."

"But The Bromgrev is the title given to the Rhambdan mass mind!" someone objected. "Are you saying that this is *not* so? That the Rhambdans are not the enemy?"

"Exactly that. I see Exmiril with a group over in 25. Exmiril, why not come around here and tell everyone the story? Okay, thanks!"

They waited a minute or two, some quite restive, for the agent to make his way to Wade's stage room.

"Is what he's saying true?" Jenny asked Savage, disbelief tinged with awe in her voice.

"Pretty much," he told her. "At least, the main facts are there. Who's who is still open to interpretation."

A creature appeared at Wade's podium. It was tall and wore a standard black uniform, but it looked like nothing Savage had ever seen before. It had a red skin—*bright* red—with a face something like a fox with the hair gone and the snout even thinner. Huge, elephantine ears projected from both sides, and the eyes were round, cat-like, but lidless.

"I was there when The Bromgrev discovered Rhambda," it began in a thin, reedy voice. "It was very, very long ago—even for my long-lived race—but I remember it well. Let me tell you of it."

Exmiril's voice took on a timbre not there before, and his eyes seemed lit by flames. So emotional and animated did he become that the listeners almost felt as if they, too, had been there . . .

2

"SWITCH TO INTERIOR!" Captain Eurosan of the Caltik Federation Trade and Exploration Ship *Admiral Gnarvan* snapped.

Swiftly, one of the three screens switched to the interior of the scoutcraft, while the other two showed an ever-nearing view of the planet below, green-blue and placid-looking.

The two crew members were still in their seats, acting normally, and Jurian, the pilot, was flying with all the skill at his command, fighting the tremendous force of gravity.

"Scout 1, Scout 1—come in! What is the trouble?"

The two in the scout paid no heed at all to the call. The continued their silent downward plunge.

"Jaxmal! Can you probe?" the captain asked the

small, frail old one who sat impassively watching the screens.

Jaxmal nodded, and the telepath shot mentally downward to the scoutcraft. Suddenly he screamed horribly, then collapsed and rolled onto the floor.

Two crew members ran over to him and picked him up. One called for water, which was already forthcoming.

In the background, the screens showed no change in the scout, except that the pilot was slowing to land in a cleared space below. The nose camera showed the features of the terrain: lush, tropical jungle like that which extended over three-fifths of the land surface of the planet.

The old one moaned, and seemed to come to. Horror was written on his face. "You—you must destroy them—and the scout," he gasped. "They—they are not—not *men*. Not anymore. Not any— *Ach!* It's trying to get at me! It's clawing at my mind! Destroy the scout and flee while you can! Do it before— Oh, gods! It's killing me!"

He seemed to collapse into a tiny heap, his blinkless eyes no longer seeing anything at all. He was dead.

Captain Eurosan wasted no time. He had served too long and survived too much to ignore a warning from a ship's telepath.

"Bridge!" he shouted into the intercom.

"Aye, Captain!" came a crisp reply.

"Arm one of our locan missiles and, upon receiving automatic sequencing instructions from the computers, destroy Scout 1."

"But Captain!"

"That is an order, sir! Get to it!" snapped the captain.

"Aye, sir! Armed and primed, sir!"

"Direct complete destruct before touchdown!"

"Aye, sir. Say—by the three moons of Klabius! It's not landing! It's heading back toward us!"

"Hit it!" the captain almost screamed.

The ship gave an instant shudder. A moment later, the screens showed a bright flash of light, then went completely dark.

Eurosan breathed again, and reached once more for the intercom. "Science!"

"Aye, sir?" a different voice rang in.

"Master Exmiril, assemble your staff. I suppose you saw?"

"Aye, sir." The tone was dry and flat, without emotion.

"I want to know what happened to those two men—and what killed Jaxmal."

"Jaxmal is dead, sir?" Incredulity was in the tone.

"It was *his* order—his dying order—to destruct. Now you have *your* orders, Master!"

Science Master Uen Exmiril stood at the head of the wardroom conference table on which he had installed a small projector. His staff flanked him on both sides. The captain and deck officers and department heads crowded around.

"You asked me, sir, to come up with a quick explanation to the problem," Exmiril began. "That I cannot do. But what I *can* offer are some films and some facts based on extremely old data—so old that it's in a *book,* published centuries ago. Then, I can guess. But this will be an explanation of the problem only, sir—solutions I leave to you."

"Go on," the captain urged.

"First, I recommend that you order this ship away with all speed before we even begin. I will explain why in due course."

"I'll accept your recommendation on that," replied Eurosan, and he gave the appropriate order.

Within seconds, they felt the engines kick in and they slid out of orbit.

"First," Exmiril said, "let's present the facts.

"One, this is a jungle world, inhabited primarily by predators. The dominant species seems to be a large, orange-colored cat, having, like all animal life on this world, six limbs. It appears to be intelligent, and can use its forward limbs in centauroid fashion to make and use simple tools. The forepaws show some evidence of crude prehensibility.

"It's a deathworld down there: every living plant and

animal seems to eat each other and its own kind. But our automated probes showed that the cat seems lord and master—its only natural enemy seems to be itself. We first believed that this was simply a high state of savagery, but we were wrong. We believe what's going on down there is a full-scale and nasty war."

There were astonished mutterings around at this. One young officer, a signalsman, asked, "Then they are sentient to a high degree?"

"Quite," Exmiril affirmed. "What we have here is the second recorded case of telepathic absolutism. By that high-sounding term I mean that we have a sentient race—quite unprecedented in form, I assure you—with the curse of telepathy."

"Curse?" put in another officer. "Telepathy is in our own people, you know. And other races are even more adept. Jaxmal—"

"Was, like almost all known telepaths, quite limited. You see, he could read only surface thoughts—and could shut them out at will. These cats read *everything*—and have no way of shutting down."

"You mean, then, that these cats broadcast and receive *all* of everyone's thoughts?" the young signalsman asked incredulously.

"Quite so," Exmiril agreed. "They have *no* natural blocks. Oh, they almost certainly didn't start out that way. Back in the past, they probably had only latent, primitive abilities along these lines. But theirs is a vicious world—and probably was even more so in the past. Their talents evolved to meet the crisis of survival—probably first as sort of a racial warning system.

"But soon, if I may hypothesize, *all* of the beings were like this. Thus, the thoughts of one member of a tribe soon became impossible to separate from those of another individual. There existed, finally, a single Mind with a great many bodies. In this way it coped with, and outlasted, its stronger natural enemies. Some time in the past, this melding became absolute on a geographical basis, probably even taking in the much less developed predators around them. At least, the cats always knew before an attack was launched, and so avoided the other predators of their world.

"Finally, what remained was a world of jungle cats, organized into tribal groupings, each with its own mass mind. Warfare of a peculiar sort was inevitable. A prisoner was simply assimilated into the mind of the victor. And so it's gone on—for how long . . . ? It must be a tremendous mental struggle.

"It caused great progress, of course. All conflict does. And it caused the logical extension of the mass mind concept: absolute assimilation. Here, let me show you some pictures taken by the drones. We isolated and followed a raiding party. Watch . . ."

They were there, those sleek, muscular orange shapes, gliding noiselessly through the dense green of the jungle. Their mouths were frothing; it was obvious that they had come a long way.

"Notice how the pack moves in almost uncanny unison," Exmiril pointed out.

Suddenly the pack halted, having spotted a family of four other animals. To a Terran these would have resembled giant gophers, a meter high, with long, pointed teeth.

One of the cats went forward. The smaller animals did not run, and made no move to fight. They remained frozen like statutes.

The lead cat went up to the closest animal and methodically tore it limb from limb. The rest of the pack joined the first, and started on a second of the gopher-creatures.

"Horrible!" someone muttered.

"Horrible, yes," Exmiril acknowledged, "but not the way *you* mean it. This chance footage gave the clues I needed, when matching it with the old data I mentioned.

"You noticed, I hope, that the prey never moved a muscle, gave no resistance at all. The cats simply assimilated the creature's lower brains into their own Mind and the Mind then ordered the things to calmly sit and be torn to shreds for the common good. Note, too, that the cats ate only two—they left the other two for when they needed them. That was the smart thing to do, not the actions of a bloodthirsty predator."

"But how does this explain what happened to our people?" someone asked.

"Why, that's simple," replied Exmiril, astonished that his listeners had not already seen the obvious. "They came close enough to one of the Mind's fields of mental domain, and were simply assimilated, having no defense. This included all of their past knowledge and experience, of course, so they could still fly the ship. The Mind obviously decided to have the ship brought in while it digested the new knowledge it gained. It was Jaxmal's probe that shocked it—you simply cannot sort out all of an individual's knowledge and experiences, particularly alien ones, in a few minutes—and the Mind decided to go on what it had and return the scout to the ship. It was doubtless prepared to try some bluff, get them back aboard, and move to assimilate the ship, too. As latent telepaths ourselves, the Mind's addition would make us like them. Those men in the scout could have done it. Then the cats would have a ship and the knowledge to fly it—to conquer, perhaps *become,* the rest of the galaxy.

"The last time a race of absolutes was discovered, it *did* take the ship, and it *did* get back. All of a planet's population had to be destroyed before *that* one was resolved. *We* were more fortunate. The Mind simply didn't think and act fast enough—such as to radio a reassuring message or something, we being just too alien for it to digest all at once. My guess is that if the entire race on that planet had finally become *one* mass mind, we'd have suffered a direct mental assault. Just luck!"

"How *was* the previous case stopped?" asked the junior signalsman.

"The Kreb were still a race then . . ." Exmiril said slowly.

"Could *we* destroy *these?*" asked the captain, after a pause, thinking like a military man.

"Probably," Exmiril replied, "but it would be difficult. The danger would be that the Mind would be waiting, forearmed with knowledge of us, next time. Faced with a common threat, however, the remaining minds would probably merge into a force potentially great enough to assimilate any ships attempting to de-

stroy the planet. Automated attack would be more than
we can manage at this stage. No, I think we just list it as
Rhambda—'forbidden'—and wait nature out."

"What do you mean, 'wait nature out'?" asked one of
his own Science staff.

"Well," Exmiril explained, "the scoutcraft was destroyed, and had only basic propulsion, anyway. Neither
scout was a physicist, and they hadn't the tools, anyway,
to build a ship. Most of you don't even understand why
the light goes on when you press the switch in your
room.

"Sooner or later, one mind will win out over all down
there—and that will mean stagnation for them. Without
competition, there will be no progress, no motive force.
They will devolve, or die out."

"I wish we'd never found it," the captain snarled in
disgust. "It's a pity that there are no more Kreb to neutralize this threat. Even with your reassuring words, Exmiril, I feel this Rhambda world is a ticking bomb under us all."

"Indeed it is," the Science Master agreed. "And we
must carefully wait until that bomb is defused, no matter how long that takes. But one thing still bothers me."

"What?" several asked in unison.

"We were in orbit for fourteen days before we sent
the scout down. Eleven hundred of us were on this ship,
some telepathic. For nine of those days we were in sta-
tionary orbit—over one mind's territory. Yet it failed to
notice us until *we* went to *it*, almost as if we were under
a shield blocking us from contact. Why . . . ?"

"Perhaps," said the young signals officer, rising to
leave, "perhaps there *are* still some Krebs . . ." A
strange smile was on his face.

The young signalsman was halfway to his room
when he became violently ill. At any other time, he
would have cursed the sex-changing of the race he had
chosen; he'd more than once resolved in the past never
to get near these accursed people again. But somehow
he didn't mind it anymore. He suddenly felt a sentimen-
tal attachment for the body he wore.

They had given him a weapon.

They had given him *the* weapon.

It had been so long, so very long since the last Unification, he thought. Plans swam in his brain, ideas fitted together like intricate pieces of a puzzle. As he retched violently over the basin, he did not even see the bile and blood, nor feel any real discomfort.

He reflected, as he threw up again, that it was a most wonderful and auspicious day all around . . .

3

"THE REST YOU can figure out," Exmiril was concluding. "The young signals officer was, of course, The Bromgrev, and once back on Caltik, he arranged a private expedition to the Rhambdan world. Instead of being assimilated by the Mind, *his* mind assimilated *it*—and unified them all. My home world was his test, the first conquest. And The War began."

Wade moved back into view. Exmiril, head bowed, left quickly, overcome with emotion. It had been hard on him.

Savage was interested in the reactions of the people in the room with him. Gayal had sobbed at the end, Vard looked very upset—the first real emotion he had displayed—while Jenny had almost squeezed his left hand off. Koldon, he noted, had shown massive disinterest.

"That's our history lesson," Wade was saying. "But, be assured. Haven was built by me of materials that could withstand the fierceness of its extradimensional environment. Being not in normal space, it is outside the range of the Mind. It cannot reach us here, and any member of the Mind who penetrated would be instantly cut off from contact with both the Mind and The Bromgrev, whose sheer mental force allows the Mind to stay unified despite massive distances and dispersions. Haven is unattackable by conventional means, unreachable even by *un*conventional ones, the only truly safe place in the galaxy.

"Haven.

"You know, now, the background of The War and of this place—and of me. We already know a great deal about you. You are the hope of your peoples. The Bromgrev, being condemned to the flesh, must fight by conventional methods; that means he can be beaten conventionally. We delivered a costly defeat to him not long ago. During the days and weeks ahead, you shall undergo training so that you can fight that battle with us. I know you will bear up under it, and that you will contribute greatly to the victory, for you all have a great stake in the outcome, and you have all seen what victory for The Bromgrev would mean for you and all of your people. Are there any questions?"

A few were asked, but nothing of consequence, and Savage called his little group together.

"Tomorrow we will begin our training," he told them. "All of you have been furnished with a great deal of background material that you will need. Study it, for tomorrow the questions and testing begin. All three of you are already in excellent physical shape"—he looked at Gayal as he said this—"and so we will be able to start out at a more advanced level than is usual. Meet me tomorrow morning at 0800 in this room."

And, with that, he left them.

Jenny was silent all the way back to their quarters. Finally he asked her what the problem was.

"It's a hell of a thing for a good Baptist to swallow," she said.

"She takes to the simulator as if she's been flying all her life," Savage observed to Koldon, who just nodded.

The subject of the conversation was Gayal, who had proven to be the best pupil in simulator flight training for being a command pilot. It had been a complete surprise; she'd done only fair in much of the preliminary testing, and her submissive manner and, to put it nicely, extreme need for social contact had led to other conclusions.

"One might almost suspect that she's done it before,"

Koldon commented, "yet I've looked deep within her and see nothing suspect. It appears that we have a natural for machines."

Savage mulled this over. "Maybe," he replied. "But for somebody who's barely in the top quarter percentile in mechanical aptitude, her complete control of the ship and her mastery of some tight tactical problems *is* amazing."

Koldon snorted. "Come, come! I've watched you using an electric typewriter with great speed, but can you really explain to me why and how those words appear on the page when you touch an apparently unconnected key? One does not need to *understand* machines to operate them well."

The training problem ended, and Gayal emerged, her face almost radiant with pleasure.

"Did I do well?" she asked, knowing she had.

"Amazing," Savage told her. "Simply amazing. It's almost like you and the simulator were one."

"That's the way it feels in there," she replied. "It is— well, hypnotizing, wonderful, like a god almost."

Now it was Koldon's turn. Although he had ridden on ships since he was small, and was certainly the most cosmopolitan of the group, he had the most trouble in training—almost the reverse of Gayal. Koldon understood everything, almost never missed a question; yet he fared poorly in the pilot's chair and did only slightly better as a gunner. The Quoark had sought to explain it, but it exasperated him as much or more than everybody else.

"Comes from knowing what everyone else around you is thinking. This telepathy is like a machine: you get to depend on it to do the work for you. Once in there, I do *not* become the machine, the machine becomes *me*—and live creatures can outthink a machine any time, if their power and speed is boosted to the machine's level."

Even so, Savage wondered about the great bear. He was a fine conversationalist, never at a loss for words, able to hold his own with experts in almost every subject. It was almost as if his failure in the simulator was compensation for such genius—*or* camouflage . . .

A few minutes later, Koldon was done. His score had improved, but it was nowhere near the expected norms. Koldon studied the printout and shook his head in disgust.

"Vard's turn, now," Savage said. He looked around. Vard was not there. "Where'd he get to?"

"He didn't do well on the syllogismic problems yesterday," Koldon replied, "and he was upset because he usually does quite well. Said he was going to run some checks through the computer room and see what went wrong."

"Bad timing," Savage growled. "There are a lot of people waiting to use this simulator, and I have to fight to get on the day's schedule. This character's kind of strange, anyway, isn't he?"

Gayal nodded. "Yes. During the entire trip here he said not ten complete sentences to us. He is a most disagreeable and unsocial person."

"The fellow's a bit kinky," Koldon agreed, "but you have to understand him. He's had no social life for years—not since becoming the agent on Fraska. He's had to seal himself away from everyone, in sort of like a self-imposed prison sentence. He's not used to dealing with people."

"Fala did so with no problems," Gayal pointed out.

"That's true," Koldon acknowledged. "But Fraska is not Delial, and the social customs and such that Vard needed and suppressed for so long a time are quite different than ours—and were impossible for him when he was an agent. Now such a life is still denied him as a refugee."

"You're quite an apologist, aren't you, Koldon?" Savage put in. "War is a leveler, and fighting it is a team job. If Vard doesn't realize this and adjust, we'll have to wash him out. Put him in a little room with communications devices like he had on Fraska and let him rot."

The Terran stalked off angrily toward the computer section, leaving the other two standing there looking at each other.

"He has quite a temper," Gayal commented.

"True," Koldon agreed, "but he's right."

"He is such a strange man . . ."

"I'm afraid I have to agree, knowing a lot more of his history than you do. But, even so, I cannot get down to the part that counts in him—his blocks are so strong that I can only read what he's actually *saying.* I suspect there's a complex and fascinating enigma in his brain, but it's beyond reach. For all the power of personality he has shown and the contradictions he's presented, one would almost think he might be quite a bit more than he appears."

Gayal studied the big bear's features. They betrayed nothing, as usual.

"Why *shouldn't* he be anything other than what he claims?" she asked.

"You know," Koldon mused, "one of The Hunter's best-trained and one-hundred-percent-blocked agents would be a perfect place for The Bromgrev."

"You don't think he is—?" Gayal gasped, horror-stricken.

"No, I don't," Koldon replied thoughtfully. "But, likewise, I don't think that he *isn't.*"

Savage stalked to the computer room nearest the training center, blood in his eye. He had just fifteen more minutes and then he would have to clear out for the next simulator group—and this ass was screwing up the works. He fondly hoped he'd never be in a situation where he would have to depend on Vard.

Savage entered the computer room, one of the smaller rooms with access to the master computers, quietly. Surprisingly, no one else was around. Vard sat alone in a center chair, helmet on, figures dancing across the screens in front of him at a dizzying pace. The Fraskan seemed unaware of Savage's existence.

Savage did not speak to him immediately. His curiosity was aroused beyond measure by the various complex figures dancing on the screen, a little too fast for him to read. But there were definitely too many equations, too many diagrams flashing on, however briefly, for Vard to be reviewing training problems.

Savage noiselessly took a seat in the back of the room

and put on a helmet, punching the required codes to tie
him in with Vard's display.

At first glance they seemed to be tactical problems,
anyway, but Savage stuck with it for a minute or two.
Something was certainly not right. It took him only a
second longer to realize it—the red and yellow bands
flashing along the sides of the picture!

They weren't problems, they were actual exercises.
The stripes denoted classified information.

They were Haven military defense contingency plans.

Suddenly the display stopped, and was replaced by a
readout in clear English—which was particularly surprising, since Vard spoke not a word of it. It read:

HELLO SAVAGE * I HAD NOT INTENDED TO BE
FOUND OUT SO SOON *

Savage quickly shot back: SO THE BROMGREV IS AT
HAVEN *

WHY IS THAT SO UNUSUAL TO CONTEMPLATE *
DID WE NOT TELL YOU THIS *

BUT ARUMAN VARD IS FAR TOO OBVIOUS AND VUL-
NERABLE * Savage objected. I JUST DO NOT BELIEVE IT *

Savage removed his helmet and walked to the figure in
the front chair. "And I still don't, Vard," he said aloud.

Vard turned and smiled, then removed the helmet.

"I lost a great deal in the abortive attack on this
place," he said casually. "And, while here, I cannot
properly coordinate the actions of my units. These will
aid me when contact is again possible in avoiding the
inevitable counterattacks."

Savage shook his head negatively. "You're no more
The Bromgrev than a cell of my body is *me*. Just when
did you assimilate Vard, anyway?"

"After the escape," The Bromgrev replied casually.
"Which, I might add, was extremely difficult to manage. The man was a total incompetent."

"So why stick your neck out now, so early in the
game?" Savage asked.

"The element of surprise is no longer of any import-
ance. It was more necessary to have this information
and to have it early. This was the easiest and most di-

rect way to it. The classified codes are absurdly easy to crack."

"So now what?" Savage asked the creature. "Hunter will make you as a doppelgänger, if I don't turn you in—so I have to turn you in. What good was all this?"

Vard's face smiled again; it was an unnatural and grotesque expression for the Fraskan. "I cannot control The Hunter in this place, so removed from the realities of the galaxy. It will be necessary to establish more suitable conditions for our, shall we say, double murder?"

"And you expect *me* to do it?" Savage growled.

"Oh, if not you, then someone. There are lots of possibilities. But there *is* the girl, you know."

Savage reached over and picked him up, shaking him violently.

"What do you gain by shaking a tenth of my toenail?" Vard managed.

Savage stopped and dropped him to the floor. The creature picked himself up slowly.

"You see? Who *really* controls the way of the worlds?"

"You're crazy as a loon," Savage snapped.

"Perhaps. Perhaps we *all* are. That was a wonderful story The Hunter told everyone at orientation a few days ago, about the evil one and the guardian. Absolutely correct—but, of course, with the roles reversed. The Hunter was isolated here forever—but for this cursed bubble that allowed him his escape. Finally, out again among the stars, he proved as mad as ever. He began raising forces to wreck the Next Race—and any Next Race he found that might be a challenge to his dreams of power."

Savage looked puzzled. "Now, how the hell could he do that?"

"Oh, by making certain the wrong things happened at critical times. The almost perfect birth control of Delial was one. An ancient planet, an extremely intelligent people—worthy successors! Now they multiply not at all, having maintained a very small stable population and continuing those numbers into the infinite future in a stagnant society. The projection now is that they have no future, only a frozen present. Other cultures—young cultures—were given the tachyonic drive to dilute them early. Too early. The discovery and development of the drive must be carefully managed and timed."

"You introduced it here," Savage pointed out. "Charley's ship."

"Oh, come now," The Bromgrev grumbled, making a gesture of dismissal with his hand. "That was a fluke— an accident. It was shot down and crashed. I assure you that they got nothing from it. The whole thing will go up in one big bang when they attempt to get at the drive; and not a shred will remain. Little by little, over years of time, people and evidence will be altered to fit a coherent but less likely form. I cover my tracks. Had you not eliminated the Kah'diz, I assure you *we* would have done so."

"Nice talk—of justice and truth and all that—from one who is in league with the Kah'diz, who enslave planets and kill millions."

Vard stood up, towering even over the tall Terran although he was less than two-thirds Savage's weight. "I am a pragmatist. I use the tools that are available to me." He spat angrily, then just as suddenly he calmed down.

"There was in your planet's past a dictator," he said, "who took over a country that was a century backward and totally impoverished, yet threatened by powerful neighbors. Inside thirty years, he built a mighty industrial nation that withstood the world. In the process, he killed off almost a third of his people—often in brutal slave labor. But the survivors and their descendants live a comfortable life undreamed of by their parents. And a safe and secure one. Would you swap misery, famine, disease, hopelessness, for the modern way of life—if that were your only choice and, if you picked the latter, it meant doing unspeakable evils?"

"That's been the argument of dictators everywhere," Savage pointed out. "Somehow it seems to work out differently. Besides, what's the moral imperative of destroying an innocent person like Vard when, with a little more effort, you could have done it otherwise?"

"This same dictator I was speaking of—well, there's a story, perhaps apocryphal, about how he liked to drive fancy cars down lonely peasant roads at high speeds. Once, while doing so, he struck a small girl. He did not stop. When asked why, he replied, 'It's only *one* little girl.' "

"That's disgusting," Savage commented, looking as if he had smelled raw garbage.

"It's your own people," The Bromgrev pointed out. "I merely illustrate. To survive in the jungle, the ends must justify *any* means. Besides, it is either me or The Hunter. You—or someone like you—will have to choose."

"And if we choose neither?"

"Then someone else will make the decision," The Bromgrev answered matter-of-factly. "There is always a lever on anyone, always someone else if all else fails."

They stood silently for a while, looking at each other. There seemed nothing more to say

"This has been most interesting and refreshing," The Bromgrev said at last, breaking the silence. "But I have accomplished what I wished to do, and the relief of this very boring existence I've been living since being here has been most welcome. Now I shall terminate this utensil's usefulness."

With that, Vard's body crumpled over, dead.

Savage stood staring at the corpse, then turned and left. But the conversation lingered in his mind as he made his way back to the two students he had left a few minutes before.

It is either me or The Hunter, a voice seemed to whisper.

You . . . will have to chose, it continued.

There is . . . always someone else . . it insisted.

But there is the girl, you know, it taunted.

There is always a lever on anyone, it reminded.

It's only one *little girl.*

Wade switched off the transceiver.

"So we know it isn't Savage," Koldon said cheerfully.

"We know nothing of the kind!" Hunter snapped back. "The Bromgrev knew it could be—and probably was—bugged, in there. That whole thing was a performance for my benefit, not Savage's. It's a taunt, a sign he's feeling his imprisonment here and an attempt to provoke me into action. Or immobilize me here in Haven. I wish I knew which!"

"A monologue, then?" Koldon mused. "How fascinating! And, if a dialogue, it calls into question one of your best men. Nice touch."

Wade nodded. "It was a challenge, all right. Come out and get suckered, or stay in while *he* can leave any old time by simply creating new components and sending them outside. No, we'll stick to the script here," Wade decided. "The final battle will be *my* choice. One of my agents *must* find out who in this installation is The Bromgrev. That Vard takeover stuff was bullshit. Vard was Vard when he *came into* Haven, so The Bromgrev's right here, thumbing his nose at me!"

"So they find out who he is," Koldon responded. "What good would it do? *He* knows who *you* are, after all, and it isn't doing him a fat lot of good."

"That's it!" Wade exclaimed, pounding his fist on the desk. "He wouldn't be here unless he had a plan to do away with me. And yet he hasn't acted, despite all the opportunity. That means he can't act in here with a certainty of success! He wants me *out* . . ."

"And then what?" Koldon asked. "You've been fighting each other for millennia and it's always a draw."

"Not this time, Koldon, not this time. A small but definitive Armageddon is looming. A decisive one. As to the how— No, no one knows that until it's time. I don't know who *you* really are, either. Or anyone else."

"The watcher watching the watcher watching—this can't go on forever, Hunter."

Wade got up from his chair and put his hand on the bear-creature's shoulder. A strange half-smile was on his face as he said, "It won't, Koldon, it won't. I know what he needs now, and time is on *my* side."

4

THEY TOOK THE shakedown cruise in a pickup ship, which meant that there was room for passengers. Savage replaced Vard at the gunnery position with little trouble, as he had trained along with them. He would not like to get into a real firefight, he thought, particularly with Koldon as backup; but for shakedowns and normal checkouts it wasn't much of a problem. Gayal, who seemed to be born to the job, was, of course, the pilot.

Jennifer made her way out from the rear compartment aft of the bridge. She had spent three days memorizing the fixed placements in a similar ship and now knew it very well. Koldon was on gunnery duty, and Savage was sitting in a lounge chair drinking a cup of coffee and reading a book.

"What are you reading?" she asked as she put her arms around him from the back of the chair and heard the book shut.

"Detective novel," he replied. "An old one, as a matter of fact, by the greatest master of locked-room puzzles: John Dickson Carr."

"You'll have to read it to me," she told him. "You *used* to read to me—until the training started taking all the time. There's not nearly enough in Braille or talking-book for blind people."

"Go back to the beginning? I could never reread a locked-room puzzle," he said. "Really louses things up when you know the answer. But," he continued, kissing her, "you'll be learning to read regular print soon enough, you know."

She was silent for a moment, a stiffness betraying an inner apprehension. "Paul," she said quietly, "I'm kind of scared. How long will it be until . . ."

"Until Valiakea?" he completed. "Not long, love.

177

With this space drive, there's more time spent in slowing down on a long trip than in actually getting there."

It was his present to her, this trip: a combination business and pleasure trip that Wade had approved. Savage himself had mixed emotions about the whole thing. On the one hand, for Jenny to have eyes, to be able to see for the first time in her life, was the greatest gift he could give her. Yet, underneath, he felt uneasy about it. It wasn't merely that he would lose her dependence on him—he felt he was big enough to accept that—but it was all the insecurities of a life of ridicule and derision about his looks.

Deep down, he was afraid that she wouldn't like him when she saw him. He feared this, and couldn't put it out of his mind.

"Coming in," Gayal's voice, somewhat metallic-sounding though the wall speakers, told them.

"Shall I strap in?" Jenny asked.

"I don't think it will be necessary," Gayal replied. "We are not in a fight or any other kind of rush. I can put us in orbit and hold, so that you won't even know we've changed position."

Jenny had steadfastly refused Savage's attempts to put a helmet on her, even though she would "see" with the helmet as guide. She tried to put on a brave front, but she, too, was a product of conditioning from birth. Deep down, she was comfortable the way she was. She *liked* depending on Paul, partly because it bound him closer to her. Blindness was a normal condition. *This* was the unknown.

"There are two dozen or so ships in orbit," Gayal's command voice cut in. "At least four are unfriendlies. What shall I do?"

"Don't worry about it," Savage assured her. "This is truly neutral territory. The Valiakeans don't like anyone fooling around with that—and within their own sphere of influence they can zap anybody who violates the truce. Besides, anybody who did so would be forbidden to use their services again—and The Bromgrev needs them as much as we do."

Koldon growled in the background, and Savage turned to see that the huge creature had removed its helmet and was lifting itself up from the gunnery position into the bridge section. "Maybe everybody else thinks it's just great," he grumbled, "but all that damned thing does is give me a bad headache."

"I've accepted Valiakean control and we are in a stable orbit," Gayal reported.

Savage reached over and flipped a switch on the panel, causing Gayal's mind to break contact with the ship's automatics. No pilot could ever do it on his or her own, and automatic and manual systems were provided to ensure that every pilot was brought out.

Gayal groaned, and awakened in the chair next to Savage. She turned off the console and removed her helmet, then brushed her hair with her hand so that it mostly covered the shaven places where the contact points in the helmet touched her skull.

Savage broke free of Jenny's hold and grabbed the transceiver mike, dialing the Valiakean hailing frequency.

"This is Haven Special in early for appointment," he reported. "Can you handle two subjects?"

"Two?" Jenny repeated. "Who else?"

"That depends, Haven," came the Valiakean answer. "We have one Haven spectrum sight installation here. That is a minor matter. What is the nature of the others?"

"Cosmetic," Savage replied. "I'll read you the data as I have it, and let you decide."

Whereupon, Savage picked up a sheet of notebook paper and read-in a long series of seemingly meaningless figures and gibberish words.

"We can handle that easily enough, although you'll have to do it one at a itme. We have only a supplemental carrier ship to service you. Business is quite heavy, as you can see."

"That's all right," Savage responded. "We'll do the supplemental first."

"Very well. We are finished early on another party and will send the supplemental over in five or six minutes."

"Fine. I compliment you on your service," Savage responded politely and switched off.

"Who's the other?" Jenny asked him.

"Me, of course," Savage replied with a laugh. "When you see me, I'll be a handsome devil."

"Just don't let them touch the most important part!" she warned.

"Only to make it bigger and better, my dear," he replied, and kissed her.

He had an ulterior motive in doing the cosmetic surgery, of course. If he went first and underwent any kind of modification, it would ease her own fears.

There was a shudder and bump through the ship. The Valiakeans were already here.

The Valiakean technician who entered the lock area looked like the same being who had serviced Gayal and Koldon on their trip in. This was just the Haven norm shape of convenience for them, however, and it might or might not be the same one, the two former visitors knew. Gayal wondered again about the power to instantly change one's molecular structure to meet any conditions. She had heard that one Valiakean survived a cataclysmic explosion and hours in hard vacuum when a ship went up.

Savage entered the Valiakean ship and went through the same procedure as had millions before him. After the examination, they stuffed him in that chilly coffin and he went black.

He awoke a few minutes later feeling, he admitted to himself, better than he had ever felt in his life. While in, the Valiakeans generally cured your minor illnesses or whatever, and even cleaned the cholesterol out of your bloodstream, plus adjusting weight and muscle tone to proper—indeed, *ideal*—limits.

Savage unhesitatingly re-entered the Haven ship.

Gayal gasped.

He was still tall and dark-complected, but with an almost perfect build. His apish ugliness, scars, and Neanderthal-like head and shoulders had been altered to the look of a rugged outdoorsman. He'd kept his short-cropped hair and it contrasted superbly with the dark complexion.

He would have driven women on Earth wild, except for one thing.

"You didn't regrow the hand!" Koldon exclaimed. "We all thought—"

Savage gave a slight, wistful smile. "I have reasons for not doing so right now," he said enigmatically. "Later on, in a future trip, I will. But the claw they gave me is still great—slips on and off the stump with no straps needed!" He showed them by twisting slightly and pulling the pincers off. He slipped it back on quickly. "All electronics now," he proclaimed proudly.

All three of the others thought he was crazy.

"Where the hell did you get the idea for the new look?" Koldon asked him. "It's certainly distinctive— and it's still you, sort of, but—er—well, straightened out, put in all the right places."

Savage laughed. "From a cover painting on a paperback of an old pulp hero," he replied. "I'll show you sometime. 'The Man of Bronze.'" He chuckled, then turned serious. "Now you, Jenny," he said brightly.

"I—I really don't—" she started to say.

He moved over to her and kissed her. "It's best," he told her. "Go ahead—and don't be scared. It's not like a regular operation."

The Valiakean stood waiting with passive indifference. Jennifer finally put on a brave front and took the creature's hand.

Once seated for the examination, the Valiakean took out some notes of some kind. Jenny could hear the paper—or whatever it was—rustle.

"You have never seen before," it said to her.

"No," she answered. "Never . . ."

"Very well," it replied. "Having looked at your eyes and the neural connectors from the plates we made as you sat here, it looks like a simple matter. However, we will not allow you to see until we take you back into the ship and do it gradually. The connections are delicate and such things must be eased in, both for medical and psychological reasons. Do you also wish cosmetics?"

"No!" she almost snapped at the Valiakean. "I—I want to see myself the way I've always been."

"Very well," said the Valiakean in a tone indicating that it couldn't care less—which it couldn't. "I will take you over to the operating area. Just lie down and be comfortable. You will be unconscious for the actual re-encoding."

Back in the ship they all waited nervously, Savage the worst of all. He kept pacing back and forth, and, despite a very comfortable temperature, was sweating. The air conditioning was hard put to rid the air of his cigarette smoke.

"Do not worry," Gayal tried to reassure him. "In my time at Haven, I have come in contact with many Terran women. Should she never have met you *before,* she would nevertheless desire you now," she said. "In fact, I would be honored to be one of your wives myself."

He looked down at her and smiled. "Don't tempt me," he muttered, and resumed his pacing. "What's taking so long?"

"It's only been ten minutes," Koldon told him. "What with examinations, interviews, and the like—"

He stopped. They heard someone in the lock.

The Valiakean guided Jenny back into the cabin. It pulled out the cot on the bridge and lay her upon it. Her eyes were covered by thick pads, apparently many layers of them, held by a thin band.

"I wish to do this slowly," the Valiakean told them. "It is better."

"Take your time," Jenny whispered, trembling slightly.

They all came as close as they could. The Valiakean turned her head away from them, toward the soft wall lighting, and removed the first small strip from each eye.

"Tell me when you perceive anything," it told her.

One by one, very slowly, the extremely thin strips started to come off. About a quarter of the way through the apparently infinite layers, Jenny gasped.

"It's—it's different! Lighter!" she breathed.

For the first time in her life, she was perceiving light itself. The Valiakean continued.

"Very good. Now what do you see?"

"Little lines—indistinct—running up and down and from side to side," she whispered. "And . . . a whiteness."

"Very good," repeated the Valiakean. "That is the bandage."

He got down to the last thin layer, then removed the one from her left eye, then the right. She blinked.

The creature held her head looking at the wall. None of the other three breathed.

"Which of you is her mate?" asked the Valiakean.

Savage answered, "I am." His voice sounded dry in his throat.

"Step forward to the cot," it ordered. "The others please stay back."

Slowly the Valiakean turned her head. Her eyes were closed, Savage saw, and there was intense fear on her face. It was as if she was refusing to see.

"Open your eyes!" the Valiakean commanded.

Jenny seemed to steep up her courage, then opened them. They were, Savage saw, a beautiful nut brown.

She looked at him, her eyes running up and down his form. She was fascinated, almost awestruck.

"Hello, lover," she whispered.

He smiled and kissed her. The Valiakean put its hand on his chest and pushed him away with unexpected strength.

"Will one of the others come forward?" it asked. "Stand beside this one, please."

Gayal stepped into Jenny's rigidly held field of view.

"Oh, you're so beautiful!" Jenny said. "That bluish tint makes you look very sexy."

Gayal laughed. "It is the color of my people. Your people have *many* colors, I have seen."

"I'm going to get into this picture," Koldon grumbled, and stepped up to her.

She knew he looked like a bear from "feeling" him, but she had never *seen* a bear, and he was a fascinating sight.

"You will be extremely dizzy until your mind adjusts to using its new tools," the Valiakean warned. "You must practice, and take it in small steps. It will affect your balance, and you will have to get used to judging depth and distance. Take it slowly. Get around with your eyes open as much as possible, but if things begin to blur or pain you, shut them for a while. In a few days you will be acting as if you were born sighted. I will go now. Others require my services."

It rose and walked quickly out of the room. They heard the lock open and close. There was a hiss and a shudder as the Valiakean ship soared away.

Nobody said anything for a while.

Jenny kept twisting her head and looking—just looking. Ceiling, floor, the three others, the furniture—everything was an object of novelty and fascination.

"Can you bring me a mirror?" she said at last.

"None around," Savage told her, "but if you come over to the side bulkhead here, it's shiny enough to see a good reflection."

She got up and took a couple of steps toward him, then almost collapsed. He caught her.

"Dizzy," she said.

But she wouldn't be put off. He led her to the floor-to-ceiling shiny bulkhead. She simply stared.

"Dumpy-looking fat broad," she said at last. "What a couple we make!"

Savage stood behind her, ready to catch her if she became dizzy.

"But we fit in the mirror together so well," he pointed out. He kissed her on the neck, and she smiled.

"There are some things still better done in the dark," she said.

STEP FIVE

1

WADE'S OFFICE LOOKED even worse than the last time, if that were possible. Savage entered and unpiled the junk from the chair so that he could sit down.

"What's the word, Wade?" he asked.

The other turned to him and put out the cigar he had been smoking. He immediately lit another. Despite the blowers and ventilation, the place reeked of stogies. Wade took the cigar from his lips, studying it.

"These have been my greatest pleasure," he said, addressing the cigar as much as Savage. "I shall miss them when I go."

"You've decided to go through with it, then?" Savage asked.

Wade nodded. "I've got to. I haven't any idea what The Bromgrev's plot is, but he will have to act soon or he'll lose almost all of his gains. The armies need him— out there, where he can command, coordinate, and control. We know it's your group, Paul. We just don't know which."

"Oh," Savage commented offhandedly, "hell, I've known who The Bromgrev was for some time. It was simple, once everything was put in its proper place."

Wade reacted as if shot. "You *knew* who he was?" he thundered. "And you didn't tell me?"

Savage shrugged. "I had to make my own decisions. It's not easy, you know. I never really thought the decision would fall to me. The Bromgrev seems to have known it, though."

"Sure!" Wade snorted. "He can pick his own time, place, and people! *I* couldn't!"

"Until now," Savage responded. "But what good does all this do us? How can you kill him, anyway?"

Wade pondered long and hard. "It's a difficult decision to tell anyone. It can be used both ways," he pointed out.

"Meaning that if *I'm* The Bromgrev, you'd be committing your own murder," Savage commented. "A nice point. You'll have to gamble. For once, you're in the same spot as all the mortals in the galaxy."

Wade looked both angry and frustrated. "Dammitall! I had to go and build the blocks on you people so thoroughly that The Bromgrev himself couldn't get through without making such cornmeal mush of your insides that he'd get no information!! I really don't have much choice, do I?" he said almost to himself, in a voice much calmer and lower than before. "If you *are* The Bromgrev, I'm delivering myself into your hands. But if you're not . . .

"Hell, Savage, it's a draw. After all these thousands of years, it's still a draw. It'll go on forever unless one of us can knock off the other. I know that—and I think he does, too. That amount of time builds up a lot of hate. I've— Oh, shit. Okay, who is it?"

"You'll have to tell me how you're going to do it, before I'll tell you *who* you'll do it *to*," Savage prodded.

Wade swallowed hard and told him. "We are creatures of pure energy," he began. "The only obvious way is to disperse that energy over a wide area too quickly for the consciousness to react and get out. And here's how we'll put The Bromgrev where we want him and do what must be done . . ."

Savage just nodded at the plan. When Wade finished, the detective said, "It won't be too hard. After all, The Bromgrev requires the same circumstances for *his* plan. We'll use that." Savage nervously lit a cigarette. "By the way, how'd you know it was my group?"

"Oh, that was easy. Each group was sent out on a training flight, one at a time. We simply watched the enemy. Oh, he tried hard to pretend The Bromgrev wasn't back, but couldn't avoid betraying it—and acting on some of the information The Bromgrev had. They needed it too badly. During others—nothing. During your flight, *bingo!*"

"I'll be damned," Savage commented. "There *is* one last thing—one last price to be paid."

Wade smiled. "I think I know it already. You're revenge-motivated, Savage. Go on, say it! It's easy to arrange."

A dangerous tone rang in Savage's voice and a faraway look came into his eyes.

"McNally," he whispered.

"It is true we're going to attack Rhambda itself?" Koldon asked Savage.

"That's right," the other replied. "Sort of the reverse of what The Bromgrev had planned for us—and a little retaliation. Look, it makes sense: destroy the home world of the cats and you deprive The Bromgrev of the mass of his best troops—himself."

"But it's impossible!" Gayal objected. "The Mind's force alone will overtake ships that get close enough to destroy the planet! Remember Exmiril's story?"

"That's true," agreed Savage, "but if you remember *all* of Exmiril's story, you'll also remember that the Mind didn't take the Caltik Federation ship. The Bromgrev was on board and was able to block the Mind without any aid. Imagine what could be done if he had cybernetic augmentation such as we use for our command ships. Amplified a million times!"

"That means The Hunter must lead the attack personally," Koldon pointed out. "Isn't that just what The Bromgrev wants? To get The Hunter out of here?"

"Calculated   risk,"   Savage   explained.   "Break Rhambda and you break the army. The Bromgrev goes back to being weaponless once again, and we become masters of our fate once more—at least until the next time something nasty like this comes up. And we'll be together, looking to see that such a weapon never falls into The Bromgrev's hands again."

"If The Hunter likes it, okay," Koldon gave in.

"Glad you agree," Savage told them both. "Because we're to crew the command ship with The Hunter on board."

Both of them gasped.

"When?" Gayal asked.

"Tomorrow. We leave at 0600 tomorrow morning. Get some sleep."

Savage was making his way back to his quarters when a young Terran woman in the dark black cloth uniform of Haven ground personnel called to him. She was nothing much—the clerical type you never look twice at in the office. Savage remembered seeing her in Food Services, but he didn't know her. She knew him, though.

"Can you come with me for a few minutes, Mr. Savage?" she asked in a high, kittenish, sexy voice.

"It's tempting," he smiled, liking his newfound romantic idol status since his shape change. He had turned down a lot of offers.

"I am The Bromgrev," she whispered.

He stopped dead in his tracks.

"Not *another* one!" he exclaimed.

She shrugged. "When it suits my purpose. The technique is laborious and quite involved, unless I am in contact with the Rhambdan Mind."

Other people—human and otherwise—were walking past them in the corridor.

"This is kind of public, don't you think?" she said, and went over to an office door, which opened automatically. The place was deserted. "I have neutralized all of the snooping devices this time," she told him. "We will not be overhead."

"What's all this about?" Savage asked her. It was difficult not to think of him as a "her."

"You've been expecting this," she accused him. "You've been waiting for it."

"Okay, so I knew you'd talk to me. So?"

"This attack on Rhambda gives me the conditions that I need," she said. "The Hunter will be in your ship. You must neutralize him, both for Rhambda and for my sake."

"Neutralize him? How the hell can anyone do that?"

"Both The Hunter and I are basically electrical in nature," she reminded him. "Call it pure energy. When the attack comes, The Hunter will be tied in to massive amplifiers within the command ship—amplifiers built for the purpose of offsetting anything I can do to stop the attack. I have observed the construction of those amplifiers."

"So?"

"I will tell you how to short them out," The Bromgrev said calmly. "Such an action will also produce unconsciousness in The Hunter—for several days, probably. Longer than I will need, certainly."

"And once I've short-circuited him?"

"You will take command of the ship and bring him to a world near Rhambda. It's a deserted rock pile on which I have a small base. It was once an observatory for another race, long ago. There we will do what has to be done."

"And what about the others?" Savage asked. "Unlike you, *I* respect individuals' lives. I once took one in anger that I had no right to take. I cannot bring myself to take innocent lives again."

"Their preservation can be arranged," The Bromgrev replied. "In fact, the way to do it is built in, for you well know that everyone is a creature like me. Just make certain that *you* are not tied in to the system when you short—and that *they* are. The ship will retain their physical bodies and care for them. Their minds will be locked into the ship's systems, but impotent to do anything about it. They, too, will be unconscious—that's the best word. 'Unable to think' is probably more accurate."

"So how do I restore them?"

"When you dock, you will disconnect them from the main amplifier circuitry, as I shall show you. They will then revive none the worse for wear, and what must be done will be done."

The conversation went on some time more, The Bromgrev sketching the details of how the system would be shorted and restored. When Savage could repeat it back flawlessly, the woman's face showed satisfaction. "It is finished, then," she said. "Go."

He left her still sitting in the office, wondering if she would collapse in death as Vard had. Probably not, he thought. She might be useful to The Bromgrev in Haven with The Hunter away.

Jenny greeted him with almost too much affection when he returned. He laughed, and picked her up, looking into those beautiful brown eyes. "So what's the occasion?" he asked her.

"I know there's to be a battle," she said seriously. "We might not see each other again for a long time."

"Then we must make tonight count, beautiful," he whispered, and they started to do so.

They made quite a night of it, but Jenny had tears in her eyes as he left the next morning.

"Please come back," she called after him.

Later, she heard the speakers throughout Haven announce, "Ship's away!" She had a grim expression as she walked back to the apartment.

Ralph Bumgartner sat smugly in the command chair of the big Situation Room in Haven. He was feeling very pleased with himself. In charge of Haven while the boss was away!

A woman, dressed in black clerical garb, entered the big room and looked around, her eyes finally resting on him. She walked confidently over to where the temporary head of the resistance movement sat.

He looked up at her and smiled. "What can I do for you, babe?"

"You can listen," she replied evenly.

Bumgartner's eyebrows shot up. "What the hell is this?" he asked.

"You are a most interesting individual, Bumgartner. I've studied you for a while. I am here to offer you a proposition."

"Any other time I'd say 'Great,' but I'm kind of busy right now," he laughed, and started to turn away from her.

A very strong grip brought him back around.

"I am The Bromgrev," she told him.

"You aren't kidding, are you . . . ?" he said more than asked.

"No," she replied. "I have need of your services. It is essential that you monitor a series of signals—particular signals—from the battle area, and that you have a ship ready for my use."

"Why should I help you, lady—Bromgrev or whatever you are? I work for the opposition."

"You work for yourself, Bumgartner," she observed. "You like the winning side. You are in it for the work, not the cause. I am about to win, and those who are with me will share in the rewards."

"Now, look here—" he began impatiently.

"Do I have to assimilate everyone in this room to prove it to you?" she asked him.

He calmed down and grew thoughtful.

"If you need me so much, why not just assimilate me?"

"You know the reason: Hunter has set up blockages in you as he did in all his agents. But, if necessary, I can operate without you."

"Okay, okay, all right," he said, throwing up his hands. "Let's talk about it."

2

THE PLANETARY DESTRUCTION force was composed of just a dozen large ships, each powerful enough to obliterate a huge mass. In addition the same principles that governed the space drive itself were directed to a different purpose: Pushing along a huge mass of rock held with tractor beams, the destruction force prepared to transform the mass into anti-matter once it had been placed in the proper trajectory to strike the target—still distant—ahead of them.

A dense fighter screen darted in and out and all

around, but they were no match for the well-planned attack. Drawn thin within a large volume, they could ill afford to concentrate their forces, for fear that The Hunter's attack was but a mass diversion to allow for systematic pinpoint attacks on major fronts.

For primary defense, the Rhambdans depended on the Mind.

To get close enough to Rhambda to transform the great mass they towed and make certain it hit, the attackers would have to be almost in orbit.

But this time things were different.

Hunter sat under a central command helmet in the special ship constructed to monitor the attack. The massive power generators in this ship were not directed at the mass, and it threw no tractor beams. Using the amplifiers, Hunter's own mind threw a shield over the entire attack force—a shield of such power that none could break it.

Gunnery was handled by Koldon and Savage, although neither had to fire a shot. The combination of fighter protection and the massed locus of the power shield had protected them from attack.

The massed squadrons of Rhambdan defense units were suicidally throwing themselves at the towed planetoid, ignoring the enemy fighter screen. It was having some effect: despite massive losses, parts of the planetoid were being chipped away. As Savage watched with his 180-degree vision, he could see huge chunks get torn out of the mass by the concentrated gunnery beams of the Rhambdan ships.

To Savage, it was also clear that they would be in position over Rhambda, even moving at the A-1 slowness demanded by the tow job, in a matter of minutes— far too quickly for the Rhambdans to take out the bulk of the planetoid.

Suddenly his view faded out. The automatics he had preset when getting into battle stations had brought him out of the circuitry almost on cue.

"What's the matter, Savage?" Gayal's concerned voice came over the ship's intercom. "Why are you no longer manning your gun?"

"Must be a malfunction of the timer!" he called out,

shaking his head clear. "I'll be back in harness in a minute. I'm not critical, anyway."

Slowly he raised his head and looked around.

Koldon reclined opposite him, still deep within the guns. Gayal remained immobile at the helm, her body strapped in the forward chair. Stephen Wade's body was similarly immobile in his chair behind hers.

Quietly Savage unstrapped himself and sat up. He got unsteadily to his feet, to which he could feel strength and circulation rapidly return.

The vessel was a modified pickup ship; aft, where the cabins would have been, though, were the amplifiers for The Hunter's effort. Because they were all powered from the engines below, Savage went over to the red and yellow cables which led from the amplifiers into the deck. Taking out a piece of coiled copper wire and a pocketknife, he wrapped the wire around two live terminals on the master amplifiers, then took it down to the two cables.

Split seconds were all he had, he knew. Once he broke the cable, the copper wire must immediately touch it, or there was a chance that the automated mechanisms would free the others before the proper actions could take place.

He sweated nervously as he cut the yellow insulation from around the top cable. Below—exposed—were the massed cables he needed.

Putting the thick, rubber-lined glove over his left hand, he grasped the copper wire, bringing it out to full length.

"Savage? How's it coming?" Gayal's voice asked, sounding as mechanical as the ship, since it was actually the verbalization of her thoughts slowed to a speed which those not cybernetically linked to the machinery could understand.

"Okay!" he called to her. "One more minute!"

He held his breath and touched the copper wire to the exposed cable.

The lights dimmed, and the ship seemed to loose even the pulsation of the engines. That was all.

He wondered if something had gone wrong. He waited for a moment, then wrapped the coil around the cable so that it would stay, and went back into the command bridge.

Everything looked the same except for the dimmer lighting.

He had a dryness in his throat. "Gayal?" he called. "What is the position of the ship?"

There was no response.

"Gayal!" he shouted, his voice echoing around the walls. "What's going on?"

Silence answered him.

The three forms on the bridge continued their rhythmic breathing but did not stir.

He went over to the manual controls and punched in. "Break off! Break off!" he called into the transceiver. "Abort." He flipped on the monitors overhead.

As soon as the Mind had been suddenly freed of its blockage, it had reached out hungrily to take the opposition ships.

It had not done very well. A few lingered, but the bulk of The Hunter's craft had gone into D. It *had* gotten one of the bigger ships, apparently, but the rest were too quick for it—a tribute to the training of their captains and their equipment. The cybernetically linked minds thought faster than the Mind.

The planetoid could no longer be held by one lone ship, and had started to move away. It was already in the gravity well of Rhambda, and so was trapped. In a short time, it would either become a new small moon of the planet or become the largest meteor in that planet's history.

Slowly, deliberately, Savage took the ship away from Rhambda, feeding-in the coordinates which The Bromgrev's surrogate had given him in the office back in Haven. Then he realized suddenly that he had not yet sent the signal. Well, that was all right, too. In good time.

The alarm bells rang abruptly, telling him he was near his destination. He looked up at the monitors and saw it—a dark planetoid in the outer reaches of the Rhambdan system. A building of some kind sat on it— a rounded dome showed plainly under magnification. A disk lock was on top of a lower building to the rear of the dome.

Savage brought the ship to the disk and settled it gently down. Then he walked back to the airlock.

Equalization was achieved in a minute or two, and he opened the lock door unhesitatingly. A similar lock appeared just outside, and he pushed that open as well.

The second lock was the building's—and it was obviously out of place. The geometry of the room and the hall that it opened on were like nothing he had ever seen before. The place had not been built for any race he knew—or could imagine.

He heard footfalls. Down the corridor plodded a sleek orange form, rather graceful, like a cheetah on the African plains. It was large for any cat—larger than any lion he had ever seen—but its squatness, box shape, and incredible muscles on all six of its limbs showed that its home world was much heavier than his.

It drew up near to Savage and halted, studying him for a moment.

"It is done, then?" asked the Rhambdan, telepathically.

Savage nodded. "I'll send the signal. You reintegrate the pilot and gunner and take them to a decent place to recover."

"Food may even be prepared to your specifications," the cat informed him.

"Good. Prepare it for three and arrange for it to be served about an hour after the gunner and pilot have had the chance to revive."

"It shall be done. The place is mostly automated; I have only to give the orders."

"How many of you are there here?" he asked.

"Just me," the cat answered. "This ensures against accidents happening to telepathic receptives who might be here."

Savage nodded, and he and the cat re-entered the ship.

As Savage switched in the signals device, the Rhambdan fiddled with the pilot's master control panel, removing it with brute strength. Savage noted that the Rhambdan's forepaws were very much like small, short-fingered hands with long, nasty claws. It used all of its assets very competently.

It struck him as odd that, after all this, it was the first Rhambdan he had ever seen.

The signal sent, Savage helped the Rhambdan remove Gayal first, then Koldon, from the ship's circuitry and from the ship physically. Both were still out, but the Rhambdan assured him that they would come around in no time.

Savage sent the cat off after situating the other two and telling the Rhambdan what needed to be done.

He stared at the still strapped-in form of Stephen Wade. It was silent, immobile except for an almost imperceptible rising and falling of the chest.

Savage strode over to a panel below his gunnery station and pressed a stud. A small compartment opened, and he removed his .38 and checked to see that it was loaded, clean, and ready to go.

Then he sat down to wait.

He soon grew impatient and uneasy. Rising, he looked out the lock, down that long, alien corridor. Nothing stirred. If the Rhambdan was coming back, it showed no inclination to return soon. That was good.

He walked back over to the still silent form of Stephen Wade, The Hunter.

Wade opened his eyes and looked straight at Savage.

"It would have worked, you know," Wade said softly. "If you'd connected the *red* cable I'd have been as short-circuited as our two friends over there."

"I know," Savage replied. "Don't think I didn't consider it. Come to think of it, what made you so damned certain that I wouldn't?"

Hunter chuckled. "Savage, if you haven't seen by now how transparent you are, you never will. *I* could still have destroyed you in that room, you know. But once I knew who— Hell, Savage, I told you *before* that you're revenge-oriented with a one-track mind. Considering what's been done to you, you *had* to decide against The Bromgrev." He stopped, and looked disdainfully at Savage's pistol. "I wish you'd brought something more reassuring than that primitive blunderbuss."

"It will do the job," Savage assured him. "Can you do yours?"

"I feel certain I can," Wade replied. "The nature of this beast is that it will head in a direct line for Earth once it's done. This will be tricky. But The Bromgrev thinks I'm caught in that contraption over there, and will have no choice but to come here personally to handle—er, to do what he plans in order to get rid of me. His ship will head here on a straight course—and I will be pulled back on a straight course. I should intersect the ship before I'm halfway home."

"You might not get out before you're caught, too, you know," Savage pointed out, scratching an itch on his neck with the claw.

"You're counting on it, aren't you?" Wade replied, and grinned. "That *is* the plot, isn't it?"

Savage said nothing.

"You know what gave it away, don't you?" Wade said knowingly. "The hook."

Savage looked at the metal claw at the end of his right arm bemusedly. "What do you mean?" he asked, knowing the answer.

"You got yourself made into Adonis but you kept the hook. It bothered me. Why would he keep that claw? I kept asking myself."

"If it is so obvious," Savage put in in an irritated tone, "why go on?"

"Because I'm going to screw you up. Other people have tried to beat me, you know. I've always won in the end. I'm going to get away with it, Savage: I'm going to kill The Bromgrev and survive to come after you."

"The Haven computer puts your odds at under 9 percent of getting out before the cataclysm," Savage pointed out. "You know that."

"The computer only conjectures about me in my *natural* form. It has no real idea of my reflexes or capabilities . . . Insufficient data, Savage. The odds are in my favor." He stopped as Savage turned with a jerk toward the door. "What's the matter?" Hunter asked.

"Thought I heard someone in the hall," Savage mumbled softly.

"Don't worry, it's nothing," Wade reassured. "I will know if anyone comes close enough to hear us."

"I have confidence in the pistol, Wade—not you."

"Suit yourself. It should be an interesting contest, really. We're so much alike."

"You've never loved anybody but yourself," Savage snapped. "You're the antithesis of humanity—in the broadest sense of that term. No, Wade, we are not alike."

"Sure we are," the Kreb taunted. "And we'll grow more alike as you go along. Law of the jungle, Savage. Look what The Bromgrev became in his battle with me. He really *was* all that is good once, you know."

"I wonder how much longer it will be?" Savage growled impatiently. "They should have left by now."

"Why should they hurry? After all, as long as I'm a prisoner of the amplifiers, verified by our cat witness, there's no rush. The Bromgrev was always orderly."

Savage gave a mirthless chuckle; then pulled out a cigarette and lit it, inhaling deeply. "You might answer me one thing, if there's time."

"Go ahead," the other invited.

"Why can't you just kill yourself? The Bromgrev could."

"No, The Bromgrev cannot. That's what you—or Bumgartner—are for. Oh, the doppelgängers, sure. Do you miss a cell when it wears off the skin? But suicide—real suicide. I don't look forward to this, you know."

"I thought it would be the highpoint of your overly long life," Savage retorted sarcastically.

"In a way. But *you've* died only once. *I* have died thousands of—maybe more—times. That backlog will hit me when I go. It will produce the most horrible set of flashback sensations imaginable. If we are indeed both mad, it is that which did it. I don't think my brother or myself could bring ourselves to do it."

Savage shrugged off the idea. "Why haven't you two simply had it out long ago—face to face?"

"Doesn't do any good. We're of equal strength and limitations. He's tried it several times, in several ways—but it's always been a draw. He beats me, then I beat him. Read your Bible. That's why he's so desperate to have pulled all this—and I'm gambling my life to end it."

"Well, it's—" Savage started, but suddenly a high-pitched screech came through the cabin sound system.

"That's it!" Wade cried excitedly. "The signal from my agents! The Bromgrev is away and in space! Do it! *Do it now!*"

Savage aimed the pistol, but hesitated.

"Do it!" Wade screamed. *"She's only one little girl!"*

Savage fired.

STEP SIX

GAYAL GAVE A low moan and opened her eyes. They refused to focus for a few minutes, then the double images seemed to merge. Koldon was standing over her.

"My head is killing me," she groaned.

"I know," Koldon sympathized. "Mine's only now getting down to a dull explosion. Just take it easy for a while."

"What happened?" she asked.

"Savage doublecrossed us," Koldon replied. "I never did quite trust that man. Hunter blocked his mind, but you could see a tremendous amount of hurt and hate mixed in his eyes. I warned Hunter, but he wouldn't believe me."

"Savage—The Bromgrev?" she gasped plaintively. "I just don't believe it!"

"I'm still not *certain* he is," Koldon told her. "Somehow, I seem to get the idea that, in the game of Hunter and Bromgrev, Savage was playing, too. But he shorted out the cybernetics—that's the only thing that could have caused what we went through."

"But—" She raised herself up, then held her head and groaned again. "But where is he? And where is The Hunter? And where are *we*?"

"Wherever we are, it's not any planet I've ever been on or heard about. The walls have that strange fluidity! And the doors! Most doors are built to accommodate the shape of the beings using them. But these . . . !"

He muttered something about hourglasses and tesseracts.

She saw what he meant. Bumgartner, Koldon, Vard, Valiakean, Earth, Savage—all alien. But the builders of this room had been so different that it was difficult to conceive of them existing in the same continuum. This was a total alienness beyond experience or description.

However, the beds, the curtains—these were "human" or real-world touches, lending some sanity to the surroundings.

"Now what do we do?" she asked the Quoark. She had never felt more helpless.

"We wait," he replied.

A small speaker crackled to life like an ancient radio. "The game is over," Savage's voice came at them, echoing around the weird angles of the room. "There is nothing left but the explanation. If you two will join me, I have food prepared."

The doorway opened impossibly, as if collapsing in and of itself until nothing was left of the folds. A long corridor was revealed.

"Shall we go?" Koldon asked.

Gayal nodded and got out of the bed. They both made their way through the door and down the hallway.

At the end, a similarly alien room had been made over into an almost conventional small dining room. It contained a table, linen, eating utensils, and dishes spread out before them. Savage was just finishing his meal. He looked up at them and smiled as they entered.

He looks older, much older, Gayal thought, almost as if he had the weight of the galaxy on his shoulders.

"Go ahead and eat," he urged them, motioning to the food. "It's pretty good and compatible with all of us."

Still they hesitated; then hunger overtook them.

Savage lit a cigarette and said nothing.

"Just what the hell—?" Koldon started, between chews.

Savage cut him off. "Eat first. Then I'll tell you everything you want to know. There's plenty of time—now."

The agony, the death, the trauma was subsiding. Already The Hunter could feel himself clear, sort, and grow. The power surged into him, and he fed deeply on the energy of the cosmos.

I am! he exulted. I am again!

He reached out and found the inhabitants of this piti-able rock they all occupied. Just four, he saw. They had fulfilled their purpose. They were no longer relevant to him, and he quickly forgot their existence.

The Pull began, that ancient geas laid upon him in times past by The Race, that curse that tied him to his planetary sphere.

Thousands of times before, he had been thus; and thousands of times before, he had resisted—in vain. Now, this time, he could choose a host from any along the route, defeating or delaying The Pull.

But he would not resist. He flew, taking the energy he needed from the stars that shone all around him. He soared confidently, triumphantly, seeing the universe as his race had seen it, joyous in the sudden return, if fleeting, to godhood.

To meet the ship, that fragile shell, which carried The Bromgrev to him.

"Right from the beginning," Savage began, "I had this feeling that things weren't quite right. But it didn't really all come together for me until one day in Wade's office, when he told me the impossible stories of your escapes. Oh, they were real and dangerous to you—but they sounded like low-grade movie thrillers.

"And they were! That's what tipped The Hunter that The Bromgrev was making his move. Suddenly I saw how The Bromgrev thought—and realized that your stories weren't the only low-grade thrillers around. *Everything* I had experienced since going on that wartime patrol was like that—set up, contrived, like we were all unknowing actors in a plot, with the author's heavy hand all around. Nothing rang true.

"I was a soldier, sent on patrol. But I was improperly briefed, and I was supplied with men who had no stomach for the mission and were ready to do anything to louse it up. Ultimately, I was faced with mutiny, and shot by a man—one of my own—named McNally. And then this same McNally made certain that my body, with its potential incriminating evidence, got back to home base."

"You were killed?" Gayal gasped. "But—you are not dead!"

"Yes. I *am* dead. I exist only because The Hunter 'met' me on a metaphysical plane and kept me from going to the place of the dead—and restored me to my body. My hand was left behind to the enemy—the only part of me that Hunter did not restore."

"Yeah, that's bothered us for some time," Koldon put in. "When you remade yourself into your version of tall, dark, and handsome, why did you keep the claw?"

Savage smiled as if at a private joke. "Hunter understood—at least at the end. It was, well, my reminder and my symbol."

"Of what?" they both asked simultaneously.

"That Hunter had limitations," he replied. "It was something—*one* thing—he could not do with a wave of his hand. It made him less than godlike, more human— and, therefore, more vulnerable. *He had limits.* It may have been silly or stupid to retain it, but, for me, it was necessary. As long as it existed, a small part of me still belonged to me." He took a sip of water and continued.

"I was part of the first step in Hunter's master plan. All of it depended on figuring out who among the trillions of sentient beasties in the galaxy The Bromgrev was. Haven and The Hunter's powers put one place off-limits to The Bromgrev's agents and surrogates—and it was the nerve center of resistance to The Bromgrev's conquests. The Hunter deliberately created a situation where only the physical presence of The Bromgrev would do."

"I think I see," Gayal interjected. "There was no way to tell who The Bromgrev was with all of those surrogate selves around to give the orders. So, rather than sifting through uncounted beings, hoping to come up with the right one, he brought The Bromgrev to him."

"Right," Savage agreed. "And I was part of the team he developed to identify The Bromgrev once he arrived."

"But why come at all?" Koldon asked. "The Bromgrev was winning, wasn't he? Why risk everything by exposing himself to danger?"

"Several reasons," Savage replied. "Specifically, the sheer scope of conquering the known galaxy. How many millennia would it take? How many lives? And what would be left? Back in Vietnam we had an officer who once destroyed an entire village to 'save' it from being taken over by the enemy. The enemy never took it over, all right—but who won? And, of course, there was the terrible hatred both had built up against each other in the eons they had been battling. A hatred, I think, transcending all bounds of logic and reason. They knew each other well.

"Also, The Hunter had been expelled from The Race and left behind, out of the godhood he coveted. The Bromgrev was the last, although degenerate, symbol of that race that cost him his glory— But, we're getting away from the answers." Savage paused to light another cigarette.

"I was part of the team The Hunter developed to identify The Bromgrev, once he arrived," Savage continued. "I discovered early on in the game that the man who killed me—McNally—didn't exist. The Hunter had arranged the patrol; The Hunter put Ralph Bumgartner, alias McNally, in there specifically to kill me and yet get my body out in one piece."

"Bumgartner!" Gayal exclaimed. "But he was the one who rescued me! I—"

"Just another pawn in The Hunter's little game," Savage cut in. "I wasn't certain until one of The Bromgrev's agents lured me to a small town for a private chat. He put forth the proposition to change sides."

"And you did!" Koldon spat.

"No. I didn't," Savage corrected him. "I never really had a side. Not one of theirs, anyway. The Bromgrev offered totalitarianism for the good of the galaxy, The Hunter offered an anarchy where he could play little tin god all he wanted. So I kept my options open until I saw what both games were—and, once I had all the answers in this game of galactic war, I started playing, too. Particularly when I saw that I had become, by accident or design, the pivot in both sides's schemes."

"How could you possibly know that?" Koldon put in. "After all, there were thousands of agents."

"The Hunter went to too much trouble to recruit me just to discard me—and The Bromgrev went to even more trouble to talk to me personally when a phone call would have done the trick as well. So already things were moving toward me as the focal point for both sides.

"Then came *you*—not just the two of you, but many more. A lot of our people, trapped on planets with the enemy breathing down their necks, made almost impossible escapes. Why? The only answer was that you were *supposed* to escape."

"I'll have you know it wasn't easy," Koldon snorted. "Gayal and I both almost got killed!"

"It wasn't supposed to be *easy*. Just—suspicious. A few of our people still got it—enough to show how hard it was. But the fact remains that so many hair's-breadth escapes, coming one on top of another, made everyone a suspect. The Hunter saw The Bromgrev in each of you—as The Bromgrev intended."

"So that's it!" Gayal exclaimed. "We were camouflage for the real Bromgrev!"

"Sure," Savage continued, "but The Bromgrev was smarter than we were. He sent all those suspects in the front door, then came in like a thief in the night, in a way totally unexpected."

"You mean *none* of us was The Bromgrev?" Koldon gasped. "Then, *who is?*"

Savage smiled. "You both should have figured it out long ago. The clues were all around—and at least one mistake was as good as putting up a sign."

The Bromgrev's ship was in sight, on its way to kill a helpless Hunter.

But The Hunter was already there. Quickly, he matched velocities with the ship and dissolved into the energy field. He sensed them all within, and saw with satisfaction that the one he had identified as The Bromgrev was indeed there.

"The War will not end with the death of The Hunter," he hears The Bromgrev say.

"I know," agrees Ralph Bumgartner. *"There is always conflict in the jungle, and this has disrupted the orderly flow. The War will go on."*

"The War will go on," The Bromgrev intones.

The War ends here, Hunter thought with satisfaction, *but they could not hear. He saw ahead the huge scoop of the engines, like the great gaping mouth of a monstrous beast. Slowly he began to change his shape, acquiring mass as he drew what he needed from the matter around him. One by one, slowly, methodically, The Hunter neutralized the safeguards by transmutation.*

"Yes," Savage told them, "both of you should have known The Bromgrev when I did."

The others were thoughtful. Then, suddenly, Koldon banged his fist on the table, shaking the dishes. "Oh my God!" he exploded. *"Jenny!"*

"Yes . . ." Savage acknowledged in a low, sad tone. "Jenny. Not from the start—at least I have *that.*"

A deep hurt was in his face and manner, and they were hesitant to intrude upon it. Finally, Gayal broke the silence.

"But—but I don't understand," she said in a puzzled tone. "How could we have known?"

"Because of *you,* curse me for a fool!" Koldon snapped in an angry voice. But the anger was directed at himself. "Look," he said more calmly, "do you remember when Jenny got her eyes? The training flight?"

Gayal nodded, but her face still betrayed puzzlement.

"Remember, the Valiakean brought each of us in turn for her to see?" Koldon continued, getting excited again. "When she saw you she said—"

"She said I was blue," Gayal recalled. "But I don't see—"

"Jenny was blind from birth," Savage reminded her. "She had no pupils. There can be no color for a blind person—not even the *concept* of color, to one who has never seen. Terms like 'red' and 'blue' have no meaning. You *were* blue and she saw you as such, but she should have had no way of knowing that blue was blue unless she'd seen blue before. Without pupils there was no way. Ergo, the only way she could have known that blue was blue was because it wasn't Jenny."

"And all this was based on that?" Gayal asked.

"Well, that was the clincher. But there were earlier slips—small ones, like mentioning the time without feeling the clock and the like—that led me to the suspicion that Jenny was The Bromgrev. And with that discovery everything fell into place for me—and saved our lives. For The Hunter would have killed us all, if he hadn't been convinced that I would do his work."

"Yes, I was wondering about that myself," Koldon said. "Why was The Hunter so sure you'd be on his side?"

Savage grinned. "He knew me well. That's why he picked me. I was bullheaded, self-centered, and revenge-minded. Never in my whole life had any woman paid any attention to me—because of my looks . . . I never had had sex with a woman I hadn't paid. But . . . Jenny couldn't see the deformed exterior: she 'saw' me in different terms, and she accepted me . . . The only spark of human warmth I had ever known— and The Bromgrev took her away from me, killed her because it was a good move. There was no other way I *could* have acted—and Hunter knew it."

"But how could The Bromgrev be Jenny?" Gayal said in an unbelieving tone. "How would he have the chance? And how could he know you two would fall in love?"

"Because he engineered the whole thing," Savage answered. "You heard of my experiences with the Kah-'diz—Charley or whatever—and how I met Jenny?"

They both acknowledged that they had.

"Well," Savage continued, "that was the next of the things that didn't add up. Charley was shot down during the attack on Earth—but why attack at all? The Bromgrev had to know that the defenses here were the strongest of the resistance, and he couldn't afford to throw all his forces into the fight by withdrawing from the conquered places. He also knew that, even if he destroyed Earth, Haven would survive. The Hunter could escape, in any event, to begin it all over again. *The en-*

tire reason for that attack was as a smokescreen to sneak The Bromgrev in!"

"Then The Bromgrev was—" Koldon began.

"Charley, of course," Savage completed, nodding. "Oh, I seriously doubt if *all* that happened was planned in advance, but The Bromgrev was a master of improvisation.

"All The Bromgrev wanted to do was to get killed in the neighborhood. Don't ask me why, but they can't kill themselves. Something psychological, I think. After death, they have a period of time—apparently a good deal of time but still finite and predictable—to find a new host body. In order to have enough time to pick a really appropriate one, he wanted to die in as close proximity to Earth as possible. The Kah'diz form was a logical one. Imagine the Kah'diz's power amplified and coupled to the unknown powers of the Kreb! It was ideal as a war identity—but not very good for infiltration."

"Then he didn't intend to crash?" Koldon interjected.

"I doubt that he thought he would get the chance." Savage lit yet another cigarette. "But when he saw an opening and got away, he realized the additional opportunities. Our defenses reported that his ship had veered in its course—he had decided to land alive, and picked my area. I'm sure I wasn't the only agent who had been contacted and primed, but I was the one closest to Haven, and The Bromgrev obviously saw many of the ways in which I was vulnerable. It was clear from his agent's conversation that they'd made a special study of me.

"After the ship plunged into the lake, he set out to find a new host—green lizards aren't exactly inconspicuous in that area."

"Then the crash wasn't as devastating as it might have been?" Koldon asked.

"No. It wasn't a crash at all," Savage explained. "When I went out to the ship, it was *on* the bottom, not *in* the bottom. The engines were shut off but the auxiliary power generators were on. It *floated* in to Earth, you see, which implies that the engines were operational. There were also the three crew members—all

dead, all strapped in. And yet the fourth survived un-
hurt: the body of the lizard we later recovered wasn't
banged up in any way. We saw, with Vard, that The
Bromgrev could take over a being when it suited his
purpose and then will it to die when that purpose was
accomplished. All three of the other crew members
were Bromgrev surrogates—he wouldn't have trusted
any other type of crew for so delicate a mission. Having
served their purpose, they were told to die—to reinforce
the crash idea.

"The Bromgrev was still swimming toward shore,
mounted on the surviving lizard, when he met old man
McBride swimming out to get his daughter. The Bromgrev worked a quick Kah'diz loyalty conversion on the
man, and had both a possible host and hideout.

"What bothered me, after the fact, was that McBride
had talked to the State Police and other authorities—he
could hardly avoid it, what with the accident and all.
That's why the lizard's body was missing: *McBride*
couldn't be the host until the interviews had been
cleared up. Of course, by the time I got there The
Bromgrev had formulated his plan, put it into effect, and
was perched on McBride's back.

"The next problem with the scenario was another
that bothered me: Why make yourself conspicuous?
Particularly when you *knew* trained agents of Haven
would be around? The answer was obvious, but I didn't
see it. He *wanted* me to discover him. He eavesdropped
on me and Jenny that morning under the guise of selling
ice cream, and found the two of us very much attracted
to each other. He knew I was the agent simply because
he couldn't read anything but my surface thoughts;
Jenny, though, was wide open. Only when the two of us
came down to breakfast did he break off contact. By
then the plan was set."

"You told me it was a whirlwind romance," Gayal
put in. "So this was all according to The Bromgrev's
plan?"

"Exactly," Savage affirmed. "Using the Kah'diz's
powers, he stepped up both Jenny's and my own emotional relationship, pushing an instant attraction into a
passionate love affair and binding us together. It both-

ered me at the time how irrationally I was acting, but I continued to act that way, never thinking that The Hunter had never blocked the *empathic* paths to my mind. Using children and implying the possibility of a morning takeover of the whole town, The Bromgrev induced quick action while making certain that Jenny stayed with me."

"But how could you have known?" Gayal sympathized. "After all, he put on such a good show."

"A *flawed* show, dammitall!" growled Savage. "I'm a trained observer and problem solver, yet I continually let the obvious slip by. If he had a force-field generator from the ship sufficient to protect him, *why did he let us through*? Why not just seal himself in the cellar until the ship was raised? Only one reason—because he wanted me to seek him out and kill him. I'm sure it was a shock that Jenny did the deed, but the same result was obtained."

"And the passion he induced . . . ?" Koldon prompted.

"Camouflage, to give some glimmer of a rationalization for the fact that we got in at all. But that, too, was a major mistake I should have noticed and did not, since it forced home the fact that my empathic channels were open and I was as open to that sort of manipulation as Jenny. It should have been a tipoff, and I missed it."

Savage paused for a second, and there came a faraway look in his eyes.

"He took her almost immediately . . ." he whispered.

Satisfied now that the ship is vulnerable, The Hunter draws from the energy around him what he needs to transmute the liner material inside the scoop to his purpose: a material that is fluid, much denser than lead, but with far less mass.

The material forms around him as he works, and begins slowly to flow into the depths of the great engines. Had the safety mechanisms not already been neutralized, the knowledge of the gaps in the lining would have been instantly transmitted to the cybernetic pilot in time for a system shutdown. No alarms ring. The ship goes on, the material oozing back into the figure-eight-shaped plasma bottle; past the high-flux density coils it flows. The material begins to slow the generated tachyons to the point where separation becomes impossible. Huge numbers of tachyons are created, having both positive and negative half-spin.

"So The Bromgrev entered Haven by the back door, while we concentrated all our efforts on the new arrivals like yourself."

"So why blow it by taking over Vard?" Koldon asked. "Surely he was perfectly hidden, and we could only *suspect* he was there."

"True," Savage replied, "and it's here that the improvised plan showed its weaknesses. As Jenny, The Bromgrev wasn't on a crew and so couldn't get outside easily. I think The Bromgrev was telling the truth when he told me, as Vard, that he was 'squeezed' in Haven. But he *did* need that information—and he accomplished two other things at the same time. One was to focus attention on the two of you, since all three of you had been kept apart from the rest of the new arrivals, and the second was to precipitate action on The Hunter's part. The non-space of Haven shocked him; I think The Bromgrev planned to have his host and Hunter's killed at the same moment, and then engage Hunter, Kreb to Kreb. For some reason, he thought he could win on those grounds—perhaps prevent Hunter from getting a new host, or force him to a host that would neutralize him. A crystalline world with a much slower time rate, for example. But he dared not take the chance in the null-space of Haven, whose properties Hunter knew and he did not. Therefore, he had to get The Hunter out of Haven.

"But The Hunter was smarter than The Bromgrev thought. Instead of rushing out in panic, he sent *us* instead—each team, in turn, out of Haven with the rest isolated inside. If those bits of information Vard stole were so vital, they *would* be transmitted to the Mind, even if The Bromgrev took pains to avoid being obvious. Subtle shifts and better organization were noted after our training flight, so Wade knew The Bromgrev was one of us. Even so, Hunter had totally forgotten Jenny. Even *I* was a suspect; he called me in to set us all up for the kill, I think, and I didn't know what to do. It became apparent to me that we would all die in whatever scheme he'd planned, unless I acted fast. So I told him who The Bromgrev was in exchange for two things.

"First, I wanted to know how he was going to kill The Bromgrev—since that would ensure that I could take steps to see it wasn't worked on *us*. And, second, I wanted Ralph Bumgartner to have to face The Bromgrev when the showdown came. I was convinced that he'd change sides readily, and as a result be the one The Bromgrev would trust to bring him to The Hunter. He would be the logical choice, since, once I discovered who The Bromgrev was, I wouldn't likely be very cooperative in the double-kill."

"And did he?" Gayal asked.

"I don't know about Bumgartner," Savage told her, "and I won't for some time. But I *did* know The Hunter's murder weapon, and ran it through the computers. They gave me the answer I expected—that any way to kill one Kreb would probably also kill the other. You see, in this crazy game of chess, *I* was playing, too."

The fluid slowed the newly generated tachyons to the point where they interacted with each other in great numbers. Matter canceled anti-matter, and the ship rapidly annihilated itself.

In the moment before cancellation, however, The Bromgrev sensed the presence. He struck out at the unseen presence leaving the ship as the ship and all matter within it canceled. The resultant energy burst dissipated that energy over a great block of space in all directions. It was far too fast and too total to allow escape. The Bromgrev struck out, trying to draw The Hunter back into the trap, to at least know that, as the pure energy forms of the Kreb were dissipated over the cosmos, the contest would end in a draw, with all participants who had died so many times truly dead.

A piercing, agonizing scream came from elsewhere in the ancient observatory. They all heard it and froze. Just as suddenly, it was over.

Savage breathed a sigh, and took out his pistol. Turning to the door, he waited expectantly, his weapon pointed at the opening. The other two remained quiet, quizzical expressions on their faces.

Seconds that seemed like hours in the eerie silence went by, and then suddenly they heard footfalls coming down the corridor toward them. Immediately the Rhambdan station attendant appeared in the doorway, eyes blazing and with a fierce expression that must have come from Rhambda's primordial past.

The creature saw the pistol and stopped.

"What have you done?" it screamed telepathically at Savage, tremendous violence and menace carried in the words.

"From the looks of you and your screams of agony, I've done exactly what I intended to do," Savage replied calmly. "I've just won The War."

The cat seemed to compose itself and took in some deep breaths. As it did, Savage said to the two, in a lower tone, "You see, the Rhambdan Mind is still The Bromgrev, even if The Bromgrev's dead. All its memories, all its knowledge remain—but not its powers."

"But —why . . . ?" the Rhambdan asked, almost pleading. "I offered the only solution to the salvation of this galaxy. The Hunter offered only the anarchy you've brought upon it, anyway."

"But it wasn't *my* idea of salvation," Savage told the creature. "You and Hunter were both so taken by the 'cosmic vision' that the people who were fighting and dying for you were merely so many expendable things, not people at all. Their goals were not your goals. What matter that a man gains the Earth, if he loses his own soul?"

"I can still kill you, you know," the cat snarled. "You are near Rhambda."

"Them. Not me," Savage reminded it. "And what good would that do you? Revenge? You? Where are your high principles then? If you kill for revenge, you will

understand what *I* have done and why—for you will be on *my* level."

The Rhambdan stood a moment more; then its features softened, the fire in its eyes seemed to dull.

"You are right," the cat said finally. "Unity is the prime directive. And now you've won. Now what do you propose to do?"

"The Hunter—" Savage prodded, "did he die as well?"

A note of satisfaction was in the Rhambdan's reply. "I sensed the wrongness in the final moment, and reached out. I caught him."

"That's all I needed to know," Savage told it. "We are now in command. *We*—those of us in this room. You know what will have to be done."

The Rhambdan nodded. "A conference, of course. And you?"

"If you can prepare the ship, we'll go back to Haven to coordinate our side."

"It will be done," the cat replied, and left.

Savage allowed it to leave, then made a whistling sound. "Wow," he said, sounding greatly relieved. "I'd *hoped* it would go that way, but wasn't sure."

After a pause, Koldon said, "But, if I understand things right, you've just killed both of the Kreb. There *is* no guardian!"

Savage nodded and smiled. "Your problem is that you're still seeing things the way *they* put them. Each represents himself as an agent of God and the other as the Devil. It wasn't true. They were only two Kreb, both devolved, twisted, and power-mad. The Hunter was certain death for us; The Bromgrev, a prolonged life under the worst kind of totalitarianism. Just look what it did to *your* world in the name of keeping things right and just, Gayal!"

"But—but—" Koldon stammered, at a loss for words. "What happens now?"

"Well, The War's mucked things up so much that it's doubtful that they'll ever be put back right. But now nature takes its own course. The Next Race—if there's to be one—develops or doesn't develop, as the jungle dictates. Whoever survives wins the game."

"But there is still an empire—Rhambda—" Gayal objected.

"Ours now," Savage told her. "Remember, the Mind is The Bromgrev—the knowledge of those untold ages—but the Mind hasn't the wisdom or power to use it. They are now withdrawing to Rhambda in an orderly fashion. The Rhambdan allies will make a quick peace with us or we'll take a combined Haven-Rhambdan force and wipe them out. We now own both sides. We must put things into a semblance of order and get things going again in the postwar period."

"But—are we—are you—up to such a task?" Gayal asked, wonderingly.

Savage shrugged, and smiled a ghostly smile. "I would gladly return to Earth to die, to join my Jenny as I should." The smile seemed more and more forced, the voice somehow distant. "But I am condemned, you see, to live forever. I haven't even the Krebs' way out, for there're none left to do the deed. My curse descends on all of you. The Hunter was right—he said we were alike."

"Well," Koldon sighed, getting up from the table, "I was always pretty much of an atheist anyway . . ."

Exciting Space Adventure from DEL REY